He could no more resist her than he could stop breathing. He tunneled his fingers into her dark hair, tearing it free from the fragile hold of the pins. When it tumbled around her shoulders, he groaned and brought handfuls of it to his lips. "You are indescribable," he told her. "Absolutely and completely unique." He inhaled a great breath of her hair. "I love the way you smell."

"I love the way you touch me," she whispered.

Elliot felt something inside him melt like ice before the sun. With a soft laugh, he wrapped his hands around her waist. "I knew it would be like this for us. . . ."

Books published by The Ballantine Publishing Group
are available at quantity discounts on bulk purchases
for premium, educational, fund-raising, and special
sales use. For details, please call 1-800-733-3000.

PRICELESS

Mandalyn Kaye

FAWCETT CREST • NEW YORK

A Fawcett Crest Book
Published by The Ballantine Publishing Group
Copyright © 1998 by Mandalyn Kaye

http://www.randomhouse.com

Library of Congress Catalog Card Number: 98-92561

ISBN 0-449-22645-X

Manufactured in the United States of America

First Edition: August 1998

10 9 8 7 6 5 4 3 2 1

Chapter 1

London, 1851

Cloaked in moonlight, she moved like a specter.

Elliot Moss, Viscount Darewood, stood within the deep shadows of the arbor, watching her ease her way along his garden path.

He admired her natural grace and unaffected elegance, qualities that had attracted him to her from the first and impressed him, especially now, when he knew she was experiencing such distress. He had observed her during the past couple of years, existing on her solitary plane in Society, unwelcome in his circles, spurned in the circles into which she had been thrust. Outwardly calm, betraying no signs of strain, she seemed to draw on deep wells of strength.

Liberty Madison was, he had decided some time ago, a rare gem in a world filled with deceivers and fools.

It was no wonder, he mused, that he wanted to

possess her. He'd made a lifetime occupation of seeking out the rare and beautiful—and possessing it.

When she was within a few steps of him, he moved from the arbor. "Good evening, Miss Madison."

Only a quick intake of breath betrayed her surprise. "My lord." Her extraordinary gaze met his. "I expected to find you inside, before a warm fire, with a snifter of cognac in hand."

"I believed the meeting you requested might be better conducted without overinterested servants nearby." He watched intently as she lowered the hood of her plain woolen cloak. "Besides," he added, "I don't drink cognac. Can't abide the stuff."

The quip won him a slight smile. "Lord Huxley always said that you were a man of discriminating taste."

"Even if he hated me otherwise?"

She didn't respond.

Howard Rendell, the Earl of Huxley, had made no secret of his disdain for Elliot Moss. Certainly Liberty, who had served for years as Howard's confidante and, if rumor was to be believed, in at least one far less proper capacity, knew the extent of her benefactor's loathing for Darewood.

She glanced over her shoulder at the darkened path. "I have risked everything by coming here. You know that, of course."

"I do."

"If we are seen—well, there will be no escape from the consequences."

Her voice had always reminded him of warmed brandy. It had a soothing, melodious quality that eased taut nerves. Tonight, however, he didn't miss the thready note of worry in her tone.

"I assure you," he said, "that I have taken precautions on your behalf. At this very moment, there are three gentlemen at Blickley's willing to swear I spent the evening besting them at faro."

She faced him once more, and in the pale light, he clearly saw the tiny lines of anxiety that marred the smooth skin on her forehead. Damn Howard Rendell to hell, he thought, but aloud he merely said, "Thank you for heeding my request, Miss Madison," as he stepped away from the entrance to the arbor. "Why don't we sit. I'm sure that my proposal of marriage, only two weeks after Huxley's death, came as a surprise to you. I imagine you have some questions you would like answered."

She seemed to hesitate. "I have just one question. Your answer will determine the length of our conversation."

"Very well."

Her fingers twisted the ties of her reticule. "You will understand, of course, that I cannot imagine why you would consider a woman known as the mistress of your sworn enemy to be an appropriate choice as wife and mother to your heirs. I would simply like to know, my lord, what possible advantage you hope to gain by pursuing this."

He should have realized that she would not be prone to mincing words. Rendell had seen more in Liberty than a sharp head for figures. Any man would be a fool to underestimate the strength of will that lay beneath her lovely surface. But, he thought with an inward sigh, malleable women were so much easier to manage. "I would think," he said, choosing his words with care, "that you would be more interested in the advantages my offer presents to you than in my personal reasons for pursuing the arrangement."

"Would you?" She looked at him appraisingly. "Curious. I hadn't considered that you might have chosen to pursue me for altruistic reasons. Mayhap I learned too much from Lord Huxley to believe you are possessed of pure motives. His lordship said you never made a move unless you were convinced that it would give you a tactical advantage."

She tipped her head slightly, and had Elliot not known better, he would have sworn that amusement sparked in her gaze.

"Do I have the right of it, my lord?"

At the probing question, Elliot felt a flare of satisfaction. He had known men who were weaker in spirit than Liberty Madison. She would, indeed, prove an excellent choice for a wife. "Perhaps," he said at last.

"I believe that I do," she said, moving past him,

the worn fabric of her gown whispering as she walked down the stone path.

He caught the faintest scent of her, something natural and light, as he followed her into the depths of the arbor. Her proximity unsettled him.

She sat on one of the low benches before she addressed him again. "So you see, my lord, given my suspicions, I cannot possibly make a reasonable decision until I am possessed of all the facts."

Elliot hesitated. He knew she was bluffing. The proposal he'd offered her was nearly all that stood between her and destitution. Still, her fire pleased him. He would not like to think that Howard Rendell had squeezed all the life from her. As a rule, Elliot found strong emotions annoying; they nearly always got in the way of reason. But in Liberty Madison, he found them singularly appealing.

"You feel I'm keeping something from you?" he asked.

"I do. I would like to know why you felt you must go so far as to propose marriage. Surely my reputation is tattered enough that such an extreme measure would not have seemed necessary."

"I have never allowed gossip to dictate my actions."

"Still, I would think that a man of your stature would be concerned about the ramifications of taking a woman like me as his wife. Surely you would jeopardize far more than you would gain."

A slight edge had slipped into her tone. Again he

had to squelch an urge to curse Rendell. He had
cursed him often enough since he had received that
damned letter from Huxley's solicitors. Only such a
bastard would arrange to continue in death a feud
he'd begun in life. Elliot almost wished Howard
were still alive. He would have enjoyed challenging
him for the affections of the intriguing Miss Madison.
It might have proved exhilarating.

As the silence between them stretched, he noted
that Liberty remained composed. Only the tight
clasp of her fingers in her lap betrayed her agitation.
He slapped his gloves against his thighs in a soft
rhythm as he considered how best to proceed.

"Do you mind if I sit, Miss Madison?"

A slight wave of her hand indicated the bench
across from her. "Please do."

Never mind that he had her at a distinct disadvan-
tage, he thought, she received him as if she were
royalty. Like any good negotiator, she hid even the
slightest hint of her desperation. And for that, she
won his undying admiration. He would give her
what she wanted, he decided, as long as she agreed
to wed him. It seemed a fair bargain. He had never
proposed marriage before and had found the
process somewhat unsettling at first. But once his
seething rage toward Rendell had subsided, he realized that the matter was quite similar to a business
negotiation. And at that, he was expert.

"I cannot proceed, my lord," Liberty continued,

her voice a silken whisper now, "until I know precisely what you want."

"What you wish to know," he stated baldly, "is why I did not simply ask you to become my mistress."

"Or why you asked anything of me at all."

If he expected her to demur at the frank nature of the conversation, he was sorely disappointed. Instead, she held his gaze with a disarmingly direct stare. He'd always been intrigued by her eyes, which were an exceptional shade of blue reminiscent of a robin's egg. "Have you such a low opinion of yourself?"

Her hands tightened in her lap, but she didn't look away. "I assure you, my opinion of myself is quite grand. It's my opinion of you that is somewhat suspect."

The statement was delivered with such sincerity that he almost laughed. There was no guile at all in her expression, and he found that alluring. Her hands fluttered against her wool cloak in agitation. "Miss Madison," he asked, "are you nervous?"

He heard her swift intake of breath. "Of course. I thought you prided yourself on making people nervous."

"If people find me intimidating, it is often because they've overestimated the truth in the stories that they've heard."

"I suppose some do."

"You, on the other hand, don't tend to believe

things until you have the evidence before you. Isn't that so?"

"In a manner of speaking, yes."

"Then I must assume that you are nervous because of what you have to say, and not at the thought of seeing me. After all"—he leaned toward her—"you could have responded to my proposal by letter, could you not?"

"I suppose."

"So, therefore, I may conclude that you have not determined my motive for proposing marriage, and that you are open to negotiation."

"Given the long history of your feud with Lord Huxley, I feel it safe to assume that I am a pawn in your game of revenge. I'm not certain what you could hope to accomplish—he is dead, after all— but I confess I do not find the idea of playing a role in it particularly appealing."

He stood on the edge of a cliff, and he knew it. With what he now believed to be her characteristic insight, she had cut directly to the heart of the matter. He wanted revenge, yes, but he wanted Liberty Madison more. And he knew he must hide that hunger to maintain his leverage. He had to present their liaison as a mutually beneficial partnership. "I assure you that it is not my intent to make you a pawn. Perhaps I should inform you that I know the contents of Huxley's will."

She frowned. "That's not possible."

"Miss Madison, I have spent the better part of the

last fifteen years plotting Huxley's downfall. You can be certain that I am well informed about his personal affairs. I have seen the terms of the will." He decided against telling her of the letter Howard had written him in the closing days of his life. He had received the cursed thing mere hours after Howard's death.

"But his solicitors promised—"

"They lied."

He waited for her to absorb the impact of the statement. "I see," she said quietly.

"So I know that he left you his entire estate except for Huxley House, which went to his nephew, Carlton, who also got the title, of course. And I know that Carlton and his mother, Millicent, have vowed to take you through the courts to challenge your right to the inheritance. It has left you in a desperate situation, and Huxley must have anticipated what would happen. Even he could not have been so dull-witted as to believe that Carlton and Millicent would simply allow you to control Howard's business holdings."

"That was not his intent."

"You think not?"

"I know not."

"Would you care to elaborate?"

"No. That is my secret, and mine alone. If your sources haven't revealed it to you, then I shan't either."

He conceded the point. "Well done, Miss Madison. I see you have mastered the art of negotiation."

"I learned it from Huxley. Even you must concede that his lordship was something of an expert in the game."

"That he was. However, given the predicament he has placed you in, why you should maintain any degree of loyalty to him is beyond me, I confess." He leaned closer so he could smell her delicate scent. "But I will tell you this. If you accept my proposal, I have but two requests. First, I will expect—no, demand—your complete and total integrity. While I am not particularly concerned with gossip, neither do I choose to provoke it. I prefer my solitude, and I do not enjoy having the eyes of Society prying into my affairs."

"And second?"

"Second, I want the Cross of Aragon."

She glanced at him sharply. "The Cross of Aragon?"

"Yes. You must know that I have made several attempts to purchase it."

"And you are convinced that it is part of Huxley's personal collection?"

"Utterly convinced. Each time my sources turned up a lead on its whereabouts, it always pointed directly to Huxley."

"There are many experts who don't believe it even exists, you know. It is questionable whether Catherine of Aragon actually possessed the cross, or if its existence sprang from and is part now of mere legend."

"It's real." As always, a surge of rage pumped through him when he considered the way Howard had toyed with him. For years, Elliot had pursued the Cross of Aragon with a single-minded determination. It meant more to him than Liberty could know—or imagine. It represented his final victory over a man who had spent fifteen years trying to destroy him. The thought of how close he was to possessing it made him light-headed. "I repeat, it is real, and Huxley owned it."

"What would you say if I told you that I am certain the item is not in his collection?"

"That you haven't looked hard enough. I have irrefutable proof that the cross is somewhere in Huxley House." He tried to tamp down the slightly fevered note that had entered his voice. "And I mean to have it."

"At any cost."

"At the cost of marriage at the very least."

"I see. And those are your only terms?"

"They are."

"I would assume, also, that you would appreciate as little trouble from me as possible."

"That would prove beneficial but unnecessary. I believe we will get on well together, Miss Madison. If you put behind you the notion I was Huxley's adversary in life, I think you will find we have much in common."

"That may be true, but still, I have some terms of my own."

"And what would those be, besides, of course, protection from Carlton's legal threats?"

"I have thought this through quite carefully."

Elliot felt a surge of satisfaction as he saw the way her shoulders squared with determination. Liberty Madison was an amazing woman, and very soon, she'd be his. With uncharacteristic benevolence, he prepared to offer her the world. "What is it you want from me, Miss Madison?"

"I would have three things, my lord. First, I'd like your promise that I may continue to direct Howard's business affairs, such that they fall to me, without your interference."

"Done."

She blinked. "No argument?"

"None. I have no interest in Howard's affairs." He didn't bother to tell her that he had intervened on her behalf nearly a dozen times since Howard's death, reassuring creditors who were uneasy with the idea of conducting business directly with a woman—and especially the woman who was said to have been Huxley's mistress. Associates whose continued support was critical to several of Howard's key investments had required a bit of salving lest they pull their funds and seek opportunities elsewhere. Liberty had proven during her association with Huxley that she had a sounder mind for business than most men he knew, so he saw no reason at all why he couldn't keep his word.

She, on the other hand, seemed a bit flustered by his ready acceptance. "I expected you to argue."

"One thing you will no doubt learn, Miss Madison, is that I rarely do what people expect."

"So I've heard."

"That resolved, there are two other issues?"

"Yes. The second is more—personal."

Only the slight way she shifted in her seat betrayed her discomfort to him.

"I would like your promise that in the event our marriage should end, for any reason, you will place five thousand pounds in an account in my name that I may have sole access to those funds for my personal use."

He could see what the request cost her. Her pride balked at asking for the money, yet her instinct for survival prompted the demand. She was in this particular dilemma because of Howard's will; understandably, she didn't wish to find herself there again. He nodded briefly. "Done."

She frowned at him. "You are being extraordinarily amenable, my lord. I am beginning to wonder if I am asking enough of you."

"You would prefer that I argue?"

"No. I am simply disconcerted by your easy acquiescence."

"Don't be alarmed. I am on the very cusp of having my own way. It tends to make me a bit giddy."

She couldn't possibly know the effect the conversation was having on him. Satisfaction was thundering through him like a torrent. At that instant, she could request the moon and he would vow to get it for her.

"Very well, then, that brings me to my third request. This is somewhat awkward for me, and I would beg you to have patience as I explain it."

He lifted his eyebrows but didn't comment. Liberty's fingers twisted the ties of her reticule so tightly, he thought she might snap them off. "You indicated in your note," she said, "that you anticipated our marriage to be a business arrangement. I would like to know precisely what you mean by that."

"What specifically are you concerned about?"

She held his gaze. "My concern, my lord, is whether or not you would expect the physical nature of our liaison to be in keeping with the standards of marriage."

With some effort, he hid his smile. "Ah."

"I do not find this at all amusing."

"I'm certain you don't."

"I assume, of course, that one day you will require an heir. I feel I should make it perfectly clear that I would view any contract between us as a strictly temporary agreement. Given that, I don't feel it would be appropriate for us to conduct a relationship that may have permanent ramifications."

"Ramifications like children?"

"Precisely."

"I see."

"I'm not sure you do." She drew a deep breath. "I am not unaware of the ways of the world. I have a very healthy understanding of how these things work."

As usual, he had to repress his anger at the thought of just where, and from whom, she'd received her education.

"And while I know that there are certain ways that may be employed to prevent the conception of a child, that is not my concern."

He was finding he didn't like the course of the conversation. The methodical way she spoke about her previous experience set his teeth on edge. Steadying his temper, he pressed on. "Are you asking if I would expect my husband's rights from you?"

"I am."

He paused to consider his next words. He had every intention of taking Liberty Madison to his bed. Once she was his wife, living beneath his roof, he would enjoy more than a simple business relationship with her. He felt certain she was a woman of extraordinary passions. She was not, as she'd so calmly stated, some inexperienced schoolgirl. She knew quite well the ways between men and women, and he saw no reason at all to deny himself the full enjoyment of her skills.

He realized, however, that the point was crucial to her. Her response to his proposal could hinge on his answer. Carefully, he said, "Madam, I would be lying if I did not say that I believe some level of mutual pleasure will come from our marriage. While you will have the option of ending it once you have procured the cross for me, I will not require that you do so."

"You won't?"

"No. I am in need of an heir, of course, and begetting an heir, as you well know, requires a wife. I see no reason at all why you won't suit me very well in that capacity."

"Do you mean to say that you envision our marriage as a more permanent arrangement?"

"My dear Miss Madison, you realize of course that marriages are not easily dissolved. As long as you and I enter the arrangement with a very healthy understanding of our own expectations, I see no reason at all why we can't forge a perfectly amicable future for ourselves."

She stared at him. "So you do not view this as a business arrangement at all?"

"On the contrary. A marriage is very much like a business partnership. It involves two willing adults who make a decision to begin a venture together. In large part, the success or failure of that venture depends on the attitudes and commitments of its participants."

"I see."

"You are correct when you say that children would greatly complicate the matter should you wish to end our relationship once you've given me the Cross of Aragon and I have solved your legal dilemma. I am therefore prepared to promise you that I will not rush you into childbed."

Liberty searched his face. "I will need your word as a gentleman that I may rely on you."

"You have my word of honor. I will take nothing from you that isn't offered."

She stilled. "Offered?"

He nodded slightly. "Were you not aware of a certain level of—tension—between us, I do not think you would have requested this promise. Still, I have given you my word. So long as you wish it, I will not force my attentions on you."

Liberty relaxed visibly. "Thank you."

"Have we covered all your concerns, Miss Madison?"

"The greater ones, yes. I would like to thank you for your patience."

"My pleasure."

"Would it be possible to have these terms drawn up in a contract?"

"I shall have it done before the end of the week."

At that, she studied him for long seconds. "You are willing to go to these great lengths simply to own the Cross of Aragon?"

"In order to fully understand, I think you must see the crosses in my collection. I would offer to show them to you tonight, but I believe you may have stayed as long as you dare. It won't be long before Carlton and Millicent notice your absence, will it?"

"No."

"Then please allow me to escort you back to your hack." He rose, then offered her his arm. "I think once you've considered all that's transpired here this evening, Miss Madison, you'll find that you've put yourself in a very fine position."

She hesitated for long seconds before she slipped her hand onto his arm. "I hope so."

"You will," he assured her. "And if you will pay me a visit early next week, I will give you the contract you've requested and acquaint you with my collection."

Slowly, she withdrew her hand. "I cannot risk being seen coming and going from your home."

"You are a woman of extraordinary intelligence and talent. If you wish to see me, you'll find a way."

"I'm not certain whether I should feel flattered or insulted."

"I would never insult my future wife, I assure you." He looped his fingers beneath her elbow and guided her down the darkened path.

"Very well, my lord. I shall arrange to visit you early next week."

"Good." He stopped when they reached the narrow gate, and nudged her chin until she faced him. "A small bit of advice." His hand still cradling her jaw, he gazed into her eyes. "In future negotiations, never underestimate your value." He swept his thumb over the crease between her lips. "You could have had the world."

Chapter 2

The world, she thought, would have been considerably easier to manage than the small empire Howard had bequeathed her.

She drew a deep breath as she faced the crowd in the auction house. The past few days had been a nightmare of crises and conflicts. Between Carlton's open scorn, Millicent's animosity, and the distrust of Howard's business associates, she'd worn herself ragged trying to appease all of them. It didn't seem to matter a whit to Howard's solicitors that creditors wished to be paid or that other contractual obligations had to be fulfilled; they refused to give her support, cooperation—or even civility.

Elliot Moss looked more appealing with each passing day. His proposal certainly offered her a solution to a vast array of problems. For the thousandth time, she suppressed a wave of melancholy when she thought of Howard and the predicament he'd left her. Making business decisions for him behind the scenes was one thing. The idea of a woman running his business openly was something else indeed. With the terms of his will, he'd practically ensured that she'd have no choice but to marry Carlton.

Though Carlton seemed to despise Liberty, marrying her would save him from the scandal of a long court battle and give him complete and immediate access to the assets that Howard had left her. And the law gave him the right to simply tuck her away in the country, where she'd be no bother to him. He would be able to afford to continue living the dissolute life he'd chosen.

Only Elliot Moss stood in the way of her complete despair.

Putting aside her oppressive thoughts, she pushed open the door of the Catheson, Ramsey & Bates auction house and stepped into the chaos.

"Miss Madison." Edgar Catheson descended on her like a bird of prey. "We've a bit of a problem."

She suppressed a bitter smile. "Only one? That's encouraging, isn't it?" Two workmen passed with an inlaid desk precariously balanced on its side. "Gentlemen, please. That needs to be carried upright. And do take better care to not scratch the finish." She waited while they made adjustments, then turned back to Edgar. "What seems to be the trouble, Mr. Catheson?"

He settled his hands on the brocade waistcoat that covered his considerable girth. "It seems the late earl's solicitors are questioning the necessity of selling the contents of the East Haven warehouse and the Edge Street office. Mr. Hatfield is provoking my staff in the showroom, and, as you well know, we cannot release the items for sale without the approval of the estate executors."

"Then perhaps Mr. Hatfield would like to explain just how I am to settle current payroll obligations when he has impounded the cash reserves." She winced when she heard the loud *thunk* of wood on wood in the distance.

He cleared his throat. "I wouldn't know."

"No. I don't suppose you would." She briefly shut her eyes in weary frustration. "Please keep the workmen from damaging the items. I will speak with Mr. Hatfield."

"There is one other matter, Miss Madison."

She glanced at him. "Yes?"

"If the auction does not proceed, we shall have to reach some agreement on the settlement of our bill. We've had the items in storage for several days now, and we'll need to be compensated."

"Naturally." She would have moved past him then, but a shadow from the doorway arrested her attention.

"Mr. Catheson." The unmistakable sound of Elliot's voice seemed to still the turbulence in the large room. "I'm delighted to be doing business with you once more."

At Elliot's arrival, Edgar's countenance brightened

noticeably. "Your lordship! We're pleased as ever to have you as a client."

"Are you?" He glanced around the room. "There are several pieces here I want, but I fear I heard you mention that there may not be a sale."

Edgar looked flustered. "It's just a small matter that needs to be resolved, my lord. I'm certain that arrangements can be made."

Liberty gave Elliot a direct look. "William Hatfield, Howard's solicitor, claims that I've no right to sell the contents of the warehouse or the office, and is intent on stopping the sale. As I do not have access to the cash holdings of the estate, I need the receipts from the sale to enable the paymaster to meet our obligations."

Liberty watched, fascinated, as Edgar sputtered. To the best of her knowledge, she'd never actually witnessed a person sputtering until that moment. Elliot studied the auctioneer with a raised eyebrow. "I'm certain you didn't intend to intimate that you wouldn't proceed with the sale per the terms of the agreement. Did you, Edgar?"

"Of course not, your lordship. But if Mr. Hatfield—"

Elliot shifted forward so he loomed over Edgar. "As it happens, I have spoken with Mr. Hatfield. He's quite pleased that I offered such a handsome sum for the escritoire and seems ready now to proceed with the sale."

Liberty frowned at him. "I don't think—"

Edgar was already pumping Elliot's hand in a vigorous rhythm. "Delightful, delightful. I was quite sure the matter could be satisfactorily resolved. I'll just see to the final details before we begin."

Elliot extracted his hand. "I thought you might."

Liberty frowned at him as Edgar hurried across the room. "I was prepared to handle that."

"I'm sure you were."

"I asked you not to interfere."

"You asked that I not dictate how you settle your affairs. You didn't specify that I wasn't to assist."

The breath left her body in an exasperated sigh. "You knew what I meant."

Elliot glanced over his shoulder. "You're far too intelligent to be stubborn over such an inconsequential matter." When he turned to face her again, she couldn't help but notice the somewhat predatory gleam in his eyes. The light of morning, she decided, did little to diminish his commanding presence. Immediately, her mind fled to the instant near the garden gate when he'd touched her face with those surprisingly gentle fingers. The skin tingled there as she thought of it.

He gave her a shrewd look. "I need a brief word with you."

She hesitated. "I thought you wanted to bid on several items in the sale."

"I've promised Edgar's partner more than their worth if he sets them aside for me. They won't be offered for general sale."

"Oh." Confused, she frowned at him. "So you were serious about the escritoire?"

"I was."

"What on earth do you want with it? It's a piece with scant value."

"You'll need it once we're wed. It was yours, wasn't it?"

"I don't think—"

He lifted his eyebrows. "Wasn't it?"

"Yes."

"Then that's why I wanted it. Now, will you come with me, or would you prefer to speak here?"

"We can't talk here." She glanced around the room. "People are watching us."

Or rather, she thought, they were looking at him. A flawlessly tailored green jacket set off his broad shoulders, while his ivory brocade waistcoat and biscuit-colored trousers would only enhance his reputation for elegance. It didn't seem to matter that his attire was not the latest fashion. His clothes uniquely suited him. As in everything else, he forged his own path.

"We are rather interesting to the majority here. Come. I have arranged to use Jonathan Bates's office."

"Did you have to threaten him, as you did William Hatfield?"

"I rarely threaten. It's seldom necessary. I find that a simple expression of my likes and dislikes generally accomplishes my purpose."

She didn't doubt it. His eyes, the uncanny green of a predator's, seemed to assess every nuance of his opponent in a fashion that had been known to crumple lesser men. "That must be convenient."

"Exceedingly." He removed his watch from his waistcoat pocket and studied the face. "The sale is about to begin. I can't think of a better time for us to slip away."

"You can't?" Her gaze remained riveted to his hands. She had seen him many times in the past when she accompanied Howard, and Elliott's hands had always entranced her. Long fingers, large palms that she'd seen hold a treasured object with a tenderness he seemed to reserve for the inanimate. Her flesh quivered at the thought of what they might feel like against her bare skin. His ability to make her heart flutter and her stomach turn upside down had disconcerted her. But she saw him so rarely, and even then only in public amidst a crowd of Howard's business associates, that she stopped worrying about having to mask her reaction to him.

Until he'd asked her to marry him.

He seemed unaware of her tension. "We won't be missed if we leave now." He pressed a key into her palm. "This is the key to Jonathan Bates's office. I'll meet you there in a few minutes."

Her fingers closed on the cold metal. Conscious that she shouldn't agree, but somehow unable to deny him, she nodded. "All right." She turned to go.

"Miss Madison?" His deep voice stopped her.

"Yes, my lord?"

"Don't look so alarmed. I'm not the enemy."

She repeated those words to herself a dozen times as she paced the length of Jonathan Bates's well-appointed office. Darewood wasn't her enemy, it was true, but could she trust him? She still wasn't certain. Despite his ready agreement to her terms for marriage, she was ill-prepared to face him in the light of day, when the arresting expression in his gaze did so much to unnerve her.

In the darkened garden, he'd seemed daunting, but not intimidating. This morning, he scared the wits out of her. Granted, it was a tingly, almost anticipatory kind of scared she felt, but nonetheless, Elliot Moss was not a man to be trifled with. He knew what he wanted, and he took it for his own.

She had the feeling that she was being drawn deeper and deeper into a web of intrigue. Ever present in her mind was her certainty that the Cross of Aragon was not among Howard's catalogued possessions. There was the vaguest possibility that he had hidden it from her, but that seemed unlikely, absurd really. But to reveal her doubts to Elliot could spell disaster; she didn't want him to marry her thinking she could procure an item she was almost certain she could not. Escaping Carlton's trap, she knew, would do her no good if she simply stepped into another one.

She had realized after their conversation in his

garden that she'd been either arrogant or stupid to think she could have maneuvered with a man like Elliot Moss. He was legendary for his ruthlessness. And at the moment, he desperately wanted the Cross of Aragon.

If she married him knowing that the cross was not in her possession, she would be deliberately deceiving him. There was no telling what he might do when he found out. While she knew that life with Carlton Rendell might be intolerable, he, at least, was a familiar entity.

"Thank you for seeing me."

At the sound of Elliot's voice, she visibly started. "My lord, I wasn't expecting to see you today."

"No doubt." He studied her with a narrow gaze. "You haven't been eating."

At his blunt statement, she blinked. "I—I beg your pardon."

"You haven't been eating."

She hadn't thought about it. "That is possible, but it isn't something you need concern yourself with, I assure you."

"The fact is, Miss Madison, I find I am most concerned with nearly everything you do. You look dreadful."

"Thank you for the compliment."

He showed no reaction to her sarcasm. Instead, he studied her face. She had to fight the urge to hide. She knew that the lines of her chin were sharper than they had been, that her eyes appeared larger and dimmer in her pale face, and that her cheekbones were more pronounced. The severe black mourning clothes she'd taken to wearing after Howard's death did little for her complexion, and she was painfully aware of the lines that had begun to appear near her mouth and eyes.

"You *aren't* eating," he insisted. "Are you?"

She glanced away from him. "I seem to have lost my appetite. I hardly notice."

"I thought so." He lifted a hand to touch her hair. "Your face looks pale, the shine has left your hair, and your clothes are ill-fitting."

"My lord, I'm afraid I don't have time today for a discussion of my person. I assumed you had a reason for seeing me."

"I am concerned about you. How many times have you argued with Carlton and his mother in the past two weeks?"

Countless, she thought. The feel of his hand on her face was setting off its usual bevy of unwanted emotions. She managed to say, with an admirable level of calm, "That's not your affair."

Slowly, he lowered his hand. "Forgive me. I find that I am unable to idly watch men like Carlton Rendell succeed. It tends to irritate me."

"What do you normally do when you are irritated?"

"Under usual circumstances, I buy something."

She gave him a surprised look. "I do that, too."

"As you can see, we are eminently suited."

"Except that I tend to purchase some trinket such as a book or a ribbon. You, I would imagine, purchase some trifling item such as a locomotive."

"Same principle applies."

She regarded him for several seconds. "Was that the real reason you purchased the escritoire?"

"One of them."

"What do you do when you cannot find something you wish to buy?"

"I smoke a cigar."

"As I thought. Howard said that you had an annoying habit of lighting one during the stickiest of situations."

"I find that it disconcerts my adversaries."

"After you smoke the cigar, are you any less irritated?"

"Generally."

"Very well, then"—she extended her hand—"I would like one." Somehow, his damnable self-control was making her nervous. She could not resist the opportunity to put him slightly off balance.

Elliot's eyebrows lifted. "One what?"

"A cigar, of course. I am finding this entire discussion enormously frustrating. You have yet to tell me what your purpose is for this meeting, and as I am not in a position to make a purchase so long as William Hatfield continues to exercise his control over my finances, I will have to find another solution. I am prepared to try yours."

He was laughing at her. She knew it. Somehow,

the notion goaded her more than nearly anything else could. She'd handled too many of his self-impressed sort in recent weeks to simply back down. She'd seen Howard smoke the wretched things hundreds of times. Surely one cigar would not hurt her.

Without comment, he reached into his jacket pocket and removed his cigar case. Snapping it open, he extracted one for himself, then extended it to her. "Help yourself."

"Thank you." She selected one from the case.

He slipped the case back into his pocket. "Would you like me to snip the end for you?"

"That won't be necessary." She bit off a good-sized chunk and spat it into the silver smoking cup on Bates's desk. "I'm aware of the procedure."

Elliot produced his silver matchbox and lit her cigar, then his. He took a long draw of the mellow tobacco as he watched her take her first puff. She cursed the sudden watering of her eyes and made a valiant effort not to cough. Damnation, the things were every bit as putrid as she had suspected.

With Elliot's narrow-lidded gaze trained on her face, she struggled for poise. He took a long draw of his cigar, then released the pungent smoke in a cloud. "I have found," he said, "that there is nothing like a cigar to encourage shared confidence."

A cough escaped her. She felt her eyes turning red. "Shared confidence?" Her voice sounded strangled.

"Yes. I find that cigars build a certain camaraderie that can be invaluable in a successful negotiation." He flicked his ashes into the bowl. "Don't you?"

She watched his fingers glide along the length of the smooth brown tobacco, then hastily drew another puff. After two sputtering coughs, she choked out, "Certainly." Her skin had turned parchment white.

"So, now that I have your undivided attention"— he waved his smoldering cigar at her—"I would like to speak to you about the timeliness of our agreement."

Another cough squeezed from her chest.

"I have spent the last several days examining your financial situation."

She wasn't certain whether the lurching sensation in her stomach owed more to the cigar or his announcement.

"And I have concluded that you and I should execute our agreement as quickly as legally possible."

"What do you mean?"

"I originally assumed you would wish to wait a respectable amount of time before we were wed."

"Of course. I am in mourning."

"But you aren't an immediate family member."

"Nevertheless, I feel that we should wait at least six months." Tears now stung her eyes from the acrid smoke.

"I'm afraid that's out of the question. Having

seen the state of your finances, I think we have no choice but to proceed immediately."

"I won't agree to that."

"Damnation, Liberty." He took a determined step forward. "I had no idea Howard had left you in such a state. There aren't even sufficient unhindered reserves to make it to the end of the month, are there?"

"The auction will help."

He ignored her. "I had believed, perhaps foolishly, that the power of my name would carry you through if we announced our engagement, but I have reevaluated my position since we last spoke."

"I don't recall inviting you to study my affairs."

He swore beneath his breath. "I don't recall asking your permission. Since you agreed to marry me, I considered it my responsibility to investigate quite carefully what was afoot. I knew you were in difficult straits. I'd already been asked by several of Huxley's associates to intervene on their behalf."

She stared at him. "You had?"

"Yes. But I had no idea the bastard had left you so desperate. You can't survive another two weeks without ending up in court. Howard's creditors are on your heels like a pack of hungry dogs. Why the bloody hell didn't you tell me yourself, rather than letting me hear it from my solicitors?"

She blinked several times. Through the hazy smoke in the room, he looked every inch an avenging angel. His dark hair, longer than fashion allowed, framed angular features that were set in an impressive imitation of granite. "I'm surviving," she muttered.

"You're drowning." He took another step toward her. "Let me help you."

"I don't need help."

Again, he uttered a dark curse. "Don't push me, Liberty. I don't want to force your hand, but if you make me, I will. You have my word on that."

Before she could answer, the door swung open and three gentlemen entered the room. Liberty quickly hid her smoldering cigar behind her back.

Garrick, the youngest of the three, looked from Elliot to Liberty, then back. "There you are, Darewood," he said. "We thought you'd left."

"Miss Madison and I were discussing a business matter, Garrick." Elliot moved away from her. "We had just finished. Liberty, allow me to introduce Sir Garrick Frost." He indicated the other two men with his hand. "These gentlemen are Owen Pickford and Randolph Collington."

Owen coughed as he bowed. The situation, she knew, was enough to shock the poor man to the tips of his ill-polished shoes. Finding Elliot Moss alone with a woman he believed to be Howard Rendell's former mistress would give fodder to the gossips for weeks. Garrick Frost, she knew from experience, was one of Elliot's closest friends. Elliot might trust him, but both Pickford and Collington were notorious rumor hounds.

Pickford looked curiously at Liberty, then back at Elliot. "They've sold off most of the quality goods. We were planning to head to Blickley's for luncheon and thought you might like to come along."

"So I would." Elliot exhaled a long puff of smoke in Liberty's direction. The acrid scent filled the air. "As I said, we were finished. Isn't that right, Miss Madison?"

As the smoke from his cigar encircled her, she felt her stomach clench again. This time, she was fairly certain it owed more to her horror at being caught in so compromising a position than to the tobacco. "Yes," she said in a choked voice. "Yes, we were finished."

Elliot produced his cigar case. "Perhaps you gentlemen would like to join me for a cigar before we leave?" He glanced at Liberty. "I'm certain Miss Madison won't mind."

Liberty gave Elliot an angry glance. She wondered if its severity was dimmed by the greenish cast she suspected was beginning to tint her skin. "My time is short, your lordship. I'm afraid I won't be able to stay."

Elliot exhaled another puff of smoke in three deliberate rings. "Nonsense. I don't expect this to take long. If you wait a few more minutes, I will see you safely settled in your carriage. I assume you didn't intend to stay for the entirety of the sale." Garrick was obviously struggling to hide his

amusement. Elliot waved the case in his direction.
"Frost, would you care for one?"

Liberty stifled a distressed moan. She was sure
that the additional smoke would finish her off.
Elliot calmly waited while each of the men selected
a cigar, then lit them in turn. In seconds, a fog of
tangy smoke settled on the room. Liberty began to
breathe shallowly as she tried to control the roiling
in her belly.

The gentlemen were laughing at a particularly
amusing story Garrick was relating when Elliot
moved closer to Liberty.

Swiftly, he crushed his cigar in the silver
smoking bowl, then anchored her shoulders in his
large hands. The scent of the crushed tobacco
swirled around them in a thick cloud. "You are
beginning to look a bit green, Miss Madison. I fear
you have contracted one of the illnesses that is so
common in London this time of year."

Owen abruptly stopped laughing. He glanced at
Liberty. "Dear lord, she does look a bit peaked."

Liberty glared at Elliot. "Do not be absurd. I am
quite well."

Elliot gave her a knowing look. "You're sure? I
don't think you look well at all." He nodded toward
the three men. "Gentlemen, what do you think?"

Garrick nodded. "You're right, Darewood. The
lady looks ill."

"You see," Elliot continued smoothly. "We are in
agreement."

"I feel perfectly well," she said through clenched teeth.

With one hand, he ground his cigar butt in the bowl again, sending another burst of scent into the air. She could not quite stifle her moan. "I think not, Miss Madison. I think you are dangerously close to a serious loss of your faculties. I believe the stress of the entire situation has done you in, so to speak."

She sagged against the desk. "It's not the stress, you idiot." She said the words beneath her breath so only he could hear them. An ominous-sounding gurgle forced itself from her chest. "It's the cigar."

"The cigar?" He tightened his grip. "You mean to say the tobacco was rancid?"

Liberty leaned toward him in defeat. "If I admit that I have never tasted a cigar before, will you please let me escape?"

"I am surprised, Miss Madison. Do you mean to say that you requested a cigar merely to shock me?"

She met his gaze with bleary eyes. "Do stop teasing, my lord. I fear I will soil your clothes."

With a soft smile of reassurance, he glanced at the three men. "Gentlemen, you can see that I need to escort Miss Madison to her carriage. She is not well."

"I came in a hack," she whispered.

"On second thought," he said without looking at her, "I think she'll be more comfortable in my coach. Frost, may I rely on you for a ride home?"

"Naturally."

"Pickford," Elliot continued, "will you please find my footman and have him tell my driver—"

"Of course, of course. I'll have your carriage brought round back." Owen hastened to stamp out his cigar in the silver bowl.

"Excellent. Collington, please alert Edgar Catheson that Miss Madison has returned home to Huxley House. He may forward the paperwork to her there. As soon as I see Miss Madison settled, I'll join you at Blickley's."

"Certainly, Darewood." The two men hurried from the room.

The moment the door closed behind them, Garrick gave up the fight with his laughter. Elliot sent him a censorious glance. "It is unchivalrous to delight in the lady's distress, Frost."

"Forgive me, Miss Madison," Garrick said. "But I think perhaps it's time you knew that there's a steady stream of smoke rising behind your head."

With a groan, Liberty produced the cigar from behind her back. Elliot pried it from her fingers and extinguished it in the bowl. "You're a wretched man," she told him.

"Undoubtedly true, but you challenged me. That always has consequences."

"I most certainly did not challenge you."

"You did. You deliberately goaded me by suggesting I had no right to be concerned about your health."

"And you goaded me by trying to bully me into

giving you your way. Had you not been so thick-headed, I would have explained that I had already reached much the same conclusion based on the threat I received yesterday afternoon."

He went utterly still. "What threat?"

She studiously ignored him. "It is plain to me now that I erred in thinking I could depend on you to help me reason through it. All you wished to accomplish this morning was to embarrass me with that horrid cigar and bully me into a hasty decision."

Elliot's fingers clamped onto her shoulders. "Liberty, stop prattling."

Garrick took the seat across from her. "Who threatened you?"

Elliot seemed to struggle with his temper. "It was Carlton Rendell, wasn't it? Damn the bastard. I'll—"

She looked from Elliot to Garrick, then back again. "I'm not sure who it was, or what it meant. I received a note."

Elliot extended his hand. "Give it to me, please."

"What makes you think I brought it with me?"

"You've been clutching your pocket all morning. I wondered what you had in there." He wiggled his fingers. "I want the note."

"Why should I let you have it?"

"Because we're going to be married—as quickly as possible, I might add—and therefore, your personal safety is now my responsibility." He paused. "Will you feel safe if you return to Huxley House?"

"It's not that type of threat. I don't think anyone means to do me physical harm."

"All right. But be aware that Thomas Adley is on my books."

"The footman?"

"Yes. If you need anything, you may depend on him."

"I cannot believe you have one of Howard's footmen on your books."

He gave her a wry look. "How else do you think I kept abreast of Howard's business?"

"Good God, Darewood, have you no principles at all?"

"None. Now, give me the note."

She hesitated for several seconds, then finally, muttering about his proprietary behavior beneath her breath, she produced a folded piece of parchment and handed it to him.

"Thank you." He deftly pocketed it.

"Aren't you going to read it?"

"First, I'm going to send you home." He glanced at Frost. "Garrick and I will get to the bottom of it, I assure you."

"I don't need you to take care of me, Darewood."

"Then all the more reason to let me." He slipped his hand beneath her elbow. "Now come on. It's time to send you home."

Garrick and Elliot supported her elbows as she

stood. Liberty groaned. Loudly. "I should hate you for this."

Elliot brushed her hair back from her face. "I offered you the cigar to see if you could be baited, not to make you sick."

"And I took it to shock you." She swayed a little as another wave of nausea threatened to overwhelm her.

"You'll soon learn that I'm very hard to shock." Without waiting for her response, he scooped her into his arms to carry her from the office.

"My lord," she said in soft remonstrance, "I must insist that you put me down. I'm perfectly capable of walking."

Garrick took her auction records from the desk. "You'll also have to learn that Darewood seldom does what he's told."

Elliot moved swiftly through the back door of the auction house, where Pickford had his coach standing. He waited while his footman jumped down to open the door and lower the steps. Turning to Garrick, he said, "I'll be back in a moment. Ask Henry to take us around the block." Carefully, he settled Liberty on the seat, then joined her in the close confines.

Garrick handed her belongings to Elliot. "Do you want me to speak to Pickford and Collington?"

Liberty nodded. She knew if Elliot demanded it, he could stop the story from spreading.

He didn't seem so inclined. "No. It's not necessary."

"Whatever you say, Darewood." Garrick shut the door before he relayed Elliot's instructions to his driver. Finally, Elliot relaxed against his seat by propping his booted feet on the bench next to Liberty. "Feeling better?" he asked.

She glared at him. "You know very well that I'm not."

Elliot unlatched the small coach window and swung it open. "The air will help."

She tipped her head back against the carriage wall. "Undoubtedly."

"Now, suppose you tell me what you know about this note." He pulled it from his pocket and read it. Cold fury swept through him as his eyes focused on the sprawling script.

"I know nothing at all about it. No member of the staff seems to know who delivered it or when. I received it yesterday afternoon." She passed a hand over her damp forehead. "I thought perhaps you might have some ideas about it."

He glanced at her through narrowed eyes. "Do you think I sent it?"

The question surprised her. "Don't be ridiculous. You would never resort to a cheap, dramatic trick. If you wanted to threaten me, you'd do it in person."

"I'm glad you have such a high opinion of my character," he said.

"I meant it as a compliment. I've no stomach for

subterfuge." The coach hit a particularly nasty rut, and Liberty groaned when it lurched sideways. "Or cigars, it would appear."

Elliot made a sound in the back of his throat as he shifted to sit next to her. "Place your head on your knees," he suggested. "It will help relieve your sickness." With firm pressure at the base of her neck, he guided her into position. "I am sorry I caused you discomfort."

"You are not."

He rubbed his thumb along the spot where her neck became her shoulder. "I assure you, I had no intention of making you ill."

"You must have known what would happen."

"I didn't. I was intrigued, I'll admit, by the notion that perhaps you'd smoked one before. I found the picture irresistible."

"And, of course, you didn't anticipate at all that we would be discovered."

He paused. "I suspected we might."

"It doesn't bother you one whit that the story will be in every drawing room in town by this evening?"

"I learned long ago not to concern myself with the work of idle tongues. Society will gossip. It's a sport as old as time. I'd rather give them something real to gossip about than leave them to their own devices. Still," he continued in a softer tone, "the issue here is who has threatened you and why."

"I simply cannot understand it. No one would

have cause to send me that except you and Carlton. Since it is obvious that neither of you is to blame—"

"Why have you ruled out Rendell?"

"Because I live in his house. If he wished to terrorize me, I would hope he could think of something far more effective than an anonymous note. He could begin by locking me in my chamber and depriving me of meals, then work his way up from there."

That notion didn't sit well with Elliot. "Has he?"

She glanced at him in surprise. "Has he what?"

"Locked you in your room?"

"I am being dramatic, Darewood. I see you've no notion at all of how to recognize a jest."

"I don't find the notion of Carlton Rendell terrorizing you the least bit amusing." He squeezed her shoulder. "Are you feeling better?"

"Some. I do not think I shall be trying to smoke cigars again for some time."

"I'm glad to hear it. It's a nasty habit."

"I thought you said you found cigars advantageous for sharing confidences."

"I do. I do not, however, particularly care for the taste of them. The first time I smoked one I was thirteen, and I reacted as you did."

"So you knew precisely what it would do to me before you tricked me into smoking it?"

"I didn't trick you, Liberty. I preyed on your weakness for a challenge."

She managed a slight laugh. He was really quite

charming when the mood suited him. "Match conceded, Darewood. Next time, I'll know to be more careful."

"I doubt it." He tempered the comment with a slight lift of his eyebrows. "But I would confess that I am not immune to the folly of accepting challenges."

"It comforts me to know you have at least one fault."

"I assure you, I have a quantity of faults." He glanced out the window to see they were turning the corner. "If you are feeling sufficiently restored, I'll leave you when Henry completes the block. He will see you safely delivered home."

She sat up. "I'll be fine, I assure you. You needn't concern yourself."

"Don't be ridiculous. You've been threatened. Of course I'm concerned."

She couldn't quite mask her relief. "Thank you, Darewood."

The carriage rolled to a stop. Elliot waited until his footman opened the door, then climbed down and turned to give her hand a final squeeze. "I will get to the bottom of this. You have my word."

"Thank you, my lord. I'll be by at the beginning of next week to pick up the contract."

Chapter 3

Liberty stared at the door knocker to Elliot's town house. Wryly, she remembered reading a Christmas serial by the popular author Charles Dickens. She'd been looking at Elliot's door for so long, she almost expected Howard's face to loom out of it spouting warnings like Scrooge's Jacob Marley. At the image, she managed a small chuckle. If Howard knew she was standing on the threshold of Elliot's home, and in fact was planning to marry him, he would die all over again.

If she had hesitated at all, her resolve had been strengthened that morning when she'd found Carlton Rendell unconscious in a chair in the foyer. One look at his florid face and too-soft features had made her shudder. He'd spent his evening, no doubt, in some gaming hell or brothel with his disreputable companions, bragging about his sudden change of fortune. He was certain that she would marry him. He'd offered her marriage or a court battle. Both had seemed like death sentences.

45

The thought drew her hand to the door knocker.

Elliot answered the door himself scant seconds later. Standing at the entrance of his home, like a lion protecting his pride, he had the same predatory look he'd given her at the auction house. "Good morning," she managed to say.

He glanced over his shoulder at his butler, an aging man who hurried forward as he straightened his coat. "Never mind, Wickers. I'll take care of it."

The flustered-looking butler skidded to a stop. "I'm sorry, your lordship. I was conferring with Cook on the menu for the day." He slid a censorious look at Liberty. "I wasn't expecting guests so early in the morning."

Elliot's firm mouth seemed to curve at the corner. "I was," he assured the butler. "And not to worry. I'll escort the lady to my study."

Wickers was either too well-trained, or too accustomed to his employer's eccentricities, to comment on the extraordinary nature of the encounter. As if he found it perfectly normal for his employer to answer his own door at an unorthodox hour of the morning, he gave Elliot a slight nod. "Very good, sir. I assume salmon bisque is satisfactory for this evening's first course?"

Elliot continued to study Liberty with an unsettling look in his vivid green eyes. "That'll be fine, Wickers. Thank you." He waited until his butler disappeared down the hall before he stepped back to allow Liberty entrance to his home. "I'm glad you're here."

"Am I too early?" She stepped warily across the threshold.

"No. I've just finished reviewing the contract." He studied her with a shrewd look. "You've had no difficulty since the other day?"

"None. Carlton and his mother have been out quite a bit. They hardly seem to notice my presence." Slowly, she pushed her black veil away from her face and looked at him. She wondered when she'd get used to the effect he had on her senses. His hair, not quite black and not quite brown, was freshly washed and still damp. Unless she missed her guess, he'd risen early to exercise—most likely to ride—that morning. He seemed a man as fastidious in his toilet as in all other matters. He would bathe after vigorous exercise. She found the notion pleasing.

She became suddenly aware of the long silence that had ensued, and, uncomfortable, she glanced around for a means of conversational escape. Her gaze found the large marble statue in the center of the foyer. "That's a lovely piece," she commented. "Howard always admired it."

"Thank you. It's one of my favorites." He indicated a set of doors with a wave of his hand. "As I assume you have limited time, I'd like to give you the contract now. We might as well discuss it in the library."

Feeling a vague sense of inevitability, Liberty took a deep breath as she stepped into his foyer.

He held out his hand. "Would you like me to take your cloak?" he asked.

Slowly, she unbuckled it. "Your solicitors must be quite efficient to have drawn up the contract so swiftly."

"I pay them to be efficient."

"Still, they cannot have enjoyed being pressed into so lengthy a task."

"To my knowledge, they haven't uttered a protest. Money, Miss Madison, is the greatest motivator in the world."

She handed him her cloak, then followed him to the library. The bitterness in his tone awakened a new fount of sympathy in her heart. She was beginning to suspect that Elliot Moss was a remarkable man whom the world had sorely mistreated. He deliberately sat apart from the world, protecting himself by isolating his life in his own self-created ivory palace. He'd built a kingdom and defied anyone to take it from him. Somewhere in the depths of her soul, a pain she recognized as deep empathy emerged to make her heart ache for him. How well she knew that feeling of utter isolation. And that feeling, that very certain and sure knowledge that Elliot Moss was, in his heart, a lonely man who needed someone to care for him, reached her as nothing else could. She was good at many things, but she was excellent at caring for people.

With a renewed sense of purpose, she preceded him down the corridor a few steps, then turned to face him. "You're a very strange man, Darewood."

He seemed to find the slight rebuke complimentary. "So I've been told," he said. "It's part of my allure."

"And no doubt part of your success." The remnant of Liberty's tension drained away suddenly. Elliot Moss had a way of making her feel as though she'd just unearthed a rare find or stumbled onto a scientific discovery. As much as she'd like to remain irritated with him, she couldn't. He had an uncanny ability to snuff out even her most ardent objections. His insistence that they hasten down the aisle should have infuriated her, but at the moment, she saw it only as the means of escape she so desperately wanted. If she managed to tell him she was uncertain she could procure the Cross of Aragon and still retain his promise to wed her, she'd feel that the victory of a thousand battles had been won.

He held open the door of the library for her. "Are you going to tell me how Carlton has been behaving since I last saw you, or will you make me smoke it out of you?"

She frowned. Smoke? How unchivalrous to refer to the cigar. "That wasn't nice."

"I'm hardly ever nice. And don't attempt to change the subject." He shoved open the door to his study at the far end of the library.

She sensed his determination. He wasn't going to

relent until she gave him what he wanted. With a disgruntled look, she said, "Very well. If you must know, he is bent on publicly humiliating me with his loose tongue and even looser morals. I found him passed out in the foyer yet again this morning, smelling like a brewery. I am certain he was with his friends last night and that I was the object of their scorn."

His gaze held hers. She saw the way the gold flecks in his eyes seemed to flicker, like candlelight, as he intently watched her expression. "It hurts you, doesn't it?" he said as he guided her into his study.

When the door clicked shut behind them, she turned to face him. "Of course. No one likes to be insulted."

"I understand."

"Do you? You didn't seem to understand it the other day. You made no attempt to cover up that unfortunate incident at the auction house. I think you're rather enjoying the gossip about me. So it is difficult for me to believe that you understand my anger at Carlton. His crime is no worse than yours."

"Bloody hell and damnation. I will not allow you to compare me with that imbecile. What I offered you was a perfectly reasonable business arrangement. Carlton is a lecherous drunk who is no better than his uncle."

"You see my dilemma. If I confide these things in you, they are destined to make you angry."

"What's making me angry is your insistence that

I am no better than Huxley in the way I've treated you."

Liberty studied him in the pale morning light. Had Carlton been in the room at that moment, she wasn't certain she could guarantee his safety. "But I agreed to *your* terms, my lord."

Briefly, his eyes narrowed as he watched her. Then he took a deep, cleansing breath. "So you did."

"I trusted you, not Carlton. So you must see that I've found something redeeming in you after all."

"I will try not to be flattered by your opinion of me."

"Oh, come now, Darewood, you cannot be unaware that I hold you in the highest possible esteem. I simply think that some of your opinions are a bit outdated, and I cannot resist the urge to educate you."

"I shall look forward to the process with the same enthusiasm I would reserve for having a tooth pulled."

Liberty laughed. "It won't be nearly as painful, I promise."

Elliot raked a hand over his face. "I concede the point, madam. Now if you've finished instructing me on my weaknesses, let me show you the crosses."

He strode across the room to unlock his safe. She watched as he removed a large velvet box from the interior. From what little of his home she'd seen on the way to his study, it was clear that his taste in decor was eclectic and complex.

It shouldn't have surprised her.

The large rooms seemed the perfect foil for his character. She'd caught glimpses of several of them as they'd passed down the long hall. Each had a distinctly separate color scheme. The foyer was a pristine black and white, dominated by an enormous white marble Greek sculpture. Shades of muted purple filled the parlor. The library was primarily blue. His study was brown. She glanced from the captain's desk to the inlaid bookcases to the Persian carpet. A pinkish brown, it was true, but still brown. Her mind drifted through the possibilities the large town house might contain. Inevitably, she wondered what colors a man like Elliot Moss would choose for his bedroom. Visions of red lacquer furniture and a crimson silk counterpane dashed through her mind. In seconds, her blush matched the very color she imagined his carpet to be.

Elliot set the velvet box down on his wide cherry desk, then indicated the clasp. "Open it," he invited.

She looked at him in surprise. "Are they all in there?"

"There are forty of them. Some are quite small. If they didn't fit in the box, I'd have a larger one made."

"No, that's not what I meant. I thought you would have at least some of them on display."

"They're quite valuable," he said. "I wouldn't

simply leave them out where they could be stolen or damaged."

"I didn't expect that you'd have them sitting out on your reading table, but I thought surely you'd at least have them in a case where you could look at them without bothering with your safe."

"I don't need to. I know what they look like."

"But don't you want other people to see them?"

"They're mine," he said with unmistakable finality.

Intrigued, she pursued the subject. "Of course they're yours. But I don't understand what good there is in a collection of things you have to keep locked in a safe."

"They last forever."

"And that's more important to you than their beauty or worth?"

"Beauty and worth fade. The crosses are made of precious metals and stones. They'll last forever. Even a fire couldn't destroy them."

"But what good is having something, even if it is forever, if you can't enjoy it?"

Elliot flipped open the catch on the box. "I didn't say I didn't enjoy them. The enjoyment is in the possession."

The statement gave her a rare insight into his enigmatic character. A driven man, his need to possess probably extended to nearly every level of his life. It was no wonder that his competition with Howard had been so fierce. They shared the trait.

With some difficulty, Liberty managed to turn her

attention from Elliot's bent head to the collection of jeweled crosses. With one of his long fingers, he traced the edge of a diamond-encrusted Maltese cross. She watched, riveted, as he circled a large ruby with his index finger. The sight of him caressing the stones sent forbidden heat coursing through her. When his fingertip slid slowly over the crest of the ruby, she had to shut her eyes briefly. As if he knew precisely what the lazy motion of his fingertip was doing to her, he gave her a look that could have melted an iceberg. Finally summoning her voice by dragging her gaze from his fingers, she said, "They're very impressive."

He picked up a particularly large cross and pressed it into her palm. "This one is the Cross of Dagmar." The cold metal contrasted sharply with his warm fingers against the flesh of her palm. "It's reported to contain a shard of Christ's Cross inside the gold."

"Do you think it does?" she asked, studying the contrast of his bronzed hand against hers.

Tracing the outline of the cross on her palm, Elliot shook his head. "If every supposed splinter of the Cross were authentic, we could build a bridge to the moon and back with them."

When he took the cross from her hand, his knuckle brushed the spot where her fingers joined her palm. Her hand was trembling when he replaced the Cross of Dagmar with one she recognized as an Egyptian ankh, easily identifiable by its rounded crest. The allure of the piece was unmistakably seductive. "Cleopatra?" she guessed.

He nodded. "A lover's gift from Mark Antony. He was evidently quite impressed with her charms."

Leave it to Elliot to bring seduction into the conversation, but she refused to falter beneath the challenge in his eyes. "I see. I suppose if her talent as a seductress was sufficient enough to bring the Roman emperor to his knees, it stands to reason that he would give her such a valuable gift."

"You think so?"

"Naturally."

"I imagine he enjoyed seeing it hang between her breasts."

Liberty fought for her composure. "He must have. She would have been bare above the waist, of course. I suppose that gave him sufficient view."

Elliot smiled. "It would depend, I imagine, on the length of the chain and the lady's proportions."

Damn him. Hastily, Liberty put the cross back in the box. "What about this one?" She pointed to a small silver pendant, praying she'd selected something less suggestive.

"Persian," he said. "The Persians worshiped Ahura Mazda, the angel or, some say, the principle of light and goodness, the creator of all things. To them, the shape of the cross symbolized a balanced life."

"So they aren't all Christian symbols?"

"No." He selected one made of bronze with an intricate design etched on the front. "This one, for example, is African. It comes from an ancient tribe in Kenya. The bronze is quite interesting. It's not indigenous to the area, and suggests far-flung trade, perhaps with the Phoenicians."

Intrigued, she peered into the cradle of his hand to study the markings. "Is it symbolic, or merely decorative?"

"Symbolic." He impaled her with his gaze. "For the Africans to whom it belonged the four tines of a cross represented the four seasons. The joining of the four seasons, of course, is universally the symbol of fertility. This one"—he pointed to the rings on each tine—"was probably part of a larger piece of adornment. Perhaps even a chastity belt of some kind."

Liberty gritted her teeth. "How very interesting."

When a spark of amusement flared in his eyes, she quickly averted her gaze back to the crosses. "But the largest crosses appear to be Christian. Is that correct?"

"Yes. The most impressive examples are the Christian ones. The Cross is so central to Christian theology, it's only natural that they would be magnificently crafted." He paused. "Like the Cross of Aragon."

Running her finger over the jagged edge of an emerald, she said, "That is what I wish to discuss with you." She picked up a topaz-and-opal cross and turned it over in her palm. "I debated whether or not to reveal this to you, but I do not think it

would be fair to you if I did not. I personally catalogued the library and all of Howard's possessions.
It's one of the many tasks I performed for him after
he hired me as Lady Rendell's companion. I have
kept the records completely up to date, and I have
never come across the Cross of Aragon or any reference to it among his things. I think he must have
sold it."

"He didn't. I would have known."

Setting the cross down, she looked at Elliot. "I
wasn't aware that you were omniscient, my lord.
Surely you don't expect me to believe that you
know *everything*."

"When it comes to the Cross of Aragon I do. Had
Howard made it available on the general market,
one of my buyers would have alerted me."

"Still, I don't believe it's there. As I said, I've
never seen it."

"Perhaps it's slipped your memory?"

Clearly, he had no idea how ludicrous the sugges-
tion was. "No. If the cross was there, I'd know."

"Carlton has already confessed to me that he
doesn't know where it is."

"You spoke with Carlton about this?"

"Naturally. I offered to buy the cross the day
Howard died."

"He didn't tell me."

"I didn't imagine he would. I do know, however,
that it didn't show up in any of the listings of the
estate's contents."

"That's because it isn't there." She pointed to the velvet box. "I wanted to see your collection this morning, just to assure myself I wasn't mistaken. There was a chance that I had seen the Cross of Aragon but had miscataloged it or not recognized it for what it was. Having seen these, I know that's not true."

"There must be over five thousand items in Howard's collection, plus the books," he persisted. "How do you know—"

"Seven thousand three hundred thirty-six," she said. "Seven thousand three hundred thirty-seven if you count the Louis the Fourteenth salt-and-peppers as two items."

If he was surprised at her abrupt answer, he didn't show it. "I see you keep a fairly exact count."

Liberty nodded, then said, "I have extraordinary recall. If the Cross of Aragon was in the library, I'd know." When Elliot said nothing, she examined the combination of garnets and sapphires in a large silver ankh.

After several long moments of silence, Elliot's hand covered hers. "What if I'm willing to risk that the cross is there?"

She fought the urge to yank her hand from his heated grasp. "You don't seem to understand. I don't forget anything once I've seen it."

"I believe you."

"In fact, there's not even a written copy of the

library inventory in existence. There's a rough ledger somewhere, but for the most part, I maintain it in my mind. Shakespeare's *The Tempest*, manuscript copy, item number seven hundred forty-three, shelf number M683.2. Like that."

"Very impressive," he said.

She gave him an exasperated look. "I'm trying to explain to you that the cross isn't there. It's just not possible."

"What if it's hidden?"

"Why would it be? If it's as valuable as you say, why wouldn't Howard keep it with the other collectibles in the library? It's the most secure place on the entire estate."

"Oh, I believe it's in the library. Hidden. All we have to do is find it."

"That's ridiculous. Why would Howard do that?"

"He liked to play games, Liberty." He looked at her for a moment, then strode around his desk and reached beneath the top drawer to activate a hidden spring. An inner drawer opened and he produced a folded piece of paper. "I received this shortly after Howard died."

Startled, she accepted the letter. "What is it?"

"Read it," he prompted softly.

She held his gaze a moment, then unfolded the note. The familiar scrawl of Howard's handwriting made her hands tremble. She almost felt his presence in the room. "This is from Howard," she said, surprised.

"So it is."

Something in the dark tone of his voice made an anxious knot form in her belly. Warily, she read the letter.

Darewood,

By now, I'm sure you've heard the happy news that I'm dead and buried. I'm sure your only regret is that you played no role in my demise. All my efforts at immortality, it seems, have failed. In the end, none of it really mattered. All that's left is a cold grave and the even colder knowledge that I carry with me the bitterness and anger of so many.

But if I have one comfort it is knowing that my task is not yet done. I have something you desire. You have, in fact, desired it from the beginning, and I know that Liberty's loyalty will keep it from you.

Had things been different, I suppose we might have been friends. Raise a cup for me now and again to acknowledge, at least, that I was your most worthy opponent.

Eternally yours,
Huxley

She felt the unwanted sting of tears as she stared at the paper. "I didn't know about this."

"I suspected as much."

She forced herself to look at him. "Is this why you proposed to me?"

"It is."

"I see."

"I doubt it."

"No, no. I do see. Howard is using me to exact his final revenge on you, and you are using me to exact your revenge on him. Where does that leave me?"

Elliot seated himself on the edge of his desk, then took both her hands in his. "It isn't like that."

"Isn't it? Can you honestly tell me that you'll have no satisfaction in denying Howard his dying wish?"

"I realize that you cared for the man, but the simple truth is, he liked to play games with the people around him." He paused, not allowing her to wiggle her fingers free from his grasp. His countenance had become somehow harder, colder. She watched, fascinated, as a myriad of emotions played across his stormy face. "But you needn't let him win, Liberty. If you felt he used you, then take control."

"Aren't you using me?"

"I, at least, have tried to be honest. I see our relationship as mutually beneficial. Howard left you with only one choice, and it's unthinkable."

"You mean, to marry Carlton to protect his business interests, don't you?"

"Why else would he have done what he did?"

The words wounded her as few others could. For weeks she'd avoided facing the idea that Howard might have structured his will the way he had to force her to marry Carlton. He must have known that the marriage would destroy her. That he would so deliberately ignore her needs to his own selfish ends wounded her heart. She had loved him in so many ways. Now, it seemed, none of her affection had been returned. And, suddenly, she no longer had the energy to care—not about any of it.

When she looked at Elliot, his tender expression nearly undid her. "Why does it have to be so hard?"

"It doesn't. You don't want Carlton Rendell, and Carlton Rendell doesn't want you. Although he's a fool." His grip tightened on her hands, and she took a stumbling step forward. "What man in his right mind wouldn't want you?"

"Elliot, I—"

He tugged at her captured hands, and before she had time to consider the consequences, she found herself wedged between his strong thighs. "Don't deny you want this, Liberty. I've sensed it in you from the beginning."

"I don't know what you think—"

"Every time I look at you, I want you." Slowly, Elliot laid her hands on his chest, then circled her waist with his arms. "Even from the start—the day I first saw you at that art auction with Huxley—I wanted you, and I have wanted you ever since."

"I've only seen you a handful of times, and on each occasion I was with Howard."

"It didn't matter. I felt the passion in you. I craved it. And you knew it, didn't you?"

"No, I—"

His hands tightened on her waist. "Did you know that each time I saw you, I could think of little else for days afterward?"

The question was too disconcertingly close to her own private thoughts. "Elliot—"

"Say it again," he prompted. "I like the way you say my name." He lowered his head until his face was mere inches from her own.

"Please, I don't think—"

"Ah, sweet Liberty. I see you're not quite ready to confess."

"There's nothing to—"

He silenced her by laying a finger on her lips. "Not to worry. I expect I'll drag it out of you one way or another. I'll look forward to the interrogation, too, I might add."

She pushed his hand from her face. "This is impossible."

"I'll make you forget him," he vowed. "I'll make you forget all of it."

"You can't."

He smiled then, a genuine smile of charm and seduction. The effect was devastating. She'd never seen his smile before, and when he gave it to her, it made the world grind to a sudden and crashing halt.

Beneath her, the floor moved. Her heart stopped beating. Her stomach fluttered. Her entire existence focused on the intensity in his gaze. "My dear Miss Madison, never underestimate me again. Carlton Rendell may not want you," he whispered, his breath a hot, moist caress against her face, "but I certainly do."

Chapter 4

He gave her less than half a second to absorb the blunt comment before he bent his head and captured her lips. She was every bit as soft and yielding as he'd known she would be. At first, he wasn't certain she'd respond to him. She stood perfectly still as he worked his mouth against hers. He lifted her hands and twined them around his neck, then pressed her body fully against the hard length of his own.

She responded instantly. Her head fit naturally into the curve of his shoulder. Her soft whimper drove him immediately to the edge of sanity. Dear God, how he wanted her. Nothing could have prepared him for the indescribable need that ripped through him. He cupped her face in both hands as he slanted his mouth against hers. With a moan, she threaded her fingers into his hair. The exquisite sensation of her softness cradling his strength made him feel simultaneously weak and powerful. His hands tightened on her waist in a possessive grip that had her gasping for breath. "My lord," she whispered against his lips.

"Elliot," he prompted. "My name is Elliot." Before she could respond, he was kissing her with a barely contained hunger. He felt almost violent as he raided her mouth. He found some solace for the unexpected depth of his emotions in the knowledge that Liberty was not some untrained innocent. She had served Howard Rendell in his home and in his bed for nearly a decade. She was a woman well versed in the ways of the world.

He moved his hands up and down her back, fitting her more closely against him. Through her thin gown, he felt her exquisite, soft curves against his hardness.

Passion pounded through him in streams of heated longing. He could no more resist her than he could stop breathing.

He tunneled his fingers into her dark hair, tearing it free from the fragile hold of the pins. When it tumbled around her shoulders, he groaned and brought handfuls of it to his lips. "You are indescribable," he told her. "Absolutely and completely unique." He inhaled a great breath of her hair. "I love the way you smell."

"I love the way you touch me," she whispered.

Elliot felt something inside him melt like ice before the sun. With a soft laugh, he wrapped his hands around her waist. "I knew it would be like this for us," he murmured.

She gasped, startled, when he lifted her onto the desk. The sight of her there, surrounded by the scattered array of his prized crosses, made him grow hard and taut. He wanted desperately to be inside of her. So desperately that he pushed aside all thought of the unlocked door, of her own vulnerability, of his common sense. At the moment, he could not have resisted her had someone put a gun to his head. Something inside him seemed to recognize that he was perilously close to his doom, and salvation lay in Liberty's warmth.

Surprise registered on her expressive face. Her lips, still swollen and red from his kisses, parted on a confused moan as he began tugging at her skirts. "My lord, what—"

The question died on her lips when he quickly pushed her skirts up and stepped between her thighs. The sensation of her soft, strong thighs against his hips was incredible. When she reached up to clasp his shoulders for balance, he bent his head to kiss her throat. She groaned, and his fingers went, unerringly, to the slit in her pantalettes.

"Elliot."

The sound of his name set off an explosion in his head. She was so giving. He had never had a woman respond to him as Liberty did. He had worried that no matter how urgently he wanted her, he would not be able to ignore that she'd once belonged to his enemy. It seemed, however, that he could forget anything so long as she kept talking to him. "That's it, Liberty. Sing for me."

"Elliot, what are you—"

He moved his hand until one finger traced a hotly intimate path along her quivering flesh. Her only response was a ragged moan. "That's it," he whispered. "There's the song."

When he found her already hot and ready for him, he nearly lost whatever shreds of sanity he had left. The feel of her softness against his fingers was the most erotic thing he'd ever experienced.

Liberty's shocked gasp told him that the sensation affected her almost as deeply. His gut tightened when he felt her small hands clamp onto his shoulders. "Elliot, this is beyond anything."

Somehow, his fragmented mind formed the thought that, yes, indeed, it was beyond anything he'd ever experienced before. Words could not begin to describe the cataclysmic effect she was having on him. "You cannot imagine what you do to me." His voice sounded raw.

"I hope it is similar to what you are doing to me, my lord."

He managed a harsh laugh as he glided his lips along the curve of her throat in a silken trail of fire. "I cannot begin to describe the sensation." He gently bit her earlobe. "At this moment, I'd die to have you."

Her breathing became ragged. At the instant his mouth settled on the spot behind her ear, he slid one finger into her tight warmth. With his hand pressed intimately to and within her, and his tongue plying at her ear, she erupted. Like a glittering explosion of light, her body tightened around him in a thousand rippling shudders.

With a soft groan, Elliot raised his head to watch. He had never seen anything more spectacular in his life. For a man who owned a good number of the world's greatest treasures, he was prepared to swear he held the most incredible one in his arms. Equally as shocking came the revelation that he was no longer concerned about slaking his own passion. Having given Liberty a taste of what it could be like between them, he was suddenly and oddly content. Patiently, he waited, absorbing the feel of her as she slowly drifted back to earth.

When embarrassment finally seemed to restore her strength, she gave his hand a gentle push. He reluctantly removed it, then quickly adjusted her skirts. Her fingers pressed to her mouth where it remained swollen and damp from his kisses. He sensed her confusion. Carefully, he lifted her down from the desk. "That was indescribable."

Still she didn't speak. She shook her head in mute denial. He reached for her hands once more. She resisted when he pulled her fingers from her mouth, but finally yielded to his firm persuasion. "Don't be afraid of the sensations between us, Liberty. You are an amazing creature of excessive passions. You should never apologize for that."

"This should not have happened. I should not have allowed it to happen."

Elliot rubbed his thumbs on the back of her hands. "You had to know. A woman of your experience must have been aware of the attraction all these years."

To his absolute astonishment, she blushed. In his experience, women who made their way in the world as Liberty did never, ever blushed. "My lord, I am painfully aware that you—that we—" She drew a deep breath. "Surely you understand why I find this deeply embarrassing."

He did not, but he sensed somehow that she was struggling. Elliot could not afford to lose the bond that had been built between them in this encounter, so he quickly sought to ease her discomfort. "Liberty, listen to me. You and I are different. We don't have to play by anyone else's rules." He tipped his head to study her. "Do your passions frighten you?"

"Yes," she admitted. "They do."

The admission gave him a powerful sense of elation. The sensations were as new to her as they were to him. Whatever Howard had taught her, she had never before experienced the shattering passion she'd shared with Elliot. "Why?"

"I do not like the way you can make me lose my good sense. It seems I am always finding myself compromised when I am with you."

"Would it lessen your fear to know that I find my own passions no less intense than your own? I desire you, Liberty. I have never tried to disguise the fact."

"No, I don't suppose you have. But that doesn't mean I've granted you permission to seduce me into giving you what you want."

The mere idea that he could seduce Liberty into giving him anything at all sent a surge of heat flaring through him. He was still heavily aroused, achingly consumed by the need she'd awakened in him. What he needed at this moment was a brisk walk in the London fog, but he could not make himself turn away from her, no matter how insistent the clamoring of his body. "I am flattered that you think I can. I assure you, I'm not so skilled a lover."

At that, she stepped away from him. He noted with no small satisfaction that she clung to the edge of the desk, as if her knees weren't quite ready to support her. "I think, my lord, it will be in our best interests if I cut short this interview. You will understand that I need some time to consider what's happened here today."

He studied her a moment, then retrieved a document from his desk. "I hope you will. When you do, I think you will find that there is absolutely no reason why you and I shouldn't enjoy a comfortable future."

"I wouldn't say comfortable, exactly." When he laughed, she frowned at him. "My lord, this is not a source of amusement for me."

"I assure you, I am not laughing at you. You

enchant me. I cannot help it that you put me in such an excellent humor."

"But you find my reticence laughable?"

"I find it charming." He raised one of her hands to his lips. "Do not fear what you've learned about yourself here today."

"I don't."

"I'm very glad to hear it. I want you, Liberty. And I generally get what I want."

She extracted her fingers from his. "Arrogant as ever, I see."

"I like to think of it as possessing a broad sense of vision. I have always favored business deals where everyone stands to gain."

"And that's how you see this marriage proposal of yours?"

"It is." He handed her the document. "Here is the contract you requested." When he placed it in her hands, he saw her hesitate before she slipped it into the pocket of her gown. The soft ticking of his mantel clock filled the air between them. He could almost hear the thoughts that passed through her mind. Finally, the sadness he saw in her eyes gave way to determination.

Squaring her shoulders, she stepped away from him. "Thank you, my lord. I shall examine it carefully."

"I trust you'll find it to your satisfaction."

"I'm certain I shall."

"Then how soon will you marry me?"

She met his gaze. "I think, Darewood, it had best be very soon indeed." She produced a folded piece of paper from her pocket. "I've received another threat."

Chapter 5

"Damn it, Garrick." Elliot paced in front of the fireplace in his study. "Damn the bastard to hell. Threatening notes. What kind of despicable cur resorts to that type of tyranny?"

Garrick Frost propped his booted feet on the coffee table. "It's Rendell, I tell you. He's an ass, and we all know it. He's trying to force Liberty into accelerating her plans. Between his threats of legal action and his offer of marriage, he believes he has her trapped. She could hide behind Howard's death for a while, claiming she wanted a decent period of mourning, but Carlton doesn't want to wait that long for the money. It's as simple as that."

Elliot studied the now crumpled paper in his hand. "She has no idea what this could mean. She handed it to me as if it were some bloody party invitation." With his usual expediency, he'd sent for Garrick as soon as he'd seen Liberty safely on her way back to Huxley House. Unwilling to alarm her, he had waited until Garrick arrived to voice his theories about the threats. Though he saw no reason for Liberty to worry unnecessarily, he had instructed his secretary to add two more footmen to the Huxley staff. Until he had her safely in his home as his wife, he wanted her under twenty-four-hour watch.

In agitation, he scrubbed a hand over his face. "The woman is hell-bent on self-destruction. I'm sure of it."

"She came to you, didn't she? That, at least, is encouraging."

"Perhaps."

"I don't suppose you've told her why you want to marry her."

"We've had an honest conversation. I explained that I want the Cross of Aragon. She made several requests of her own, and I granted them."

"How tidy for you. She never made you tell her you're bent on destroying Howard's reputation?"

Elliot frowned at him. "She mentioned it."

"And you denied it."

"Don't press me, Garrick."

"I wouldn't dream of it."

Elliot squelched an irritated retort. Garrick knew him too well and was stubbornly persistent in getting his own way. Experience told him his best strategy was to change the subject. "Have you had any success in the past two days?"

Garrick gave him a shrewd look that said all too clearly that he wasn't done with the conversation.

Finally, he dropped a stack of papers on the coffee table. "I have. Here's the information you wanted."

"Did you have any trouble?"

"No. Grimes was quite cooperative."

"How much did you have to pay him?"

"Fifty pounds."

Elliot scooped up the stack of papers. "Fool. He could have had five hundred."

Garrick waited while Elliot perused the papers. "Is that what you expected?"

He flipped a page. "For the most part. Howard's ventures aren't nearly as stable as they appear. I've known that for some time." After Liberty's departure, he had told Garrick that he thought the person who was threatening Liberty was one of Howard's associates—someone who had too much to lose if Carlton seized control of the estate and drove the business into the ground. Elliot had complete files on all of Howard's investors, but this particular problem required a more substantial analysis. Gerald Grimes, Howard's chief clerk, was proving to be an excellent source.

Elliot's expert eye narrowed on a figure. He flipped back several pages, did a few mental calculations, then flipped forward again. "Ah."

Garrick unfurled from the sofa. "You've got that look in your eye," he said as he advanced toward Elliot.

"What look?"

"The one that says I'm going to have to keep you from murdering someone."

"Oh. That one. Never fear, I'm not ready for blood yet. Come here and see this." Elliot separated the pertinent sheets of paper, then let the others drop to the coffee table. When Garrick reached him, he pointed out several figures.

"Elliot, I have probably explained to you at least a half-dozen times that those numbers might as well be Greek. I don't know how to read them. I could look at them for hours and still have no idea what they mean. I assume you've found a possible culprit."

"Not a culprit, perhaps, but certainly evidence that all is not well with Howard's investors. Look here." He pointed to a column of numbers. "These represent the supposed payments Willis Braxton has made toward the investment loan Howard gave him on a mining interest."

"And?"

"And these"—he showed him the next sheet of paper—"are the interest payments Howard made to his investors on the same project. Look at the date when the payments stopped."

"The last payment was the week Howard died."

"That's correct."

"Perhaps it's just an oversight. Liberty may have forgotten about the loan."

"That's not like her. I would guess that someone

is attempting to bankrupt the Braxton mine by redirecting the financing."

"But why?"

"To apply pressure to Liberty. I know enough about her to suspect she had no idea that Howard was passing money under the table. He would have kept a second set of ledgers, and someone wants to make absolutely sure that those ledgers disappear."

"Even if it means threatening her."

"Precisely. I'd wager that our culprit wants to see her married to Carlton as quickly as possible. It's the only way to ensure that all this gets swept under the carpet."

"Surely this would be a drastic measure."

"Definitely not. Since Howard's death, every investor, every banker, every businessman in London has been on her heels like hounds on a fox. To date, nothing has made her yield to the pressure. Despite the fact that over half her employees have deserted her, and that she gets no respect from the staff or the partners, Liberty has managed to keep Howard's empire afloat. Whoever is threatening her is losing patience and time."

"Then what do you propose we do?"

"I'm going to pay a few visits this afternoon. If Howard's investors are this nervous, someone will talk."

"Grimes certainly seemed willing enough. Is there anything I can do to help?"

"Yes. Find me a clergyman and get me a marriage license. I'm not willing to wait any longer to make Liberty my wife."

The following evening, Elliot stood in the cold mist, his temper hot enough to ward off the chill. He'd spent a frustrating day on the heels of Howard's cohorts. Thus far, he'd learned more than he'd ever wanted to know about the man's business practices, and was still no closer to knowing who was threatening Liberty.

Which, he decided as he pulled his cloak closer to his body, would not have been nearly so irritating if the woman had the least inkling of how to stay put. Since her visit with him the previous morning, she'd run his men into the ground. Thus far, she'd overseen a livestock sale, attended an investors' meeting at Howard's shipping company, and had at least three interviews with bankers. There was a two-hour period where she was engaged in a quite proper visit to a Bond Street bookstore, but all told, she'd conducted more business in a day than most men completed in a week.

He'd received regular reports from Huxley House and, until this evening, had been willing to stand aside while she put her affairs in order. A half hour ago, however, he'd returned home to find an anxious Thomas Adley pacing in his foyer. Liberty, it seemed, had tired of the more conventional business environment and had taken up thievery as a pastime. She'd used the servants' entrance to escape

Huxley House for tonight's misadventure. According to Adley, a hack had left her at the residence of Willis Braxton, where she'd broken a rear window and let herself into the library. Adley had pull-footed it to Elliot's town house to fetch him.

Now, standing in the cold, watching the bob of a single candle flame in the darkened library, he contemplated whether he wanted to wring her neck or turn her over his knee. Or both. He cast a furtive glance down the street, then hoisted himself over the garden wall. No sense in delaying the inevitable. First he must get her out of there. Then he'd decide how to chastise her.

Sliding in through the now open window, he dropped soundlessly to the carpet. Liberty was so absorbed in the papers she'd spread on Braxton's desk, she didn't notice his presence in the room. Elliot took several seconds to study the profile of her bent head. With her dark hair pulled into a simple braid, she looked very young and very guileless. She wore the same simple black gown she'd worn when he last saw her. Its plain lines emphasized the curves of her figure, while the stark color made her eyes look wide in her pale face.

He regretted that her illusions about Howard Rendell would soon be dashed. Her persistent reliance on the good she found in human nature was her most endearing flaw, and he hated to see her lose it.

He heard the sound of carriage traffic in the

nearby alley and realized there was no time to lose. Disaster would strike if Braxton discovered them here. He approached the desk in three easy strides. "Liberty."

She started so violently, she almost dropped her candle. "Darewood. Name of God! You frightened ten years off my life."

"Then we are even." He snuffed out the flame between his thumb and index finger, leaving them in moonlit darkness. "You will never know the anxiety you have cost me this last half hour."

"What are you doing here?" She glanced at the smoke now trailing from her wick. "You've snuffed out my light."

"Damn right I have. That candle was visible from the alley. You could at least have pulled the drapes."

"Well, I'm sorry. I'm not in the habit of breaking into people's homes."

"That, at least, is a relief."

"I suppose I don't have the right of it yet." She pursed her lips as she studied him. "You, on the other hand, seem quite adept."

"I am."

Long seconds passed with only the relentless ticking of the clock and the lingering sound of horse's hooves on the cobbles to punctuate the stillness. "And I don't suppose you're going to explain why?"

"No, I am not. Now, tell me, what in the hell do you think you're doing here?"

"You needn't be so irritable. As it happens, I have a very good reason. I think that Willis Braxton may be the man sending me those threats."

"So, naturally, you decided to travel to his house—alone, I might add—in the middle of the night and let yourself into his library."

"I needed to look at these papers."

"Did you even once consider the danger you might be in?"

"Don't be ridiculous. I'm sure I'm not in the least bit of danger. Braxton may be dishonest, but he wouldn't hurt me."

"You cannot be sure of that."

She shrugged. "Besides, by my calculations, he won't be home for at least another hour. That gives me plenty of time to discover what I need to know. You forget, I only have to see the papers once to memorize them."

"How fortunate."

"There's no need to be snide. They're really quite revealing. Look."

He glanced quickly at the alley, assured himself that they were still alone, then bent over the desk. Her warmth seemed to circle him in a lilac-scented cloud. "We don't have time to examine them, Liberty. We need to leave. Now."

"If you hadn't extinguished my candle, I could show you what I mean." She felt along the top of the desk. "Perhaps I can find my matches."

Elliot was scooping up the papers from the desk. "You won't need them."

"I'm not finished with these yet."

"You are." He stacked them into a neat pile.

She stayed his hand. "I'm not." She tapped one of the top ledger sheets with her finger. "Look here. I'm almost certain Braxton was running Howard's money through false accounts."

Elliot glanced down the alley, then snatched up the papers. "A brilliant deduction. Where did you get these?"

"Now see here, Darewood, what gives you the right—"

Quickly, Elliot pressed his hand over her mouth. "Liberty, I swear, if you say one more word, I'm going to tie a gag around your mouth. Braxton is on his way here right now. If we do not leave immediately, he'll discover us. Now, where did you get these?"

Her eyes widened. "He's here?"

Elliot tipped his head toward the window. "In the alley." He saw awareness dawn in her eyes. "Precisely. The papers, Liberty?"

"From the safe." She indicated the open liquor cabinet to her left. "It's inside the cabinet."

Elliot strode to the safe, deftly replaced the papers and decanters, then clicked it shut. "Let's go."

"But, my lord—"

"Liberty, I am not prepared to argue with you. If Braxton is running the stolen money through his accounts, he's probably prepared to go to extraordinary lengths to disguise the fact. You've already said you think he is the one threatening you. If I have to toss you over my shoulder to get you out of here, I will."

"How very modern of you, my lord. I suppose next you'll be threatening to drag me by my hair."

He took a menacing step toward her. "Damnation, Liberty—" When Willis Braxton's noticeably loud laugh sounded from the alleyway, Elliot gave her a meaningful look. "Are you coming peacefully or not?"

Her mouth remained set in a stubborn line for a few moments. Then, she finally relented. "Lead the way."

By the time they were seated in his carriage, Elliot was seething. They'd barely escaped detection in the garden. Willis had decided to take a midnight stroll through his pansies, and Elliot had been forced to corner Liberty behind the hedgerow, where he'd shielded them both with his dark cloak. At least, he'd mused, black was her wardrobe color of choice. Had she been wearing a paler shade, Willis would certainly have seen them in the full light of the moon.

"I trust," he said, "that you have some measure of a reasonable explanation for this."

"Naturally." She sat across from him, her hands folded in her lap.

"I'm waiting."

"Good heavens, Darewood, you cannot believe that I have any intention of explaining myself to you."

"Madam, in case it has escaped your attention, you are my fiancée. Unless you succeed in getting yourself killed in the near future, you'll soon be my wife. I like to believe that gives me some right to comment on your activities."

"Damned arrogant of you, Darewood."

"Don't swear at me. It's unbecoming."

"You swear at me."

"You give me cause."

"And you think I should marry you? Really, I cannot imagine what possible benefit there is to being wed to such a boorish man. As it is, you've already broken your word. You promised that you would not interfere in my business affairs."

He used his walking stick to rap on the roof of the carriage. It set immediately into motion. "I do not consider breaking into Willis Braxton's house in the dead of night to be a business activity. Now, you will explain this to me, or God help me, I'll carry you back to my house and keep you there until Garrick fetches someone to marry us."

"You needn't be so prudish. We weren't caught, after all."

"Only by the slimmest of luck."

"But we weren't."

"That is not the point."

She studied him for long seconds. "You enjoyed this, didn't you?"

"That is immaterial."

"You did. I can see it in your eyes. Tell me, Darewood, when was the last time you enjoyed an evening out more than you have this one?"

"There are many ways to describe what I experienced tonight, but 'enjoyment' is not one of them."

"But you weren't bored?"

He exhaled a harsh breath. "Damn it—"

"Never mind trying to deny it. You've sworn at me more in the last ten minutes than you have since I've known you. That's telling enough."

Frustrated with her lack of cooperation, he reached for her shoulders so he could haul her onto his lap. At her startled gasp, he pressed a hard kiss to her mouth. She resisted him for several heartbeats, then finally leaned into him with a soft moan that inflamed his senses. He crushed her to him, wrapping both arms around her. Driven by his lingering fear, he could not get close enough to her. The feel of her in his arms tore at his insides, demanding, aching, needing. The knowledge that she belonged to him, and the mere thought of how much he could have lost tonight, drove him to a new level of desperation.

Liberty yielded to the firm persuasion of his kiss. Her soft body melted into his, and Elliot plundered her mouth until his lungs screamed for breath. His hands roamed restlessly over her shoulders and back, then stroked her heavy, silken hair. She tasted like fire and honey and excitement. He could not delve deeply enough to satisfy his craving for her. When she arched her head back and whimpered his name, his blood seemed to plunge to a spot below his waist.

With a soft oath, he shifted her on his lap, then fumbled for the neck of her gown. "Liberty, I need you."

"Elliot—"

The same thready note of disbelief he'd heard in her voice when he'd last touched her echoed inside the confines of the coach. She wanted him. He knew it. Deftly, he unbuttoned her bodice. When his fingers slipped inside to caress the tops of her breasts, she gasped. Tight hands clutched his head as a tiny moan escaped her lips. He tore his mouth from hers to gaze down at her exposed flesh. In a whisper-soft caress, he rubbed the pad of his fingers over the full upper curves of her breasts. Her corset held the tender flesh confined, awaiting his touch.

"You're beautiful," he whispered. "Cream and satin."

"You are the one who is beautiful, my lord." Her fingers stroked his hair. "I swear I will never understand what you do to me."

"In time you will. It's not necessary to understand it, Liberty. Merely enjoy it." He lowered his head to kiss the soft curves. "Enjoy it."

She clung to his hair as he caressed her with his

mouth. With one hand, he supported the back of her head so he could lean her more fully into his touch. The feel of her shivering against him, the sound of her pleasured gasps, the fevered way her hands pulled at him, excited him beyond belief.

She was his for the taking. He didn't doubt it for an instant. And in that certainty, he found the strength to lift his head and begin buttoning her dress.

Liberty met his gaze with confusion. "My lord—"

He pressed a finger to her lips, then continued his task. "Our time is short, my sweet. As much as I want you"—he shifted deliberately against her, then delighted at the way her skin flushed with heat— "and never doubt that I do—I will not have it like this. Not in the confines of a carriage like some sordid tumble with a wench." Howard Rendell may have treated her that way, he thought, but damned if he would. Liberty deserved better.

When he finished with her bodice he helped her sit up, then rubbed his thumb over the swollen curve of her lower lip. "Now, sweet, you will tell me what you were doing here."

She squirmed on his lap, causing him a significant amount of discomfort. It was no more than he deserved, he supposed, for starting something he wasn't ready to finish. "Hold still," he said. "I'm not releasing you until you tell me what I wish to know."

Her expression turned wary. "Is that why you

kissed me? Did you think to distract me enough to give you an explanation? I feel compelled to remind you, sir, that you gave me your word as a gentleman that you would not press me into a physical relationship with you."

"No. I gave you my word as a gentleman that I would not take anything you didn't offer."

"Are you suggesting that I seduced you? I did nothing of the sort."

"Madam, would it surprise you to know that you can seduce me simply by meeting my gaze across a room? Or that you have only to look at me with those extraordinary eyes to elicit an immediate response?" He studied her in the moonlight. "For that matter, if you wish to know why I kissed you tonight, I did it because I have not been able to forget what it felt like the last time I saw you. I couldn't resist."

That seemed to mollify her. She muttered a soft "Oh."

"In fact, I think that if I do not have you very soon, I shall probably go mad with the wanting of it."

"My lord, really—"

"Really." He pressed a soft kiss to her lips. "Now, if you aren't going to tell me what I wish to know, then perhaps I will have to seduce it out of you. I'll admit, the notion is not altogether unpleasant."

She took his hand in hers, then shifted from his

lap to sit next to him. "That won't be necessary. What is it you wish to know about tonight's
misdeed?"

His hand enfolded hers in a tight grip. "Are you
all right?" he asked far more harshly than he'd
intended.

"Of course I'm all right. Though I'm in imminent
danger of suffering bruises from the grip you have
on my fingers."

He couldn't make his hand relax. "You frightened me," he confessed.

She gave him an astonished look, then laid her
small hand against his face. "Oh, Elliot, you were
worried about me."

"Bloody hell, what did you expect?"

"I'm not sure. I thought perhaps you were worried there'd be a scandal."

"I don't give a bloody damn about a scandal. I'm
more concerned that you've no more sense than to
charge into Braxton's house while thinking he
might be threatening you."

Her gaze narrowed. "You don't think it's Braxton, do you?"

"I don't."

"But, Elliot, the figures. If you could see them—"

With a harsh sigh, he reached for a sheaf of
papers on the opposite seat. "I have seen them. I've
seen a good bit more, too."

"I don't understand."

He handed her the papers. "When you gave me

that note, I immediately began to investigate. As it turns out, there are several people who would have good reason to threaten you, Braxton among them. After careful consideration, however, I have ruled them out."

"But why?"

"Look at the papers." He reached to light the lantern. "The story is there."

Without comment, she broke the seal on the papers and began to read. After several seconds, she gave him an accusing look. "This is a financial analysis of the current state of Howard's businesses. Why do you have it?"

"Because I decided the best place to start was with the facts."

She paled visibly. "How long have you had this information?"

"Since yesterday morning."

"Does Braxton know you have it?"

"I wouldn't doubt it."

"Then don't you think he might be desperate?"

"Only if he were the one sending the threats."

"And you don't believe he is?"

"No. I don't."

"This is my life, Darewood. I'd appreciate it if you'd be a bit more forthcoming."

Elliot released a long breath as he reached for her hand. He had dreaded this moment for the better part of the afternoon. The more deeply he and Garrick delved into Howard's affairs, the more the

evidence suggested that Elliot himself was responsible for the threats. Beyond that, he had no answer.
For whatever reason, she had not immediately
suspected him, but the facts against him were
quickly mounting. He was loath to share them with
her until he could prove his innocence in the matter.
"Howard made several enemies, as you well know."

"You among them."

He winced. "That much is true."

"But none of his enemies would have reason to
threaten me. The only people with anything to lose
are Howard's investors. It must be one of them. If
Braxton truly was cheating Howard, he'd have sufficient reason to fear discovery."

"Unless, of course, Howard knew about Braxton's deceit."

"That's impossible."

"The figures don't suggest that, Liberty."

"I cannot believe that Howard would deliberately
cheat his investors. Why would he?"

"For the same reason he sent me that letter. For
the same reason he put you in a position where you
might be forced to marry Carlton. He was a greedy,
manipulative man."

To his surprise, she didn't flinch. "It still doesn't
explain where the threats are coming from."

He chose his words with care. "The obvious
source, of course, is the person with the most to
gain."

She frowned in concentration. "That brings us

back to where we started, with Carlton and you. I swear, this is enormously perplexing. I still think it was Braxton."

His sense of relief was heady. He had to draw several breaths before he could think again. It occurred to him that it would not be such a bad thing for Liberty to stay on the wrong trail awhile. If he could persuade her to spend the next few days analyzing the figures she'd seen tonight, he might convince her to stay out of trouble until he had her safely married. "It could be," he conceded.

She warmed to the idea. "Do you think so? I never trusted him. I told Howard that, but he wouldn't listen to me."

"He is most definitely not trustworthy."

"Oh, I'm glad you sensed it, too. Howard said I was being overly suspicious, but there was something in his eyes I found disconcerting."

"Perhaps when you've had time to sift through the information you gathered tonight, you'll find your answer."

She shook her head. "I don't think so. I am still missing something. It's like a giant puzzle in my head. I am not yet sure what pieces are missing, but it becomes more clear each day."

His hand tightened on hers as the carriage rolled to a stop at the servants' entrance of Huxley House. "Just trust me a bit longer, Liberty. All will be well, I assure you."

"I suppose you are right." She glanced at their twined fingers.

He gave her hand a gentle squeeze. "I have a request to make."

"Another? Really, Darewood, you are being quite bold this evening. First, I am supposed to stay put while you ferret out my tormentor, and now you desire more?"

Much, much more, he thought. So much more, you'd melt into me if I told you what I wanted. Deliberately, he cleared his throat. "I would like you to accompany me to Lady Asterly's soiree tomorrow evening."

"A party?" She looked at him in amazement. "I don't think that's appropriate."

"As you know, Pearl is quite fond of you. She asked me to escort you."

"Elliot, surely you know what will occur if you walk into that party with me. Gentlemen like you simply don't bring women of my status to Society parties."

"I don't give a fig what gentlemen do, and after tomorrow night, neither will anyone else." He drew a steadying breath. "Pearl is expecting us to wed tomorrow evening in her private chapel."

"Tomorrow evening? Is that possible?"

"Quite."

"But, Darewood, you cannot wish to wed me in so public a setting. You know the gossip that will ensue. Have you lost complete control of your senses?"

"I am quite sane, I assure you. If you think it through, you will see it's for the best. A public wedding will make it clear to your tormentor that he will, henceforth, have to deal with me. I think the threats will come to a stop."

"Well, aren't you impressed with yourself."

"I am realistic. Whoever he is, he wouldn't dare challenge me. The best way I know to ensure Society's cooperation is to give it something to gossip about."

"I don't suppose I've any hope of talking you out of this?"

"None."

"What if I refuse to attend?"

"As it happens, I anticipated that. I'll abduct you if you make me."

"I should have known."

He pressed a kiss to the back of her hand. "Don't sound so disgruntled. I've actually done you an enormous favor."

"I'm afraid to ask what."

"By compiling the information in those papers for you, I've saved you the trouble and potential embarrassment of stumbling on it yourself. I am not quite finished with the papers, I'm afraid. I'll turn them over to you tomorrow night when I call for you. The figures will give you the leverage you need to make your business dealings less of a struggle."

"How very romantic, Darewood. I doubt many women receive financial ledgers for engagement presents."

"I assumed you'd prefer them to jewels."

"Perhaps you're not as backward as I once thought."

"Thank you for the compliment."

Liberty extracted her hand from his when his footman opened the door. "Once again, you've gotten your way. I suppose I should resent you for it."

"In time, you'll see that it's best."

"Don't expect me to thank you for interrupting my visit at Braxton's. I could have handled it myself."

"I'm certain you could, but in the interest of my mental health, I'd like your promise that you won't attempt something like this again without warning me first."

She climbed down, then turned back to face him. "I'll have to think on it."

"I'll call for you at eight tomorrow evening."

"I'll be ready. In the meantime, however, I give you my word that I will not let Carlton terrorize me."

Before he could respond, she fled into the house. He muttered a dark curse beneath his breath. If he found so much as a hair out of place when he fetched her tomorrow, he'd personally tear Rendell's throat out. And enjoy every minute of it.

Chapter 6

At five minutes to eight the following evening, Liberty closed her eyes and silently counted to ten. Carlton and his mother sat across from her, Howard's solicitors, William Hatfield and Peter Shaker, sat on either side. She'd summoned them to tell them she wouldn't be returning to Huxley House after she left with Elliot tonight.

A sense of acute relief had washed over her as the hour of her freedom approached. She was suddenly aware of how draining the past weeks with Carlton and his mother had been and how weary she was of the tremendous burden Howard had placed on her. Her discovery of Willis Braxton's business practices and Elliot's insinuation that Howard had known about them had distressed her. The more she analyzed the numbers she'd seen in Braxton's books, the more she thought that Elliot's suspicions were correct. She found herself suddenly exhausted. She hoped the evening ahead wouldn't prove too stressful. "My lord," she said quietly, "I don't have much time."

He grumbled as he indicated her black silk gown with a flick of his wrist. "So I see. The black's a bit depressing for an evening out, don't you think?"

She didn't bother to respond. "I have something to tell all of you which is going to change things significantly."

Shaker, Howard's longtime business adviser as well as his solicitor, studied her with glassy eyes. "Do you plan to try to delay your marriage to the earl, Miss Madison?"

She almost laughed out loud. "You might put it that way."

Carlton snorted. "No chance of that. I'll have the license by tomorrow morning."

Millicent snapped her black fan shut with a sharp flick of her wrist. "I cannot understand why you are insisting on making this a problem, Liberty. You got what you wanted from Howard when he died." Her thin mouth curled at the edges. "God knows you were paid well enough for it."

Liberty felt a surge of anger but suppressed a retort. It would accomplish nothing, she knew. Carlton patted his mother's hand. "Mother, that's not necessary. We all know what Howard did and why he did it. All that's necessary now is for Liberty to marry me. Once that happens, and the investors know that I am firmly at the helm of Howard's businesses, we'll have no difficulty at all in obtaining the funds we need."

Liberty's temper slipped a notch. "Are you saying that you intend to spend whatever time is necessary to ensure that Howard's ventures remain profitable?"

"Don't be ludicrous. I never understood why my uncle insisted on handling the mundane affairs himself. That's why gentlemen pay comptrollers and solicitors." He glanced at Hatfield and Shaker. "Isn't that so?"

Shaker succumbed to a sudden coughing fit while Hatfield tried, once more, to smooth the way. "I do not believe the issue here, your lordship, is a question of qualification."

"Of course it is," Millicent snapped. "No one believes Liberty can actually run the businesses. There's not a soul in London who wasn't aware of her relationship with Howard. She must be insane to think she can now step in and expect to have complete control over his assets."

"It's what the earl intended," Hatfield supplied. "That's why he had us draft the will as we did."

Millicent's lips pressed together in a thin line. "And you allowed it. What were you thinking? The man left everything but his title and home to his mistress, and you never bothered to intervene. I assure you gentlemen, she didn't work *that* hard."

Liberty had heard enough. With a frustrated sigh, she rose. "I don't have to listen to this."

Carlton was out of his chair and beside her in a

few quick strides. His fingers closed on her shoulders. "Now see here. For weeks I've allowed you to humiliate me. You've told me what I can spend, and how I can spend it. You've refused to pay the bills, making it increasingly difficult for me to obtain credit, and you've insisted on treating me like an errant schoolboy. You're going to have to marry me, Liberty; you know it. Otherwise, I'll drag you through the courts until I get what I want. Is that why you let Howard use you for all these years? To be tossed out in the street?"

Had the situation not been so absurd, it might have made her angry. As it was, she felt an insane urge to laugh. She clenched her teeth together so hard that she felt her temples throb. Carlton's hands tightened on her shoulders as he continued: "I don't know what you hope to accomplish with these constant delays, but it isn't going to work. You have one choice and one choice only. Marry me now, or I will force you."

"I suggest," said a lethally cold voice from the doorway, "that you drop your hands."

The sound of Elliot's voice did strange things to Liberty. Her stomach fluttered, as it always did when she stood too near him, but this time, the sensation was accompanied by another, more potent feeling of recognition. It was almost as if her weary heart knew she could drop her guard when Elliot stepped into the room. His physical strength and the strength of his character would shield her, and to her surprise, she welcomed the comfort. She hurried away from Carlton.

"Good God." William Hatfield rose to his feet. "What are *you* doing here?"

Elliot advanced into the room, his full coat swirling about his legs. Liberty had a fanciful vision of a pirate forcing his way onto a hostile ship. "I'm afraid," he said, dropping the stack of papers he held onto the table, "I'm here to deliver some rather distressing news. At least, you'll find it distressing. Personally, I greeted it with quite a bit of pleasure."

Millicent had begun fanning herself again. "I can't believe you'd barge in here like this. Carlton, why was this man allowed to pass the front hall?"

Elliot calmly unbuttoned his greatcoat, ignoring the question, and tossed it on the back of the sofa before seating himself. Glancing at Shaker and Hatfield, he indicated the two chairs they'd vacated. "Gentlemen, please sit. This won't take long."

Hatfield dropped into his chair with a dull thud. Shaker removed a white handkerchief from his pocket to mop his brow. "This is highly unusual," he muttered. "Highly."

Carlton gave Liberty a surly look before he returned his gaze to Elliot, who was unwinding the cord from the stack of papers. "I could have you thrown out," he said.

"I'm sure you could." Elliot laid the papers on the table once more.

"What are those?" Carlton asked, pointing to the papers.

"Liberty will tell you." Elliot leaned back in his chair. "She knows what they are," he said quietly, an amused look in his eyes.

She gave him a slight smile. He had deferred to her in order to restore the dignity Carlton and his mother were intent on destroying. When he had promised to give her the papers, she'd known what the gesture meant. They represented her financial security and independence. Elliot had seemed to sense how much she needed the assurance they offered as she prepared to marry him. The information in them gave her sufficient leverage to build a life for herself no matter what the future held. That was a gift Howard had never given her. The past few weeks had shown her how frighteningly dependent she'd become on him.

The grand gesture had endeared Elliot to her in a new and meaningful way. Despite her teasing to the contrary, she recognized that beneath his gruff exterior was a man who valued her, and tonight's dramatics reinforced the notion. He had no reason to present the papers to her in so public a setting, other than to give her worth in the presence of people who held her in the lowest possible esteem.

Millicent gave Liberty a look intended to fell her. "What are you talking about, Darewood. She knows what?"

"Those papers," Liberty said quietly, "contain all

the information the viscount needs to ensure that Howard's ruin is complete. They are a financial analysis of the balance sheets and ledgers."

William Hatfield had turned pale. "Good God."

"However," she continued, "the set he has there also includes some personal information about Howard that would ensure that no investor in the world would continue to stake the ventures he originated. We have sufficient capital assets to repay our debts, but our income would all but disappear."

Carlton exploded. "That's impossible."

"No," Liberty explained. "It is what I have told you from the beginning. The investors were crucial to Howard's success. Your behavior since your uncle's death has destroyed whatever respect you might have earned from his business colleagues. None of them are likely to put significant amounts of their capital in the hands of a man who cannot even control himself around a pair of dice and a bottle of whiskey."

Carlton rose from his chair with an angry oath. "How dare you speak to me in such a manner. Do you have any idea what I can do to you?"

"Nothing," she said quietly as she crossed the room to stand behind Elliot. "Because his lordship and I are about to be wed."

Ten minutes later, Elliot was still battling an overwhelming sense of satisfaction as he studied her across the space of his carriage. She'd squashed Carlton like the cockroach he was.

He found her intoxicating. For days, his mind had dwelled almost continuously on the image of her face as she'd climaxed in his arms. Even last night, when she'd scared the wits out of him with that stunt at Braxton's, he'd been unable to resist her. An insatiable craving to see that pleasured look again, to finish what they'd begun, had him fighting a near-constant state of arousal. The idea that tonight she'd belong to him had driven him like a madman all day. Garrick had been unmercifully cheerful about Elliot's wedding preparations. Soon, he knew, he'd have to have a word with him—he was enjoying Elliot's discomfort far too much.

Yet, about one thing at least, Garrick was right. Elliot's life had, until recently, been predictable and boring. He had found his pleasure in acquiring and owning things. He could not remember the last time he'd allowed himself to enjoy the company of another individual without pursuing a hidden agenda. With Liberty, he could. And he devoured the pure pleasure of it like a man starved.

She was watching him with a wary expression as they made their way through the heavy traffic. "I am glad you are enjoying yourself, Darewood."

"I am, though I confess I had not expected you to wear black to the wedding."

She indicated his evening clothes with a wave of her hand. "You are."

"I'm supposed to."

"And you are always so ready to do as you're told," she quipped.

He tipped his head to her. "Point well taken, Liberty. Still, I cannot help feeling that you still have serious reservations about this evening."

"Don't you?"

"Actually, no. I'm quite certain of what I want." He studied her in the dim carriage light. "I've been certain of it since the day I proposed to you."

She seemed unaware of his sudden tension. "I envy you, then."

"Surely it is not that bad. This is a wedding, not an execution."

"My lord, have you no idea what this is like for me? I have agreed to marry you because the man I thought was my friend left me with intolerable choices. I feel that I've betrayed Howard with this decision, but at the same time, I cannot help feeling that Howard betrayed me. The more closely I examine his business affairs, the more I feel cheated. As if that isn't enough of a burden, I find that when I am with you, I seem to lose all sense of myself. If you were in my shoes, would you not feel a bit of trepidation?"

He studied her features before he shifted to sit next to her. She stiffened but did not pull away. "I am sorrier than you know that this has hurt you."

She gave him a surprised look. "That almost sounded genuine."

"Despite what you might think, I am not entirely incapable of compassion. I regret that I have given you no reason to see that."

She drew a deep breath. "No. I am the one who is sorry. I have made my decision and I will abide by it. I am not myself this evening, and I must ask you to forgive me."

"Have you received another threat?"

"No. I was alone today. Frankly, I was relieved."

"If that scene I witnessed in your salon was typical of what you've experienced since Howard's death, I can certainly understand."

"You can?" Her eyes were wide and uncertain.

Elliot could not resist the urge to enfold her small hand in his. "Yes. No one likes to be insulted, Liberty."

A flicker of amusement chased away some of the shadows in her eyes. "I must ask, Darewood, how you purport to know that. I daresay there's not a person about town who'd risk the consequences of insulting you."

"You think not?"

"They live in fear of you, and you like it. Don't bother to deny it."

The words left him feeling oddly unsettled. Despite a long-cultivated disdain of other people's opinions, he couldn't shake the desire for Liberty to understand, at least in part, what drove his passions. "It hasn't always been that way," he said quietly.

"People are shaped by their experiences. I am no different."

"I didn't mean to suggest that you weren't human, merely that you appear to have mastered the flaw better than most."

He rubbed his thumb against the back of her hand. "I will confess, I've been preoccupied these past few days. I hadn't thought of discussing this with you, but I think I should before we exchange vows."

"You're going to lecture me, aren't you?"

"No."

"You aren't going to tell me that I should have known a woman has no business trying to conduct Howard's affairs? That I should never have gone to Braxton's last night? Tell me, how long did you stay angry at me after you dropped me off?"

"All night."

"Are you still angry?"

"No."

"Why not?"

"Because after this evening, I'll be able to keep an eye on you. There won't be a repeat of last night's adventure."

"Is that truly the heart of it? Or are you relieved that you will finally be in a position to convince me that I should surrender the burden to someone far more capable and equipped?"

"I cannot think of a person more capable for the task you've set for yourself. If anyone is more equipped, it is merely because Society is not ready to accept that you're smarter than most of the men you deal with."

She looked at him with a mixture of amazement and distrust. "And here I'd accused you of primitive thinking. I had no idea you were so progressive, so modern, Darewood."

"Frankly, neither had I."

That won a small laugh from her. "You amaze me, my lord."

"I do hope so. It is my intent to continue to amaze you on a regular basis."

If she caught the innuendo, she ignored it. "If I admit that I have, perhaps, misjudged you"—she leaned forward as she lowered her voice—"will you stop looking at me that way?"

A dark curl of hair had tumbled from her coiffure and lay in tempting disarray against the white curve of her shoulder. He had to force himself to pull his gaze from the tendril so he could answer her question. "What way?"

"That predatory look. You looked at me the same way in the carriage last night. It seems that unfortunate incident in your study is ever present in your mind."

"It is." He felt, rather than saw, the heat fill her face.

"I confess it makes me very nervous."

"That is what I wish to discuss with you, Liberty."

"Good Lord. You don't want to talk about what

happened, do you? I'm not altogether certain I could survive the embarrassment. I still cannot believe I allowed you to make me forget myself. I meant what I told you the other day, Darewood. I do not wish our marriage to be complicated."

"No." Her hand still lay in his, so he trailed a finger across the bare spot at the base of her wrist, locating her pulse, and pressed the pad of his thumb against it. "That's not what I wish to discuss, although I assure you I'm far from done with the issue. Right now, however, I want to talk about Howard."

She stilled like a bird in a trap. "Don't you think that is a bit inappropriate, given that we are on the way to our wedding?"

"Actually, I cannot think of a more appropriate time."

"I do not wish to discuss my relationship with Howard with you."

He increased the pressure of his fingers so her arm rested against his thigh. "And I don't expect you to. I thought, perhaps, you might understand my position a bit better if I discussed *my* relationship with the man."

Liberty extracted her fingers from his, then asked, "What do you mean?"

"Haven't you wondered why I have pursued Howard's destruction with such single-minded passion for the past fifteen years?"

"I—how do you know Howard hasn't already told me?"

"He wouldn't dare."

"But you would?"

"The story is mine to tell, and mine alone."

"What if I don't believe you?"

He carefully considered the question. There was every chance she wouldn't. What he had to say would cast aspersions on a man who had been her protector for nearly a decade. "Then that is your choice."

"But you think that I will?"

"I think that you and I communicate on a different plane from the rest of the world. I understand you. You understand me. It bodes extremely well for our future together."

"Should I take that as a compliment?"

"Definitely. I say that very rarely."

She hesitated. "Why do I have the feeling I'm not going to like what you have to say?"

"Because you are determined to find the good in the world around you, even when all the evidence is to the contrary."

"That's ludicrous."

"Is it? If you had the slightest bit of healthy cynicism, you'd suspect that those threats were coming from me."

"But they're not."

"No, they're not. But you should suspect it."

"You aren't making any sense."

"My point is this: What I'm about to tell you is an unpleasant tale of greed and deceit. I wouldn't tell it at all except that I believe it will make our future less rocky."

"You're going to say something awful about Howard, aren't you?"

"I'm going to tell you the truth. It isn't always pretty."

"I've been forced to realize since the day you showed me Howard's letter that he was, perhaps, not the man I believed him to be."

He heard the bitterness in her tone, and it caused an unexpected wrenching in his heart. "Disillusionment is always painful."

She met his gaze. "He was all I had," she said quietly.

And the statement strengthened his determination. She may have loved Rendell, but Elliot must have her loyalty now. He must know that she wouldn't betray him. Raking a hand over his face, he prepared himself for the telling of it.

"It began," he finally said, "in the winter of 1835. I was studying at Oxford, and my father was clerking for Howard Rendell." He heard her breath catch.

"Howard employed your father?"

"Yes. I see he neglected to tell you even the barest facts of the story." His tension had nearly become a living, breathing force in the close confines of the carriage. He wondered if she sensed it.

She folded her hands in her lap. "I suppose he did," she said quietly.

"I was able to go to Oxford because of my father's title. The Darewood name is one of the oldest in England. Still, had it not been for Howard's financial assistance, I could not have afforded the fees. For that, I suppose, I should be grateful."

"He did that somewhat commonly. He was known for his generosity to his employees."

"Was he?" He could not keep the bitter tone from his voice.

"Yes."

"Odd, he never felt that way toward my father. During my time at Oxford, my father and I regularly corresponded. Howard, it seemed, was trusting him with more and more responsibilities. By the year before I completed my courses, my father was Rendell's personal secretary."

"I never knew."

"I expect Howard wished to keep the matter quiet."

"He was always so open with me on other issues, I find that quite odd."

"Still, isn't it clear to you that something significant must have happened to cause the enmity between us?"

"Yes," she admitted.

"Did you never question Howard about it?"

"I did."

"And he never told you, did he?"

"He said that something had transpired between him and your family, but I knew no details." Her face puckered into a frown. "Why wouldn't he have told me?"

"Because you'd have loathed him."

He waited while she absorbed the statement. "Everyone makes mistakes," she whispered.

"True. Everyone does not, however, compound those mistakes by destroying the people around them. Like King David and Bathsheba, the sin became larger than its immediate circle."

"And that's what you believe happened to your family?"

He heard the dread in her tone and welcomed it. He had worried that she would discount his story out of hand, but she had known Howard better than perhaps any other person in the world. If anyone would know what kind of treachery the man was capable of, it was she. Elliot consoled himself with the knowledge that Liberty must bear some level of resentment that Howard had kept her as his mistress for ten years, yet refused to give her his name. He had, instead, left her for his nephew in a neat little package. The depth of the betrayal would have hurt her deeply and, as he should have realized sooner, made her more open to the truth. Her presence in Braxton's library last night seemed to suggest that she was already accepting the ugly truth for what it was.

"Howard," he said quietly, "had an affair with the

wife of an investor. The woman and her husband used the affair to blackmail Howard. He could not afford for his business associates to learn of the indiscretion. They would have seriously questioned the sanity of a man who would jeopardize not only his fortune but his personal reputation for the sake of a married woman, and fled from him. He would no doubt have lost much of the capital that investors had provided. To keep the scandal quiet, he persuaded some of his friends to invest in a few of the couple's schemes. Howard not only lost a considerable amount himself but also was responsible for friends and associates losing considerable sums. The ensuing scandal threatened to destroy him."

The carriage rolled into the traffic queue on St. James. "Howard needed someone to take the blame. He chose my father."

Beside him, she gasped. "No. He wouldn't do something like that."

"Wouldn't he?" He met her gaze again. He saw the hurt in her eyes and ruthlessly pressed ahead. "That isn't even the end of the story, Liberty. After accusing my father of embezzlement, he dismissed him, shamed, humiliated, and penniless. My mother had to take in washing to support them. I was at Oxford at the time and did not learn until months later precisely what had happened. In his correspondence, my father told me that Howard had generously retired him after so many years of service."

He uttered a harsh curse. "God, what a fool I was to believe him."

"You couldn't have known."

"I *should* have known. I naively believed that a man like Howard Rendell was above such despicable behavior. It wasn't until I was about to finish my studies that I received an urgent letter from my mother reporting that my father had fallen ill.

"I raced home, only to find that both my parents had succumbed to cholera—no doubt due to the living conditions in the hellhole where they had been forced to move." Her expression was stricken. "Even in death it was easy to see what a toll the last months had taken on my father. He looked emaciated. My mother's hands were chapped and raw from being submerged in the lye-filled water she'd used as a laundress."

Liberty closed her eyes as her lips moved in a silent prayer for their souls. "I am so sorry."

He felt almost oblivious to her now, lost as he was in the memories. "Like a fool, I believed I could turn to Howard for help. At the time, I had no idea what had transpired between him and my father."

"There must have been a misunderstanding. I cannot believe that—"

"There was no misunderstanding." He could not prevent the harshness in his tone. "Howard knew precisely what was happening. He refused to see me, refused to answer my letters. Through his solicitors,

I learned about the accusations against my father. When I searched my parents' papers, I found a letter explaining all that had transpired."

"How old were you then?"

"Nineteen. I had nothing but my education to help me make my way in the world. Because of the smear on my father's name, I was unable to find employment. No one would help me. Finally, I took a job handling cargo for an East Indian freight company. From there, I made myself what I am today."

Gently, she laid her hand atop his. The simple contact sent fire racing through his blood as he thought of crushing her in his embrace. She seemed unaware of his inner struggle as she softly stroked his hand. "I am sorry you had to endure this."

"But you don't believe it?"

"I cannot believe Howard would willingly do something like that. Even—" She broke off.

"Even though his ledgers suggest other areas of deceit?"

She shook her head. "It goes against all I know of him. He was a very caring man."

He pressed harder. "Would a caring man have left you in the intolerable position that Howard did?"

She quickly masked the flare of hurt in her gaze. "Howard was not a cruel man. His faults lay elsewhere." She leaned closer to him. "What matters to me is that you believe it. It hurt you tremendously, Elliot. You should have told me."

The compassion in her gaze astonished him. People had felt many things for and about him, but compassion had never been among them. The experience was so unique, he could barely credit it. "I did not tell you to elicit your sympathy."

"Did you tell me to make me angry at Howard?"

"No. I felt it would help you better understand that I am not completely insensitive to your situation. We share an uncommon bond, you and I. We both have been injured by Howard's greed."

She studied his face for long, nerve-racking seconds. Elliot had the distinct impression she was trying to see into his soul. As if she had finally found what she sought, she relaxed against the back of her seat. "You may not have wanted my sympathy, Elliot, but I fear you shall have to endure it. You are a most remarkable man, perhaps because of all you've survived to become who you are."

"I did more than endure it," he told her. His hand turned to hold hers in a bruising grip. "I grew stronger for it. And I swore to myself that never again would Howard Rendell have the final victory."

Chapter 7

When Elliot escorted her up the stairs of Lady Asterly's town house a quarter hour later, she was still contemplating the extraordinary story. Her heart ached for him in a way that changed everything for her. "Are you certain," she asked, "that Lady Asterly wants to go through with this?"

"Absolutely certain." He waited while she unbuckled the clasps of her cloak. "Since I told her the news of our engagement, she has been ready to expire from curiosity and glee."

"But surely she knows how much gossip this will cause." She barely refrained from adding "as do you." She couldn't believe that, after so many years of relative privacy, Elliot was willing to make his affairs known to the world. He was inviting comment on his person and his motives, and comment was bound to lead to speculation. In time, he'd have to face new questions about his father's relationship with Howard.

Elliot seemed not to notice her discomfort. "She's

reveling in it, I assure you. There is nothing Pearl likes more than to be at the heart of a good rumor."

"Something private and small would have sufficed." She saw the determined look in his eyes as she silently passed him her cloak. "This seems a trifle too dramatic."

"I thought the drama would appeal to you."

Liberty glanced at him in surprise. "You did?"

"Naturally. You have quite a feel for dramatics, Liberty." He lifted his hand to touch her hair. "With that streak of fire in your hair, it's almost a given."

"My hair is a very ordinary brown, my lord."

"No, Liberty, it is not." His fingers burrowed deeper until they touched her scalp. "Like the rest of you, there's nothing ordinary about it."

"I do believe you are trying to flatter me."

"I am trying to be agreeable."

"Flattery is always a good start."

"I believe," he said as he drew her hand through the bend of his arm, "that you and I will fare quite nicely. Ready?"

She nodded. "Should I warn you now that this is my first dinner party? I've never attended a formal affair like this."

"The object"—he paused to hand his cloak and hers to the waiting footman—"is to end the evening with no silverware left at your setting."

Liberty gave him a startled look. "Are you teasing me?"

"This is an evening for firsts, is it not? I happen to be possessed of a very healthy sense of humor."

"I had heard it was limited to the ill variety."

With a slight groan, Elliot pressed his hand to the small of her back. "I see I shall have to endeavor to correct your perceptions. Shall we go in?"

Still, she hesitated. "I hope you are prepared for the type of reception we're going to receive."

"You need have no concerns on that count. You are my guest. You will be treated accordingly."

She was quite certain he didn't understand. "My lord, you must see that you are about to invite comment on both your person and your wisdom. I'm not sure it's wise for you to—"

"Liberty, I have made it quite clear to everyone assembled that I will not tolerate an affront."

"Or there will be consequences?" she guessed.

"Precisely."

"Do you get everywhere in this life by threatening people?"

"Only when I find it necessary."

"You would not think it would be so terribly difficult for a gentleman who has systematically built a financial empire to carry off one simple evening with a woman like me. I am, after all, merely an employee of the late Earl of Huxley."

Elliot stopped just outside the door to Lady Asterly's drawing room. "What do you mean?"

She glanced furtively at the door. How could she make him understand what she was feeling? Howard, she was beginning to realize, had robbed her of far more than her reputation. While she struggled to appear confident and poised, a hint of fear slipped through her armor in unguarded moments. "They will say awful things."

His gaze narrowed. "I know. I can spare you the sting of them, but not the reality."

The empathy she saw in his gaze captured her heart. She realized that he once had faced the same insecurity.

She struggled for control. "I am merely the former employee of the late Earl of Huxley, my lord. Any one of them will tell you that I'm hardly worthy of your protection or respect."

Beneath the fine cut of his black evening jacket, his shoulders squared. He gave her a direct look that seemed to see all the way to her soul. "Never," he said quietly, "say that again."

His blunt tone surprised her. "It is true."

"It is not. You may not have been born to luxury, and you may have made some choices that cast you onto the fringes of Society, but if I have learned one thing, it is that the measure of a man is not in his station but in his honor. You have my respect. Never doubt it."

At the soft admission, she shivered. "I don't know what to say."

"No response is necessary. You are very accustomed to steering your own way through the world.

I think, however, that you will find tonight easier if you leave it in my hands."

"Trust you to take care of everything? Is that the point?"

"It is."

"How many brides, I wonder, hear the same thing on their wedding night?"

Elliot managed a half smile. "Most of them aren't wearing any clothes by the time the conversation progresses to that point."

She felt her face flush but refused to look away.

With a slight nod to the footman, Elliot indicated that they were ready to enter the assembly. "That is why I hope you will allow yourself the pleasure of the evening without dwelling too closely on the past."

The door swung open to reveal the glittering interior of Lady Asterly's dining salon. Scattered about were brilliantly clad ladies and gentlemen of Society. Gems glistened in the candlelight. Satins and silks rustled in the still air. A sumptuous buffet filled the air with tantalizing scents.

And had it not been for the firm pressure of his hand at the small of her back, Liberty would have fled.

Thirty sets of eyes focused on their arrival. To her left, Liberty heard an audible gasp as an elderly woman recognized them, then sank onto one of the sofas. She sensed the sneering expressions before she saw them, felt the escalating tension as they stood motionless just inside the door. Elliot's efforts, it seemed, had managed to quell the possibility of a direct cut, but nothing could have dimmed the impact of their arrival.

Beneath her fingers, she felt his forearm tense and sensed his anger. Fortunately, all were diverted by the sound of Lady Asterly's imperious voice. "Clear the path. I cannot see my own guests."

Like a parting curtain, the assembly pressed back against the walls. Lady Asterly sat at the far end of the room, ensconced in a wheelchair. Despite her awkward position, with one leg propped up, she had a bearing that even the queen might envy. She viewed them for long seconds through her quizzing glass before her wrinkled face shifted into a smile. "I see it's my very dear friends Viscount Darewood and Miss Madison. Come here." She pointed at Elliot. "You are late, my boy."

An audible sound of relief rippled among the guests. Garrick hurried forward to meet them. "What kept you, Moss? Are you enjoying the benefits of a grand entrance?"

Elliot glowered at him. "You seem to have lost some of your touch in spreading goodwill, Garrick. The reception has been noticeably chilled."

"I did what I could. Tongues are still wagging about that bit with the cigar the other day." He lifted Liberty's hand to his lips. "Miss Madison, may I say what a very great privilege it is to see you here tonight. You look stunning."

She gave him a grateful smile. She was all too aware that the severe black of her dress stood in stark relief to the brightly colored clothing of the other women. "Thank you, Mr. Frost."

Elliot gave Garrick a warning look. "Flirting with my bride is not in your best interest, Frost."

Garrick pressed a hand to his chest in an innocent gesture, but his expression was pure devilment. "Darewood, you cannot believe that of me."

"Then release her hand," Elliot insisted.

Liberty glanced at him sharply. "There's no need to be rude, my lord. Mr. Frost is merely being friendly."

"Give him half a chance, and he'll gladly show you how friendly he can be." The amusement in his voice took some of the sting from his rebuke. Garrick was a notorious rakehell, but his loyalty to Elliot was unquestioned. Friends since childhood, the two were closer than brothers, and not a soul in London was unaware that Garrick had Elliot's unwavering support.

Perhaps that was why she felt such a quick rapport with Garrick. He, too, understood Elliot's silent pain and sought to lessen it. She liked him immensely.

"Darewood," Pearl Asterly commanded, "stop dillying with Frost and come here. You've yet to greet me properly."

Elliot obediently pressed Liberty forward through the crowd. "Forgive me, madam. I thought perhaps you'd overlook my tardiness when you saw my reason. I had to make an extra stop to fetch Miss Madison to you."

Elliot greeted Lady Asterly with genuine affection. He kissed her gloved hand, then gave it a gentle squeeze before turning to Liberty. "I thought," he told them both, "you'd be very glad to see her."

Lady Asterly patted his cheek. "You know I am, of course. Besides, you've managed to make my party the talk of the town. This will be all over London by tomorrow noon. I do so love to be the focus of gossip."

Elliot laughed, a rare, genuine laugh. "So you do, madam. I'm glad I could oblige you. You'll have to forgive Miss Madison, however," he said in a conspiratorial whisper. "She isn't used to seeing me so agreeable."

Pearl snorted. "Who is?" She glanced at Liberty. "Come here, dear. I haven't seen you in far too long."

Elliot urged her forward. "Stay with Pearl." He mouthed the words in her ear. "I'll fetch you a chair. Try to enjoy yourself, hmm?"

Liberty took the remaining step into the circle of affection. Lady Asterly greeted her by seizing both her hands. "My dear, I am so glad you allowed Darewood to bring you. I know Huxley's death has been a tremendous strain on you."

Liberty sank gratefully into the brocade chair Elliot had procured for her. "It has."

"I want you to tell me everything that has happened. I missed so much in my confinement."

Elliot gave Liberty's shoulder a brief squeeze as he passed. "I shall leave you to your visit. I have some business to attend to."

"Young man," Lady Asterly said grimly, "need I remind you that this is a party?"

"No, madam, but neither must I remind you that I am most at ease when conducting business. You wouldn't want to see me frustrated, would you?" With a broad wink, he strolled away.

"Insolent pup," Lady Asterly muttered. "Don't know why I put up with him, other than the fact that my ego benefits from having such a handsome gentleman attend to me."

As Elliot moved away from them, Liberty regarded him with a worried expression. The hard set of his jaw didn't bode well for a pleasant evening. He made his way through the throng of guests, stopping occasionally to speak. Unless she missed her guess, he was making known his displeasure at their reception. The strained expressions that followed his brief conversations confirmed her suspicions. Pearl patted her hand to recapture her attention. "You look distracted, dear."

Liberty gave her an apologetic look. "I'm sorry, madam. I seem to be preoccupied with what's still to come this evening."

Lady Asterly tipped her head to one side. "Are you worried about the gossip?"

"Gossip and its consequences are rarely pleasant."

"Hmm. Howard taught you that lesson, I suppose."

Liberty glanced at her in surprise. "What do you mean?"

"He left you vulnerable, dear. It was unfair of him to leave you to carry the burden of his choices."

"I enjoyed my life with the Earl."

"I'm certain you did. Still, an honorable man would have protected you better."

"He was very good to me."

"He used you," she said with characteristic bluntness. "It's all right, Liberty. You needn't defend the man to me. Howard was a dear friend, but he had his flaws. The largest was greed."

Something began to unravel within Liberty. Twice in one night, someone—first Elliot and now Lady Asterly—had struck at the core of the matter. The longer she had to think of what Howard had done to her, the closer she came to anger. Elliot's story tonight had been both unsettling and confusing.

She didn't want to resent Howard, but as evidence continued to mount against him, she couldn't seem to prevent the rising tide. Pearl was watching her closely. Liberty forced herself to meet her gaze. "May I confide in you, your ladyship?"

"I'd be hurt if you didn't."

The chance to tell the whole story, to talk it over with a caring soul, was like a balm to Liberty's heart. Slowly at first, then with increasing conviction, she repeated the events since Howard's illness and subsequent death. Through the telling of it, she was acutely conscious of Elliot's gaze on her as he wended his way through the room. The hum of conversation surrounded her in the stuffy interior of the salon, but still, she sensed rather than heard the low rumble of his voice as he spoke with the guests. Their earlier curiosity about her presence had not abated, she knew. They still stared as they passed. Whispers were still exchanged behind gloved fingers. But gradually, as she poured out her heart to Lady Asterly, she was able to put the focus of the crowd from her mind.

"Dear God," Pearl Asterly said at last. "That's horrible. Howard left you with little choice but to marry that reprobate nephew of his."

"That was the way it seemed. I would like to believe that he was doing what he thought was best. Still, he must have known I couldn't possibly hope to maintain his estate without benefit of a husband."

With a snort, Lady Asterly replied, "Never underestimate Rendell's devious nature, Liberty."

She looked at her in surprise. "Your ladyship, I believed that you and Howard—"

"So we were, but my friendship with the man extended nearly thirty years. I feel I knew him better than almost anyone on this earth, and you may take my word that he was plotting something, even while he lay dying. Howard's mind would

have been the very last part of him to stop func-
tioning." As if she sensed Liberty's internal struggle,
she reached for her hand. "My dear girl, do not
allow the situation to distress you so. Howard
trusted you implicitly. He valued your judgment
and advice, just as he valued your affection. He
would have known you had it within you to make
the right choices."

"And you think I've done that by agreeing to
Elliot's proposal?"

Lady Asterly found Elliot's dark head with her
gaze. "Were I in your shoes, I would give serious
attention to the determination Elliot Moss is
showing in his pursuit."

"He wants only the Cross of Aragon, and I am
not even sure Howard owned it. In fact, I am almost
certain he did not."

"My dear, you are an exceptionally intelligent
young woman. You have told Moss that you are not
sure you can procure the cross for him, have you
not?"

"Yes."

"And yet he pursues you anyway. Why do you
think that is?"

"I"—she glanced at Elliot and found him watching her—"I don't know. I hadn't considered it."

"Only because you have been so distraught that
you are not thinking clearly." Lady Asterly indicated Elliot with a nod of her head. "There is more

to Darewood than meets the eye, I assure you. He is a most enigmatic man, and if he has decided he must have you, then he will let very little stand in his way."

"I do not like the idea that I am little more than prey in his quest for possessions."

"Even if that were so, there is no reason you shouldn't benefit from the liaison yourself."

Liberty's heart fluttered a bit as she thought of the possibilities. Over the course of the last half hour, she had watched Elliot in the crowd. Society seemed to welcome him. She'd lost count of the number of beautiful women she'd seen clinging to his arm and sending him longing glances. His presence was commanding. From the moment he entered a room, he became its focus. But she sensed in him a loneliness that echoed her own, and it did dangerous things to her heart. What drew her to him, she realized, was the inexorable sense of belonging she felt when she was with him. He made her feel valued, prized in some way. He listened to her. He talked with her, not at her. He respected her opinion. And he caused her heart to race and her skin to tingle, no matter how much she might like to deny it.

"Moss is an extraordinarily powerful man," Lady Asterly said. "You cannot tell me you haven't noticed it."

"I have, of course. Who would not?"

"And tonight, in any case, that power is all yours."

Her throat felt suddenly constricted.

"You know, of course, that he's spent the better part of the last half hour terrorizing my guests into accepting you into their circle?"

"I feared that." She felt the unmistakable magnetic pull of Elliot's gaze on her face. Unable to resist, she turned and sought him. This time he leaned against the far wall, apart from the crowd, watching her with his unreadable green eyes. There was an intensity in his gaze that forced her heart into her throat. She could not make herself look away.

"I would wager by now that Moss holds the potential fortunes of at least a dozen of my guests in his breast pocket. One word from him could send them crashing to their doom. They wouldn't dare cross him, and he has made it quite clear that he will accept nothing less than the utmost respect for you." She leaned back in her chair. "My dear, think very hard about what you want to do with that much power."

Before Liberty could respond, Lady Asterly's butler sounded the supper bell. The guests moved toward the dining table in a wave of satin and silk. Liberty sat in stunned silence as a footman wheeled Pearl Asterly to her position at the table.

Elliot bore down on her like a falcon seeking prey. "Did you have a pleasant conversation?"

His voice made her shiver. "I—yes, yes, we did. Thank you for asking."

He held her chair while she rose, then spun it back into its original position with a deft turn of his wrist. "I am glad."

"Did you finish conducting your business?" she pressed.

She almost felt the cloak of determination that settled about him. "I believe so. I will know at the end of the evening."

On impulse, Liberty laid her hand on his black sleeve. The slight contact seemed to make the air between them crackle. Elliot's gaze drifted to the spot where her pale fingers lay against his evening jacket. Her breathing turned shallow as she absorbed the heat of him with her palm. "It was not necessary," she managed to say, "for you to intervene on my behalf. I know what people say about me."

His gaze remained on her hand. "I found it extremely necessary."

"I didn't mean that it wasn't appreciated"—she waited until he met her gaze—"merely that I knew you were under no obligation."

He smiled at her. The gentleness of it nearly threatened to undo her. The breath lodged in her lungs. Her heart missed its next beat. Her fingers tightened inexorably on his arm. "My dear Miss Madison," he said, "you've no idea the extent of your sway over me, and I find the notion singularly intoxicating."

"You do?"

"Absolutely."

He led her in to supper without another word, and Liberty found, to her very great and pleasant surprise, that she enjoyed herself immensely. The Swedish ambassador sat on her left, and an elderly member of the House of Lords on her right. She conversed with both of them on their respective interests, and found herself feeling almost light-headed after so many weeks of despair. Several times she felt Elliot's gaze resting on her. Twice she met it. The lambent heat in his eyes carried to her down the length of the table, and once, she saw a flash of such blatant possession, she nearly tipped her wineglass.

By the time the ladies rose to leave the gentlemen to their port and cigars, her knees felt slightly weak. The combination of the wine, the conversation, and the tension she'd felt growing between her and Elliot made her heart flutter so violently that she feared she'd disgrace herself by collapsing at her seat. She hesitated briefly as she gathered her wits.

In the instant before she rose, a striking red-headed woman, dressed in dazzling diamond-accented white satin, stopped by her chair. Earlier in the evening, Liberty had seen Elliot embroiled in a heated conversation with the woman, whom Lady Asterly had identified as Vivian Woolrich. During supper, Lady Woolrich had cast several antagonistic looks down the table toward Liberty. Now, in close proximity, Liberty could feel her animosity. It marred the classic perfection of her face, adding years to her carefully maintained beauty. "Perhaps, my dear Miss Madison"—her voice held an unmistakable venom—"you did not know that *ladies* leave gentlemen to their cigars."

The emphasis, and its implied meaning, plunged the room into a nervous silence. The blatant challenge in the comment failed to shock her. In the years she'd spent in Howard's employ, she'd heard nearly every insult Society had to offer. This one, in truth, was tamer than most.

Sensing Elliot's watchful gaze on her face, Liberty slowly rose from her chair. "Perhaps your ladyship is unaware that ladies do not listen to the common gossip of the gutters."

The other woman's face colored. Garrick Frost materialized at Vivian's elbow. "My lady, I've decided to forgo port this evening in favor of a hand of whist with you. Will you walk with me to the card room?"

Vivian hesitated as, across the room, Elliot centered his gaze on her face. For breathless seconds, danger hung in the still air. Finally, when Liberty feared a confrontation was unavoidable, Vivian lifted her chin in defiance and slipped her hand into the bend of Garrick's elbow. "Gladly," she snapped.

In seconds, Elliot stood behind Liberty. His warm hands closed on her shoulders. "Sorry," he whispered. "It won't happen again."

Briefly, she allowed herself to enjoy the pleasure of his reassuring strength. "I fear, my lord, that you delude yourself. It will no doubt happen dozens of times."

His fingers tightened. "Not if I have anything to say about it. Vivian's a shrew. I'll not let her upset you."

The guests were beginning a slow exodus to the card room. Liberty remained in Elliot's protective shadow. The experience was utterly new for her. Howard had never shared her outrage at the injustice of it all. In fact, he had often chastened her for allowing the barbed comments to sting, and over the years, she had cultivated the appearance of casual indifference. That Elliot had chosen to give her his protection was a startling display of loyalty. He believed her to be Howard's humiliated mistress, yet his earlier words about honor had revealed the depth of his feelings.

Suddenly, she felt a great surge of affection for this man who had weathered such a difficult storm. She waited until most of the guests were out of earshot before she covered one of his hands with hers. "My lord, I assure you, I am almost immune to the Lady Woolriches of the world."

His skin felt hot beneath hers. "I am glad. If you find yourself needing retribution, however, you have only to ask."

She decided to redirect his underlying tension before he thought to confront Vivian in the card room. "If you are in the business of arranging revenge, I will confess I would like very much to exact a bit on Sirs Drake, Frampton, and Wainscot."

His eyebrows lifted. "What have they done?"

"You know, of course, that in the week following Howard's death I nearly succeeded in purchasing a coal mine in Manchester."

"So I heard."

"My efforts were foiled when Drake convinced Frampton and Wainscot to withdraw their financing. The flow of income from the mine would have been a blessing. As it was, the efforts I put into purchasing it were lost due to Drake's distrust of my abilities."

Elliot turned her to face him. "And you were embarrassed?"

"I had made several promises based on the projected income of the mine. I was forced to renege on them."

"First rule of business, Miss Madison. Never count cash until you have it in hand."

"I was taking a desperate gamble, something I thought you'd understand."

"I do." He studied her a minute, his eyes twinkling. "Do you like to gamble?"

"I wouldn't say I enjoy it, but I will do it if it's necessary."

He glanced at Daniel Drake's balding head, visible amid the milling crowd. "Would you be willing to gamble if it meant besting Drake, Frampton, and Wainscot?"

"Gladly."

He smiled. "That raises an interesting question I've been meaning to ask you. How well do you play cards?"

Liberty finally understood his meaning. Elliot, she was learning, was a man of infinite complexities. She never would have imagined that he possessed so deep a sense of irony. With a slight nod of assurance, she laid her hand on his sleeve. "Extremely well."

Her answer seemed to please him. "I have been struggling for some time to determine just what I might give you for a wedding present."

"I thought you gave me Braxton's ledgers."

"That was merely a betrothal gift."

"I see. Now you have decided to give me revenge on Drake, Frampton, and Wainscot?"

"No. I could, but I don't think you'd appreciate it quite as much as the opportunity to earn it yourself."

"My lord, are you suggesting what I think you are?"

"I am suggesting, Miss Madison, that a card game might provide you with a fitting opportunity to win back your mine."

"What a charming offer."

"I thought you'd feel that way."

On impulse, she went up on her tiptoes to kiss his cheek. "Never let anyone convince you that you aren't a nice man, Elliot." She slid her hand into his. "Shall we join the others in the card room now?"

"No. I am afraid we will have to exact your revenge later." He squeezed her fingers. "We are expected in the chapel."

Chapter 8

Elliot slanted her a cautious look as they entered the small chapel. Pearl's guests were seated in silence, watching Garrick consult with the Reverend Adam Patterson. The room was elegantly decorated with great bowls of floating orchids and rows of candles. White satin bows festooned the pews and, Elliot noted with satisfaction, Vivian Woolrich was absent.

He wished he knew what Garrick had told the guests when Pearl had instructed her staff to escort them to her chapel. The room was legend enough. To his knowledge, Pearl had never allowed another soul to enter it. She'd had the ballroom of her town house converted and sanctified as a chapel when her son had returned, unharmed, from the war on the Continent. She had given her word to God, she'd explained to the cynics, that her son's life was more than worth the sacrifice of her ballroom.

It was an elegant room with stained-glass windows and hand-carved pews. It had a certain warmth to it that had appealed to Elliot when Pearl first had shown it to him. Her guests, he was sure, were speechless at finding themselves in church when they'd been expecting a night of card play and drinking.

At the moment, however, he was more concerned with Liberty's reaction than the assembly's collective surprise. Her gaze darted about the room as if she wished to flee.

Elliot accepted a bouquet of orchids from a housemaid and gently pressed it into Liberty's hand. "Madam." His low voice was meant for her alone. "You are not contemplating leaving me at the altar, are you?"

Her gaze flew to his. "What have you done?"

With one hand, he brushed a stray curl from her face. Deliberately, he ignored the eyes focused on them, the fluttering fans, and the whispers. "Before you go looking for sentimental heroics where there are none, be fully aware that this arrangement serves my own purposes." He indicated the assembled guests with a slight tilt of his head. "By midnight tonight, all London will know that I've made this uncharacteristically extravagant gesture, and I shall be saved a considerable amount of time and effort entertaining all the curiosity seekers."

"I see." Something dangerously close to tears clouded her eyes. He hoped to God she wasn't going to start crying. He had no idea what he'd do if she did. "So I am to assume that you planned all this merely to ensure that the gossip about our marriage is kept to a minimum?"

"You are correct. If Society spends its time gossiping about our wedding, they'll have no energy left to discuss our marriage."

"I don't think it's going to work, Elliot."

He frowned. "You don't think I've created a significant enough distraction?"

She shook her head. "Not that. I don't think you're going to be able to convince me that you did all this to save yourself from bother." She brushed a stray tear from her eye. "You may have the rest of them convinced that you are a cold, unsentimental man, but you haven't fooled me one bit."

His skin felt paler. "I haven't?"

"No." Drawing a deep breath, she turned to face the minister down the length of the center aisle. "You haven't. You have shown me respect, Elliot. It's all I could have wanted and more."

An hour later, Liberty sat at the dressing table of her new room in Darewood House, the extraordinary events of the evening still tumbling through her mind. The wedding had been short, simple, and grand. Garrick had acted as Elliot's best man, while Pearl Asterly had attended Liberty. During the service, she found comfort in the deep assurance of Elliot's voice. He repeated his vows with no hesitation; his quiet strength seemed to suffuse her. Ever present in her mind was the incredible knowledge

that he'd chosen this course in front of the very
people who'd scorned him. Despite his own experience, he'd chosen to make them fully aware that he
would tolerate no slight of his new bride. He'd
given her value.

And she could never repay him.

By the time the ceremony ended, even the most
staid of Pearl's guests were offering their heartiest
congratulations. Elliot had promptly escorted her to
his carriage, murmuring something about tying up a
few loose strings before joining her at Darewood
House. With a brief kiss, he'd bundled her into the
carriage with instructions to his driver to see her
safely home.

She'd been in a quiet state of confusion ever
since.

She arrived at Elliot's home to find his staff
expecting her. Instructions had been given for the
placement of her things, miraculously transferred
from her small rooms in Huxley House. She was
greeted with great ceremony by Wickers, Elliot's
butler, who could not seem to offer her enough service. The housekeeper ushered her up the stairs and
into the magnificent chamber that had belonged,
Liberty was told, to every Viscountess Darewood
since the fifteenth century.

Inside, her clothes hung in the wardrobe, her few
personal items were laid out on the dresser, and
what might have been called a nightgown, had it
contained a few more yards of fabric, was lying

across the bed. It all seemed terribly intimate. And irrevocable.

A soft knock interrupted her musing. "Come in."

A young maid, dressed in the pristine attire Elliot provided for his entire staff, entered her room. "Good evening, your ladyship."

The title sounded foreign. Formerly, she'd been one of the staff. She felt awkward and uncomfortable with the formality of it all. "Hello."

"His lordship is waiting for you in the library. He's just returned."

Liberty drew a deep breath. She wasn't sure whether to be relieved or concerned. "Thank you."

"I'll fetch a footman to escort you."

Liberty was already walking to the door. "No, that won't be necessary. I know the way."

"But, my lady, I think his lordship would prefer—"

She paused. This etiquette business was new to her. Members of the house staff didn't worry with such trappings as escorts down dark stairways. She drew a deep breath. "I suppose you're right." The girl looked vastly relieved. "What is your name?"

"I—it's Emily, your ladyship."

"Emily." Liberty nodded. "Emily, I think this would be as good a time as any for me to tell you that this is as strange to me as it is to you."

"Strange, ma'am?"

"Yes. I'm certain you know who I am."

Nervousness flicked across her features. "Your ladyship, I wouldn't—"

Liberty waved a hand in agitation. "Please, I'm not sure I can go on this way. Until four hours ago, I was a virtual servant in the Earl of Huxley's house. I lived in third-floor quarters. I took my meals alone or in the kitchen. I'm going to have some trouble adjusting to all this, and I'd like your help."

"My help, your ladyship?"

"Yes. I know enough about household staffs to know that if his lordship told you that he and I were going to be married this evening, you have been discussing it since he left. Isn't that correct?"

"He doesn't like us to gossip, my lady."

Liberty hid a smile. "I'm quite sure he doesn't."

"And I think you should know that we never do—not outside the house, anyway. His lordship wouldn't tolerate that one bit. We get paid well for working here, and we are all happy. No one would like to be dismissed for gossip."

"I understand."

"But it was shocking news he gave us. No one was expecting his lordship to marry."

"And especially not to marry me?"

Emily blushed. "Your ladyship—"

"It's all right, Emily. I understand." She couldn't quite keep the bitterness from her tone. For ten years she'd suffered the disapproval of Howard's staff. Nothing, it seemed, had changed.

"No, your ladyship, I don't think you do. Begging your pardon, but his lordship's instructions were most precise. He told us before he left this evening that he'd finally found a woman he trusted enough to be his wife. He gathered us all in the front hall and said that he knew you'd be fair and honest in your dealings with us, and that we should give whatever loyalty we owe him to you."

"He said that?" Elliot was turning out to be full of surprises.

"Yes, ma'am. His lordship couldn't find enough good things to say about you, and we were all looking forward to having you here. It's been quiet for too long."

"Dear God." Liberty wiped a hand over her face. "The man is certainly an enigma, isn't he?"

"Ma'am?"

She shook her head. "Never mind. I will join the viscount in the library now, if you would be so kind as to provide me with an escort."

She peeked her head out the door. "I've already got Jim. He'll be glad to walk down with you."

The adoring look that passed between the young footman and Emily was unmistakable. Liberty found herself simultaneously warmed by the obvious affection and chilled by the idea that, once again, she'd found herself in a house where she would never belong. They might respect her, but she would have no friends among them. An aching sense of loss filled her as she realized that Howard truly had robbed her of everything.

Saddened, fatigued, she walked in silence beside Jim to the library. Elliot glanced up from his desk when she entered. "Thank you, Jim," he told the footman. "That will be all."

The door whispered shut behind him. Liberty stood in the large room feeling suddenly over-whelmed by the enormity of the situation. "You're home," she managed to say.

He pushed aside the large stack of papers on his desk as he rose. In several long strides, he made his way across the room. "I am. I'm sorry I had to leave you alone for so long."

She dropped into a small chair. Like the man him-self, his furnishings, though vaguely out of style, gave the unique impression of utterly belonging. Her head tipped back against the wood.

Elliot's gaze narrowed. "You look exhausted."

She managed a slight laugh. "This has been a long day for me."

He moved to the beverage cart. "Would you like something to drink?"

"No."

After pouring himself a glass of water, he took the seat across from her. "You found your things in order?"

"Yes." Dear Lord, they sounded like strangers at a dinner party.

"The room is to your liking?"

"It's lovely."

"You're satisfied with Emily as your maid?"

"Yes."

"You're sure?"

She gave him a pointed look. "As I've never had a lady's maid, I'm not entirely sure what I'm supposed to do with her. She seems pleasant enough, but it'll take me a while to learn the way of it."

With a muttered oath, he surged out of his chair and began pacing the library. She felt the raw energy in him. She forced herself to remain utterly still in her chair while she waited. Emily's words still played in her mind. As she considered the almost unbelievable events of the night—the attention he'd paid to the details of their wedding; the speech he had given his staff on her behalf; the deliberate way he'd handed her a salve for her pride in front of Carlton and his mother; and, even more astonishing, the story he'd told her of his father— she found herself dangerously drawn to him. She could not afford, under any circumstances, to surrender herself to him. To do so would give him the power to destroy her. She couldn't let it happen again.

Elliot seemed unaware of her internal struggle. He was too absorbed in thoughts of his own. "I don't want it to be like this between us, Liberty. We sound like strangers."

"I'm sorry."

"Don't apologize." The words sounded harsh. He drew a deep breath, then said more quietly, "Please, don't apologize. This is as awkward for me as it is for you. I've never had a wife before. I'm not certain what to do with one."

"Then we're at evens, my lord, since I've never had a husband."

Some of the tension visibly drained from him. "Do you think it would be possible for us to go back to the way we were? I thought we'd developed a decent rapport."

"You would."

His expression told her that he knew full well she was referring to the physical chemistry between them. "I would like us to be friends. I thought we'd agreed on that."

"We did."

"Then do you believe it possible for us to start this conversation again?"

"That's not necessary." She folded her hands in her lap. "Now that we have the niceties out of the way, why don't we just move ahead. You may begin by telling me what you've been about since I left you at Lady Asterly's. You haven't been creating more trouble, I hope."

"I have been trailing after Carlton Rendell in an effort to ensure that he knows you now have my protection."

"That must have been pleasant. He's always such a stimulating conversationalist."

"You should have told me"—his voice turned inflexible—"that Carlton planned to wed you tomorrow at noon."

"It would have changed nothing."

"It would have changed the civility of my encounter with him."

"My lord, you simply must learn that you cannot go about threatening people into—"

He held up his hand. "Liberty, do you have any idea what Carlton intended to do to you tomorrow?"

"I assumed he'd arranged some private ceremony. It wasn't as if he particularly cared how the event came off. His only interest was in the transfer of the funds."

Elliot muttered something beneath his breath. "One day, you will have to learn that people rarely have honorable intentions—especially men." He studied her face. "You have no idea, do you?"

His tone made her stomach flutter. "Of what?"

"Arranging a special license isn't necessarily a simple procedure. The purchaser has to present a compelling reason for the haste. Since Victoria has been queen, the law has been difficult to manipulate. It seems that Her Majesty was tired of seeing so many marriages performed in haste at Gretna Green. At her direction, the authorities now require certain waiting periods and credentials before they will issue a license. In our case"—he waved his hands between them—"the credentials I gave were several hundred pounds in the hands of the right men."

"I see."

"Carlton, obviously, didn't have the same luxury. His credit is nonexistent. He has no cash, and there's not a soul in London who doesn't know it. By informing his bankers that he planned to wed you, he was able to extend his debts, but no one was going to give him the funds to procure a license."

"But he got one," she insisted. "I saw it."

"Oh, he got one. He used the best possible reason there is for a hasty wedding. He told the authorities that you were pregnant with his child."

Liberty took a shocked breath. "My God."

"Garrick discovered it this afternoon. I thought that it would be prudent for us to dispense with that particular bit of unpleasantness as quickly as possible. I don't think that any member of Society, given my long-standing feud with Howard, would believe that I would willingly marry you if you carried Carlton's child. A very public ceremony, one guaranteed to be on the lips of every gossip hound in the city by midnight tonight, seemed most efficient."

Liberty dropped her head into her hands. "My God."

"I am sorry," he said quietly, "that you had to learn of this. I would have liked to spare you from it."

"I cannot believe this."

"Liberty." When he spoke her name, his voice was very close to her ear. She glanced up to find him standing next to her chair. "I know you would have preferred to avoid the scandal. If it is any consolation to you, so would I, but I felt this was best. I chose not to discuss it with you before the ceremony because I saw no need to cause you any additional anxiety."

The words did not come easily to him. Elliot Moss was a man who generally chose his course and pursued it, damning any and all consequences, yet his concern for her seemed genuine. Again, she remembered Emily's words. "My lord, will you answer me one question?"

"Anything."

"Did you, indeed, tell your staff this evening that you were marrying me because you trusted me?"

His eyebrows lifted in surprise. "I did."

"And did you mean it?"

"Yes." Exhaling a long breath, Elliot reached for her hand and guided her to the sofa so he could sit next to her. He brushed a curl away from her face, leaving a trail of goose bumps on her flesh. "Had things been different in our lives, you and I might have been friends."

"Had I been a man, you mean?"

At that, his lips twitched. "I assure you, I much prefer the feminine package."

She dropped her gaze to the strong line of his jaw. "Despite my rather tedious tendency to find the very best in everyone?"

He made a small sound in the back of his throat that might have been a laugh, yet she was certain the look she saw in his eyes had nothing to do with amusement. "I suppose I shall have to learn to overlook that most unfortunate aspect of your character, madam. Though I confess, at times I will probably find it trying."

Liberty lowered her gaze. She felt suddenly awash with fatigue and disillusionment. All the pressure of the last few days seemed to settle on her breast like a leaden weight. "So long as we are being candid, my lord, may I ask one more question?"

"Of course." He swept the pad of his thumb along the line of her jaw.

"This is difficult for me."

"I understand."

She couldn't concentrate with the feel of his fingers, warm and strong, nestling in her hair and lightly resting on her scalp. The memory of his touch the last time he'd held her had her insides quaking. When she thought of what lay ahead, of how it would be to see him like this every day, indecision tore at her heart. When he'd told her the story of his father's disgrace, something in her had gone irrevocably into his keeping. Tonight, she ached to ease the loneliness she saw in his eyes.

He'd given her more than he could possibly know. She could not remember the last time she'd felt valued. Tonight, he had gone to incredible lengths. He had restored her dignity and given her a measure of worth she had never previously enjoyed. In a thousand ways he'd shown her, and the world, that she mattered to him. She held the gift to her heart like a priceless treasure. No matter the cost, no matter the folly, she could not deny Elliot Moss the only thing she had to give him.

The choice, she realized, was not entirely about physical attraction. He expected, of course, that she was considerably experienced in these matters. What she wanted, what she hoped he wanted, was not merely her presence in his bed. It was the sure knowledge of companionship.

Tonight, he'd walked into an environment where he felt singularly uncomfortable and orchestrated his own return to the public eye, all on her behalf. Whatever his reasons, and she suspected they ran far deeper than his thirst for the Cross of Aragon, Elliot had chosen to make her the center of his considerably daunting attention.

Instinctively, she sensed that he had shared a hidden part of his soul with her tonight—something he did not easily give. He had chosen to entrust her with a painful bit of knowledge, and she would cherish it for the rest of her life.

"Liberty?" His voice sounded mysterious, intent. "I am waiting."

Slowly, she forced herself to meet his gaze. The heat she saw there awakened an answering flame in her belly. "Given our discussion of the physical nature of our relationship, I would like to know—"

Elliot cupped her face in both his hands. "Know what? Why do I touch you like this?" His thumb grazed her lips. "Why do my eyes burn when I look at you? Why does my body grow warm"—he leaned so close to her that she tipped back against the sofa—"at the first scent of your hair?" His nostrils flared when he drew in a deep breath. "What is that, anyway? Lilac?"

"Lavender." The word came out on a strangled breath.

With painfully gentle fingers, he caressed her face. "I'm becoming addicted to it."

His voice had dropped to a low rumble. Liberty felt it reverberating in her blood. "My lord—"

He bent his head. "I gave you my word I wouldn't force you into childbed, Liberty." His mouth slanted over hers then in a kiss that was quick, heated, devastating. When he raised his head again, her breath felt constricted in her lungs. "And I will keep it. I will not, however, deny that I want you almost beyond reason."

She trembled. "That's not what I wanted to know."

He started to drop his hands, but she covered them with her own. "I simply wanted to know if you are prepared to promise that I will feel that same indescribable sensation I experienced the last time."

He stared at her, astonished. "What are you saying to me, Liberty?"

Pressing a butterfly kiss to his cheek, she asked, "Are you ever going to stop talking and kiss me, or will I be forced to seduce you?"

He choked. "Would you?"

"If you wanted me to." There was something so utterly irresistible about the look on his face that Liberty could not glance away. "I'd prefer, however, that we seduce each other." She guided his hand to her bodice. "Please touch me, my lord. I have waited the longest time."

She pressed his hand to her breast at the same instant he caught her close to him. With a muttered exclamation of triumph, he reached for her shoulders so he could ease her onto his lap. Through the thin silk of her gown, she felt the hard contours of his thighs. The sensation was intoxicating. Elliot pulled her against his chest as he pressed a kiss into her hair. "Trust me, Liberty. All I ask is that you trust me."

Her last thought before he covered her mouth with his own was that he had the warmest body in the world. His hands held her immobile against him as his mouth wreaked devastation on her senses. With firm insistence, he played at her lips until she opened for him. His tongue swept inside to dance and mate with hers in a rhythm that left her breathless.

The feel of his firm mouth on hers, his large hands stroking up and down her back, combined to devastate her senses. Bit by bit she felt her individuality draining away. Soon, she didn't know where he started and she began. When his fingers moved to her bodice, she gasped at the feel of them against her breasts. Through the fabric of her gown, his strong fingers caressed the sensitive curves. With a will of their own, her hands stole around his neck.

Elliot muttered a small groan of approval as his fingers released the first button of her gown. "That's it," he told her. "Let me take you there."

Need rushed through her. Suddenly, she could not be close enough to him. The memory of how she'd felt, how she'd ached for him, drove her to a sudden urgency that had her tugging at his clothes. The sensation was like a drug, powerful and addictive. Her mind seemed to shut down as she slipped one hand inside his tailored jacket. She wrapped her arm about his waist and pushed herself against him in an attempt to alleviate the unbearable tightness in her breasts. With a soft exclamation of haste, Elliot wrenched open three more buttons.

The feel of his fingers on her bare flesh was as utterly devastating as she remembered. Her breath stopped and her heart slammed against her rib cage. A moan wrenched from her throat. Elliot lifted his head to trail a path of kisses along her jaw, her throat. Her head fell back against his waiting hand as his tongue delved into the hollow at the base of her throat. Liberty clung to him, needing an anchor.

When his warm lips glided across the curve of her breast, her body tightened. "Yes, love," he whispered. "That's precisely what I want. I ache for you."

She shuddered in his arms. His mouth teased the mound of her breast against the restrictive confines of her corset. With one hand, he began working at the hem of her gown. When his fingers closed on her calf, she gasped. "Hurry."

He pulled her closer to him. "This time, there's no rush. We have all night."

"I don't want to wait all night."

His breath exploded in a sharp gasp. "Did no one ever tell you that patience has its rewards?"

"And haste has its value." She caressed the nape of his neck. "Kiss me, my lord. It seems as though I've waited an eternity to feel your lips again."

Her fingers threaded into the silken weight of his dark hair as his lips covered hers again. When his tongue danced with hers, she sucked it into her mouth. Holding him like this felt so good, so very, very right, that she refused to entertain the notion that it might not be.

When his fingers finally reached the ties of her pantalettes, she sighed in relief. He bent his head to nuzzle the curve of her breasts above the neckline of her gown. She felt the texture of each individual silken hair on his head against her flesh. "My lord, please—"

He shifted so quickly, it stole her breath. In the blink of an eye, she was no longer sitting on his lap but stretched beneath him on the sofa. The exquisite feel of his weight pressing her into the cushions was almost beyond bearing. With one hand he cupped her breast while the other traced a trail along the bare skin above her pantalettes. His face was taut, with a look of such stark longing that it made her heart pound erratically. "Say my name, Liberty. Please say it."

In that instant, she could deny him nothing. "Elliot."

At the sound of it, he uttered a harsh groan, then covered her mouth once more. This time, he devoured her lips with a ravenous hunger that awakened an answering flame within her. She ached for him. Every lonely place in her soul seemed to cry out for his touch. Elliot offered a salve for the wounded places in her being. For these few moments, she could treasure the very comforting thought that someone wanted her.

Elliot's eyes glowed like smoldering green coals when he lifted his head to search her face. "Tell me you want this. Tell me you want it as much as I do."

She wrapped her arms around his shoulders and sighed in surrender. "I do. Perhaps I should not, but I do."

With a harsh groan, he wrapped one hand around her thigh, then lifted it to his hip. The sudden shift in position left her open and vulnerable to him. She felt the hard ridge of his passion pressing into her, sensed the urgency that now drove him.

And she welcomed it. If, for even a moment, she considered the consequences of fully yielding to him, she would put a stop to this madness. He already owned her heart. If she gave him her body as well, she would have nothing left. But the bridge was already crossed. Her need of him overrode every other consideration.

Elliot's fingers made quick work of her gown. When the silk-covered buttons refused to yield, he popped several of them free in his haste. Her hands moved to assist him as he pushed her bodice down to her waist. Above the restriction of her corset, her breasts moved with the rapid rise and fall of her breath. "Elliot"—she clung to his shoulders—"I cannot bear this much longer."

He pressed a kiss to the hollow between her breasts, then pushed aside her clothing. When her nipples were bared, they rose taut and flushed beneath his gaze. He muttered soft words of praise against her skin as he covered one sensitive peak with his lips.

That exquisite, driving pressure had begun to build again in her belly. With eager hands and trembling fingers, she pushed at his clothes. He suckled at her breast even as he struggled to remove his jacket. Liberty grabbed fistfuls of his lawn shirt to tug it free from his waistband. Finally, her hands slipped inside to touch his bare flesh. At the contact, Elliot's body grew tense. She felt his hardness press against her most intimate spot, and instinctively, she arched into him.

Breathing deeply now, he tore open his trousers. "I meant to go slowly," he gasped as he freed himself. "I meant to savor you."

She could no longer resist the temptation to touch

him. Her hands went immediately to that part of him that was aching for her. "I have no patience, either." Her own breathing was ragged. "I feel the storm rising."

He covered her lips with his as his hands slid beneath her skirts to ready her for him. With a firm and insistent pressure, he parted her thighs to fully receive him. The feel of his blunt shaft against the opening of her body sent waves of heat soaring through her. Instinctively, she knew that she would not feel whole until Elliot lay sheathed in her body. With a shuddering moan, she arched her back at the same instant he thrust into her.

Chapter 9

When he felt the fragile barrier give way, he stilled, shocked. With a startled cry, her eyes flew open. "Dear God," he muttered as he considered the unthinkable. "You haven't—"

Liberty covered his mouth with her hand. "My lord, I beg you, please don't spoil this now."

Being inside her was every bit as incredible as he'd known it would be. She was exquisitely hot, exquisitely tight. She sheathed him like the finest silk. With each movement of her body, she tormented him. In a deep corner of his mind, he reeled with the knowledge that all that passion belonged to him alone. Howard had never touched her. No one had ever touched her. "Are you all right?" he managed to ask. "Did I hurt you?"

The pressure was building inside him. The urge to move within her was almost unbearable. The feel of her stretched around him caused a coil to tighten in his loins. Her hips swiveled against his in unconscious need.

She stroked his shoulders with her soft hands. "I feel strange—not as I thought I would. It didn't hurt last time."

He swore beneath his breath as he began to withdraw. "Damnation. I never imagined—are you in much pain?"

Her legs tightened around him. "No, no. Don't leave. Please don't leave."

Immediately, he cupped her face with his hands. "Madam—"

Liberty shook her head. "Please. I have the very distinct impression I shall expire if you leave me." Her body clenched around him as an uncontrollable shudder tore through her.

His groan was guttural. Dear God, she'd surely drive him to Bedlam. "Don't do that. I can't control myself when you do that."

"I can't help it." Her body flexed again.

A primitive wildness broke the last barriers of his carefully cultivated restraint. "God help me, Liberty, neither can I." With strong thrusts, he moved in her.

Liberty clung to him as they climbed higher and higher toward that same shattering plane where nothing in the world seemed to matter. He felt the passion in her, felt the way her flesh bunched and flexed beneath his fingers, felt the way she stretched to accommodate his length. She arched her hips to meet each thrust, as if she welcomed the flow of energy between them.

In the mirror above his mantel, he caught sight of his face. His expression was a harsh combination of shadows and angles when he felt the storm overtake him. As urgently as he wanted to see her soar, he could no longer deny the clamoring need in his body. He threw back his head on a low oath. "I cannot wait," he said. His voice sounded wrenched from his chest.

Liberty pushed herself against him. "Now, Elliot. Please, now."

With a final groan, he arched his back as his body erupted inside her. The feel of his warmth spilling into her, filling her womb, drained him, body and soul. She clung to his shoulders, buried her face in his chest.

With a final groan, he collapsed on top of her, his weight pressing her into the sofa. His hands stroked a lazy rhythm on the bared curves of her breasts.

Minutes passed before he lifted his head to meet her gaze. With her eyes still unfocused, her lips still swollen and damp from his kisses, he could almost forget how he'd brutally ignored the signs her body had given him. In his own selfishness, he'd hurt her. "Are you all right?" he managed to ask.

She nodded. "I am fine."

No recriminations there. The realization filled him with guilt. She didn't even seem to know that she should be railing at him for his callousness. Tenderly, he brushed her hair from her damp face.

"I hurt you. You should have told me you were not experienced."

He saw her contented expression fade. Her gaze turned wary, then shuttered. "Would it have changed things?"

"I don't know," he admitted. He searched her face for long minutes, then rose with a muffled curse. Quickly, he refastened his clothing and tossed a woolen shawl from the sofa over her half-naked form. He had been a fool this evening. She had given him an amazing gift, and he had crushed it. With self-recrimination heavy on his soul, he lifted her against his chest. "I have handled this badly. I see that now."

Liberty squirmed in his arms. "Elliot, where are you taking me?"

"To bed."

He felt her scrutiny as she studied him. "You are upset with me because I didn't tell you Howard was not my lover."

How he hated the reticence in her tone. His breath felt ragged, his heart torn to shreds. Self-loathing rushed through him in a wave so intense that it threatened to fell him. "No" was all he could manage to say. He kicked open the door of the library and strode toward the stairs.

She began to struggle against him. "Do not bother to deny it. I can see that I've angered you in some way."

He paused to meet her gaze. "I am not angry at you. I swear it."

"But you—"

He gave her a hard squeeze to interrupt her. "I hurt you." His voice was a low rumble. "Had I known, it still would have hurt, but I could have lessened it, I think."

"It wasn't so bad. I actually enjoyed the better part of it. It wasn't as shattering as it was last time, but overall, I'd say the experience was quite pleasant."

With a groan, he crossed the foyer. "It should have been more than pleasant. If I had been able to control myself, I could have spared you most of the discomfort. Are you certain you're all right?"

"I am."

He mounted the stairs in long strides and did not speak again until he set her on her bed. With deft fingers, he began removing her gown. When she flinched at his touch, he felt a fresh wave of guilt. "I won't hurt you again."

"I know."

He would have removed her corset, but she stayed his hands. "Elliot, please, stop."

His hands stilled. "You don't want me to remove your undergarments?"

"I want you to talk to me."

His breath came out in a slow hiss. He was terrified of the turbulence that tumbled through him. The last thing in the world he wanted was a lengthy, and no doubt tearful, confrontation where he would, with his usual lack of tact and delicacy, stomp on her feelings. He'd already injured her physically this night. What was worse, he was acutely aware that he'd failed to keep his word. He'd promised her he would not rush her to childbed, but in his adolescent haste to possess her, he'd failed to protect her. If she persisted in engaging him in an emotional conversation, he'd no doubt make the damage complete.

But he could not turn away from the silent plea he saw in her eyes. Mentally he braced himself as he moved to lie beside her on the bed. In his mind, he replayed every piece of advice he'd ever been given on handling the fair sex. Garrick swore that sensitivity was the key. Elliot searched his soul for a new reservoir before he finally said, "You have shocked me tonight, Liberty. I find you are always discovering new ways to disconcert me. Like a fool, I made several suppositions about you which I now find are not true. In my haste, I hurt you. If I have any anger at all, I hold it for myself. I should have known better."

She turned readily into his embrace. He stiffened momentarily but then lifted his arm to circle her shoulders. "Will you allow me to explain?" she asked.

"You have nothing to explain."

"That's not true. I never tried to correct your impression of me."

"I wouldn't have believed you." Even as he said the words, he cringed. God, what a fool he was.

"Probably not."

Had he not known better, he'd have sworn she was teasing him. The reasonable part of his brain, however, realized that in her distress, she could not possibly know what she was saying. She must be aware of the insult he'd paid her tonight—indeed, throughout their acquaintance. He'd treated her like a courtesan, not an untouched young lady. Even tonight, he'd ravaged her on the sofa of his library without thought or consideration for her own comfort. He'd been so out of control, he supposed they were lucky to have made it as far as the couch. "Damnation, Liberty, you should have made me listen. Do you know what I might have done to you tonight?"

"You would not have hurt me."

"You have an exceptionally high level of faith in my honor."

"I do. You didn't like the thought that I was Howard's mistress, but you respected me all the same. You wouldn't have hurt me. I'm certain of it."

He was silent for long seconds as his hand absently traced a pattern on her bare shoulder.

"Elliot?" she finally said. "Would you like to know how I met Howard?"

"In a thousand years I never would have imagined discussing Howard Rendell on my wedding night."

"Does that mean you don't want to hear the story?"

He rolled abruptly to his side. Propping his face on one hand, he gazed down at her. In her eyes, he found none of the anger he had thought would be there. Disarmed, he frowned at her. "It means that you are under no obligation whatsoever to tell it to me. If this were a business deal, I'd refer to it as a profit sinkhole, cut my losses, and run."

"One day you're going to have to learn that not everything in life yields to the rules of business."

"I'd rather not."

At that, she laughed. "You can't always have your way, you know."

The sound of her laughter set off an odd explosion in his chest. He simply could not allow himself to believe that she might actually have forgiven him. "It's much more pleasant for everyone when I get it, however."

"Elliot, are you teasing me?"

Good God. Relief roared through him. If she thought he had the fortitude for a jest, she held him in much higher regard than he deserved. Warily, he trailed a finger along the line of her jaw. "I think what I am doing is delaying the inevitable. In case you hadn't noticed, I'm not particularly adept at conversation."

"Who told you a thing like that?"

"Nearly everyone I've ever met."

"Then they simply haven't taken the time to

know you better. I find your conversation to be quite enlightening."

"Only because you share my interest for account ledgers."

"And you share mine for ridiculously insignificant detail."

By some miracle he couldn't begin to understand, it was becoming readily apparent that she wasn't enraged with him. The notion left him feeling oddly unsettled. Unsure of himself, he retreated behind his usual facade of nonchalance. "Then we shall no doubt bore our friends to death. Soon, you'll find there isn't a soul in London willing to attend one of your parties."

Clouds gathered in her eyes. She shifted slowly away from him, dragging the sheet with her. When she was seated facing him, with the sheet tucked around her breasts, she pushed her tangled hair back from her face. "There won't be any parties, Elliot. Surely you know that."

She had to be the world's most baffling woman. "I wasn't serious, you know."

"I am. You cannot expect your friends to accept me, even as your wife. You weren't alone in your suppositions about me. They were shared by the rest of your social circle."

"Liberty, I assure you, I've no desire to discuss my social circle tonight. If you want to know the truth, I don't have a social circle. The ton tolerates me because they fear me."

"That isn't true. You're one of them, and just because they shunned you once doesn't mean they don't accept you now."

He lifted one shoulder in a shrug. "Frankly, I don't care whether they do or not."

A frustrated sound escaped from the back of her throat. "I don't think you understand. I've lived with this for ten years. I know what it's like."

Narrowing his gaze, he studied her face. She was a confusing mix of vulnerability and confidence. Unable to resist the need to touch her again, he trailed one hand along her thigh until it settled on her hip. "Why don't you tell me?"

"Why? So you can exact retribution?"

She had no idea how dangerously close to violence he felt as he considered how difficult the last ten years must have been for her. Not only had she been scorned by Howard's circle, he now realized, but the Huxley staff would have turned from her as well. There was no place in the servants' hall for a woman believed to be the employer's mistress. With little effort, he could picture her alone in her too-small quarters, seated by an inadequate fire with only a book to keep her company. The thought filled him with a rage to avenge that he had to struggle to subdue. Finally, he managed to say, "Something like that."

"I haven't asked you to be my avenging angel, you know."

"You married me, Liberty—for whatever reason. That gives me certain rights."

Her eyes rolled heavenward. "Once again, I see you are living in the Dark Ages. This isn't the twelfth century. I don't expect you to suit up in armor and come riding to my rescue."

"Is that what Howard did?"

"In a manner of speaking."

"You were how old?"

"Sixteen. I was working as a seamstress. I was a dreadfully poor one, I might add. I fear you're going to find that my wifely skills are horribly lacking. I can't sew. I can't cook. I can't play the pianoforte. I can't even arrange flowers."

He trailed one finger back and forth against her stomach in the barest of caresses. "Ah, but you can calculate the profit margin on an investment and compute compound interest. I've always found that incredibly attractive in a woman."

A bubble of laughter seemed to slip past her guard. The sound pleased him. "Elliot, you're incorrigible."

"I've told you before, you and I have a unique understanding of each other. Wherever this road we've embarked on may take us, I hope we can at least be friends."

She nodded. "I hope so, too."

"Now, you were working as a seamstress?"

"Yes. I was orphaned as a child. I was raised

in the West End Home for the Holy Innocents, where they trained me for employment."

"Rather than educating you to use your memory, they taught you stitches?"

"In case it has escaped your attention, young women don't have many employment choices. My unusual memory was a liability. Most employers prefer servants who quickly forget all they see and hear."

"But you realized you had it?"

"Of course. That's how I learned to read and write. I had only to look at a book once to absorb its material. The reason I met Howard, in fact, was because of an abandoned copy of the *Gazette*. I had made my last delivery for the day when I picked up a copy of the paper. There was an auction posting, and in the inventory was a jeweled powder casket."

His eyebrows lifted. "You wanted the casket?"

"I wanted to see it. I have very few memories of my mother, and none of my father. But one thing I do recall is sitting on my mother's lap while she dipped powder out of a jeweled casket. I must have been very young, not more than two or three at the time. I've no idea why the memory is so clear, except that I recall watching her in the mirror as she applied the powder."

He considered it for a moment. "And you remember the casket specifically?"

"Yes."

"Do you recall anything else about the room?"

"No. Only the casket."

"Hmm."

"What does that speculative look in your eyes mean? You think you've discovered something?"

"It's probably nothing," he said. "We are most likely to remember things that are out of place, or somehow odd to our usual surroundings. With your exceptional memory, I would think that all the details of the room would be clear to you. As they aren't"—he shrugged—"who knows what it might mean. As you said, you were quite young."

"So I was."

He deftly diverted the conversation back to its original course. He wanted more time to consider the idea that had begun to form in his mind. "So you met Howard because of the auction?"

"Yes. I knew I couldn't possibly hope to get in, but I couldn't resist trying. I found the house that night, then waited outside in the cold for an opportunity."

"And there was Howard."

"And there was Howard," she said quietly. "When he alighted from his carriage, he dropped his watch. It rolled to a stop right in front of me. I retrieved it for him, he thanked me, and for reasons I've never understood, he asked me what I was doing lurking in the shadows."

"You told him about the powder casket?"

"Yes. He seemed so interested. I rarely had the opportunity to converse with anyone on more than the most basic of topics. I couldn't resist the lure."

"I imagine the attention of a man of Howard's stature would have been overwhelming for any young woman."

"I told him that I only wanted a glimpse of the casket, that I had hoped I could find a way into the house for the barest of seconds just to see if I recognized it."

"What did he do?"

"He told me to wait in his carriage while he arranged it; then he disappeared inside. He was gone for almost a half hour. I considered fleeing several times. I was wise enough to know that a woman my age had reason to fear a man like Howard, but my desire to see the casket overrode my better sense. When he finally emerged, he had purchased it for me."

Elliot's gaze narrowed. "Didn't anyone ever tell you that accepting a gift like that carries certain ramifications?"

"Of course. And I wouldn't have taken it except that I recognized it. If it is not my mother's, it is exactly the same design. I wouldn't have forgotten something like that."

"You told Howard this, naturally?"

"Yes. I explained the nature of my memory to him, just as I did to you. That's when he offered me employment as Millicent Rendell's companion. She had just come to live with him following the death of Howard's brother."

"You weren't reticent about moving into his home?"

"Anything was better than where I was living. I felt I could adequately protect myself. As it turned out, there was no need. Howard wasn't interested in an improper relationship with me. With his permission, I educated myself by using his books. I learned his business by assisting him with his correspondence. At first, I wrote a letter here and there. Then, he asked me to inspect a ledger. Bit by bit, I became intimately involved with his affairs."

"That's when you began traveling with him."

"Yes. I enjoyed Howard's company, and I believe he enjoyed mine. He particularly enjoyed the benefit of my memory. You can understand why having a complete memory of all his business records in my head made me somewhat indispensable to him during negotiations."

"Of course."

"So we spent a considerable amount of time together." She dropped her gaze. "And the world drew its own conclusions."

"The world has a persistently bad habit of doing that." Elliot reached for her hand. It felt small and vulnerable in his larger one. "I cannot imagine the hurt you have experienced, but you cannot imagine the depth of my regret for you."

Her eyes met his once more. "You say the most remarkable things, my lord."

"You are the only one who thinks so."

"Then I am not the only one who has been sadly misjudged."

Elliot stared at her. He felt as though he were at the edge of a precipice. What had passed between them tonight was a remarkable step. He would not, even to own the world, contribute to her hurt. "Liberty"—he pressed a kiss to her palm—"I've never been good at speeches. This kind of repartee, particularly, eludes me. I can never rescind the things I've said to you, but I would like you to know that I hold you in the highest regard. If at all possible, I'd like us to find a way to make our marriage work. I believe you may even find the experience pleasant."

She stretched out along the length of him. "I think perhaps we have both made mistakes. I would like very much to correct them." She trailed a hand along the line of his hip.

He covered her fingers with his own. "What are you saying?"

She met his gaze. "There will be time enough to sort through the muddle in the coming days. We're married, after all. I assume you've no plans to leave the country soon?"

He shook his head. With a soft smile, she pressed a kiss to the base of his throat. "Then I would very much like to set aside our differences, at least for tonight."

He took a moment to absorb the incredible. "You cannot mean—"

"I mean"—she aligned herself with his body—

"that you promised me unspeakable pleasure. I would like that promise fulfilled by morning."

He tensed against her. With startling insight, he realized he'd never done anything in his life to deserve the remarkable gift he'd been given. Not only had he found a woman who seemed to understand him, but for some completely incomprehensible reason, she desired him as well. He fought an internal battle as he struggled to make sense of it all. She slipped one leg between his in a bold move made all the more arousing by his knowledge of her innocence. The caress snapped the threads of his control. With a harsh groan, he rolled her beneath him. "Bloody hell, madam. Are you trying to kill me?"

Liberty's laugh stole a piece of his heart. "Not tonight, I'm not."

She would be the death of him.

That chilling thought occurred to Elliot as he neatly executed another series of intricate stretches. He had risen at dawn, as he always did, to exercise his mind and body in the special room he'd had constructed in his house. Long ago, he'd adopted the Chinese principle of mental and physical health through the martial arts. Until today, the rigorous routine had always provided a certain solace. While he pushed his physical body through the regimen, his mind could, at least temporarily, escape the pressures of his life.

This morning, however, no matter how hard he pressed, no matter how long he continued the brutal pace, his thoughts remained firmly fixed on the image of his new bride, sleeping above stairs.

He shoved his sweat-dampened hair back from his eyes as he continued. God in heaven, what had she done to him? He had only to think of the way she'd responded to him to feel his body stirring. That realization gave him a new burst of energy. He twisted his shoulders forward, then flexed his back until he felt the pull all the way to his heels.

Still, one thought remained. Howard Rendell had never touched her. He reversed the stretch. No one had ever touched her. His muscles strained against the pulling sensation. And even if it damned him to hell, he realized, no one else ever would.

His lack of restraint had shocked him. He had never lost control with a woman, yet he'd taken Liberty three times in the night, and each had been as mind-stealing as the last. Even that morning, he'd barely won the battle of will to make himself leave her. He'd awakened hard and wanting her. For a man who'd made routine his way of life, the thought of breaking it—for a woman, no less—was almost incomprehensible. But he could not ignore the emerging fact that for the first time in almost twenty years, the life he'd built for himself left him feeling dissatisfied.

Liberty Madison was a dangerous woman. And, God help him, she was his dangerous woman. The only way he could hope to survive was to reinstitute order in his house. He had to be certain he remained in complete and utter control. Under no circumstances could he afford the slightest level of vulnerability. That would put the balance of power neatly in her hands.

True, she disarmed him with the way she seemed to understand his oddities. His bluntness did not put her off, nor did his penchant for possession. Given that, it was no wonder she had managed to unsettle him. It seemed only natural, now that he thought about it with a clear head, that the events of last night would have disturbed him. He could not have imagined the bizarre circumstances of her relationship with Howard, nor how deeply it would affect him to learn the truth. In the light of day, however, he would be able to put everything back into its proper perspective.

Perhaps once he had regained the upper hand, he might allow himself some deeper level of affection for her. But for now, he knew he must set about the task of binding her to him, mentally as well as physically, until there was no chance of her desertion. He would have her complete loyalty, and with it, her heart. Then, he assured himself, all would be well. Peace and order would return to his world.

"My lord?"

She would never know what it cost him not to react to the sound of her voice. "Good morning, Liberty." He executed another stretch.

"Am I disturbing you?"

She had no idea. "Of course not." He swung to face her. "I'm simply going through my morning routine." She looked alarmingly fresh in a gown of simple blue muslin. For the first time he realized that he had not recently seen her attired in any color other than black.

"I won't keep you, then." She watched, openly curious, as he shifted his body. "I merely have a question about how you'd like me to proceed."

What he'd like, he thought as he cursed the growing tautness in his groin, was for her to remove her gown and stretch out beside him so he could taste her flesh again. "Proceed with what?" He could scarcely believe the train of his thoughts. He couldn't seem to get enough of her, be close enough to her. Deliberately, he pulled his body into a difficult position.

"With the inventory of Howard's collection," she said. "I assume you wish me to locate the cross as quickly as possible."

To his shock, he realized that he hadn't thought about the item since yesterday afternoon. He was too preoccupied with the advantages of having her in his bed to concentrate on the location of the cross. "I—yes, of course."

She seemed to fidget beneath his scrutiny. It cheered him to know that she, too, was uncomfortable with the nature of their first morning together. She laced her fingers as she studied him. "I thought so. There are workmen here ready to transfer the items from Huxley House. I don't know where you'd like them placed."

"I've had shelves installed in the ballroom." He sat and pulled his knees against his chest to disguise the growing bulge in his trousers. "Will that give you ample space?"

"Yes. I'm sure it will." She hesitated, then indicated the door with a wave of her hand. "I'll give instructions to Mr. Wickers."

"That will be fine. Give me a moment to bathe, and I'll join you."

He watched as she quit the room in a flutter of blue muslin. She was nervous. He had seen it. It would take several days, weeks perhaps, before they settled into a routine, but he assured himself that they would. They were both reasonable, intelligent people. Peace and order. That was all he needed.

Chapter 10

It was utter chaos.

Liberty stood atop the stairs in stunned disbelief. A sudden chill edged its way through her gown. The draft, she realized, was flowing through the large front doors, which stood open as a seemingly endless parade of crates and parcels were carried through the foyer.

They were in the midst of a siege.

She had fled Elliot's exercise room over an hour ago feeling flustered and heated. The way he'd looked at her had brought back every searing memory of the night before. He'd made love to her for hours, drawing out her pleasure to a point of ecstasy that bordered on agony. The memory of what he'd said to her and done to her threatened to snap the slender thread of her composure. For the first time, she began to understand fully just what people had been whispering about behind her back.

And the state she was in certainly didn't help her cope with the storm that settled on Darewood

House immediately after she spoke with Wickers. Now she looked down on a scene of frantic activity, suddenly spotting Elliot. He was dressed in buff-colored trousers, a loose white shirt, and an emerald green brocade waistcoat. She recognized the cut and pattern of his waistcoat as one fashionable several years ago, but the fine tailoring emphasized his narrow waist—a waist she knew owed nothing to the corsets his peers had taken to wearing in recent years. He appeared frustrated as he dragged a hand through his wet hair. Her heart warmed when she saw him rescue her fishbowl from a footman. He cradled it in his large hands as he looked for a safe place to set it. He seemed more accessible now, more the man she knew and less the enigmatic combination of lethal strength and raw energy she'd seen in the exercise room. Perhaps it was the clothes that gave him an added level of civility. She wasn't sure, but the sight of him holding her fishbowl made her question her earlier perception. He didn't appear frightening at all. Actually, he looked a bit comical. She hurried down the stairs to his side. "Thank you, my lord. I'll take that."

He jerked around to face her. "Liberty. I didn't expect you to supervise this. Wickers can handle it."

Lord, he looked good to her. She wondered why she hadn't noticed it when she'd first seen him that morning. His dark hair lay in damp waves against his face. "I assure you, I had no intention of missing today's logistical accomplishments. I will confess

that I doubted your ability to have the contents of
my room and Howard's library moved so quickly."

He ignored the quip as he studied her for a
moment. "I should have asked you earlier—how
are you feeling this morning?"

Liberty blushed but held his gaze. "Quite well.
You?"

She saw something flare in his gaze as he took
the bowl again, and set it on a crate, bent his head,
and kissed her.

She experienced a sudden rush of pleasure and a
new awareness: Kissing Elliot seemed as natural as
drinking water from a cool spring. The intense inti-
macy of the night before hadn't prepared her for
this fresh, sweet response to him. When he lifted his
head, she had to blink several times before her eyes
would focus.

"And I, too, am quite well," he told her, his lips
twitching with amusement. "Thank you."

Liberty smiled as she stepped away from him.
She was vaguely aware that two of his footmen
were watching with unabashed curiosity. "I'm glad
to see you aren't unduly put out by the chaos in
your foyer," she said, a twinkle in her eye.

He glanced at two burly men carrying an enormous crate marked FRAGILE. "I was prepared. Have
you had a chance to inspect the shelving?"

"Yes. It will work quite well. Thank you."

Elliot's butler, looking harried as always,
approached them. He held a vase in one hand and a

tiny pewter candlestick in the other. "I trust all is going well, Mr. Wickers," Liberty said.

He beamed at her. "Well enough, your ladyship. If I can keep these simpletons from destroying everything in the house, that is." He winced when a loud noise echoed from the library.

Liberty pointed to two workmen who were arguing over the placement of several large crates. "Gentlemen, please. The crates can go there in the corner." When she returned her attention to the butler, he'd passed the vase to a footman for placement in the ballroom. Liberty took the petite candlestick from his hand and slipped it into the pocket of her day gown. "Mr. Wickers, I trust that between us, we'll be able to keep the noise to a minimum?" she asked above the din of hammering and sawing that poured from the open doors of the ballroom. "I'm sure his lordship would like to work today."

"Certainly." Wickers bowed to Elliot. "I was on my way to find you, your lordship. Your solicitors are in the study. They claimed they needed your immediate attention."

Elliot gave Liberty an apologetic look. "I'm afraid I'll have to leave you on your own."

"Not to worry. Mr. Wickers and I will manage quite nicely, I assure you."

"I'll leave you to it, then." He glanced around once more. "I don't envy you the task."

"Have a good morning, my lord."

Elliot tucked a tendril of hair behind her ear. "And you," he said before he strode away. Her skin still tingled from the brush of his lips on hers. The touch of his fingers seemed to heighten the effect. She found herself especially warmed by the way he seemed to enjoy touching her. Taking a deep breath, she realized that she had crossed more than one threshold last night. She'd taken an irrevocable step into Elliot's life. Determined, she faced the butler. She would not let Elliot down.

For the next three hours, they worked and sorted and organized the growing inventory. No sooner did she feel they had something of a handle on the task, when another row of carts would arrive with still more items to uncrate and store. By midday her back ached, her face was streaked with dust, and she'd seen all of Howard's prized possessions that she could stand. She dropped a jewel-encrusted signet ring that had once belonged to Henry VIII in its box and shut the lid with a decisive snap. "That's enough for today," she told Wickers. "The rest they can stack in the center of the floor, and we'll get to it tomorrow."

Wickers glanced at her. "Are you feeling fatigued, my lady? Perhaps you'd like to rest awhile?" He'd spent the better part of the morning trying to talk her out of helping with the work.

"No. I am going to see if his lordship has any fur- ther need of me this afternoon; then I've several errands to run." She untied her work apron. "Thank you for your help, Mr. Wickers."

"It was my pleasure." He pointed to the door. "I believe you'll find his lordship still in his study. I would have been informed had his solicitors left."

Liberty picked her way across the cramped ballroom, through the accumulated debris. In the front hall, an immense pile of invitations and calling cards lay on the foyer table, along with an odd assortment of flowers and trinkets. Deliberately, she averted her eyes. She simply couldn't bear to sort one more item. The library, in startling contrast to the foyer, was a haven of peace. She leaned back against the solid oak door to momentarily enjoy the silence.

"Good morning, Viscountess."

At the sound of Garrick Frost's voice, her eyes flew open. "Mr. Frost. I wasn't expecting you."

His mellow laugh warmed her. "I don't doubt it. I'd wager, in fact, that you weren't expecting any of this." Garrick lounged on one of the long sofas with his feet propped on the low table. A silver coffee tray sat in front of him.

Liberty moved to take a seat across from him. "Well, not so quickly, anyway. He really is quite remarkable, isn't he?"

"Darewood? Yes. Yes, he is."

She lifted the pot. "Did you want coffee?"

Garrick, she noted, appeared to be in need of the stuff. Unless she missed her guess, he had not yet shaved that morning. His clothes looked a bit disheveled, and his eyes had a bleary cast that spoke of too little sleep and too much liquor.

When she put the pot down with a heavy thunk, he winced. "I have been trying to summon the energy to pour the stuff for the last half hour."

Liberty handed him the cup and saucer. "I'm glad I could be of service. I suspect it's the least I can do, as I caused your lack of sleep."

He managed to smile at her above the rim of his cup. "My lack of sleep is entirely Darewood's fault, I assure you. Why I continue to tolerate the man is beyond me."

"Because," Elliot said from the doorway to his study, "I've made you a fortune in investments, and my association with you allows you to live the kind of rakehell life you enjoy." His wry smile disappeared as he glanced at Liberty. "Good God, you look dreadful."

"I see your manners have not improved," Garrick drawled.

Elliot did not take his eyes from Liberty as he strode across the room. "Damn it, Liberty, I did not intend for you to be in there doing physical labor. I employ people for that."

She shrugged. "If I put the items away, I will know where they are when I need them. Besides, I could not think of a better time to search for the Cross of Aragon than while the contents of Howard's study and library are being individually delivered."

At her mention of the cross, he frowned. "You don't have to find it today, you know. It isn't as if I've put you on a timetable."

"I've put myself on one," she said blandly, unwilling to discuss the ramifications with him. The only way she could hope to survive was to find the cross quickly, surrender it to him, then allow him to make the decision about her future. The longer she stayed, the more dependent on him she became. She was determined not to let that happen.

Elliot strolled across the room to seat himself next to her. "I won't have you working yourself into exhaustion. Given your regrettable lack of appetite over the past few weeks, I doubt it would take much to send you into consumption."

Garrick laughed. "Good Lord, Darewood, you sound like a mother hen."

Elliot frowned at him. "And what business have you got turning up at my house at this hour dressed like that?"

Garrick winked at Liberty. "Don't let this bother you. He's always irritable in the morning."

"I'm always irritable," Elliot insisted, "when I have to spend my time forcing people to take care of themselves."

Garrick took a long sip of his coffee. "He's so very benevolent. I've often wondered why he didn't pursue the priesthood as a profession."

"Quiet, Frost."

At the memory of the very unpriestlike way

Elliot had driven her mad last night, Liberty had to fight not to blush as she asked, "Are you through with your solicitors?"

"For now." Elliot glanced at her gown. "Are you seeing the dressmaker this afternoon?"

Garrick nearly choked on his coffee. "Lord, Elliot, do you think you can find one more way to insult her?"

"I am not insulting her. I am merely asking a question."

Liberty leaned back against the cushions. "I fear in this case," she assured Garrick, "he's quite right." She glanced at the worn fabric of her dress. She had never allowed Howard to provide her clothes. Instead, she'd used her own earnings to purchase the necessary garments. Fortunately, her needs had been few. She'd been painfully aware this morning, however, that she was woefully unprepared to fill the role of Elliot's wife. The gown she wore today was the best she had. The men had chivalrously avoided mentioning the patch on the skirt, of course. But obviously Elliot had seen it. She said, "One of the many things on my list to do this afternoon is to see the seamstress. I shall endeavor not to bankrupt you, my lord."

"Buy whatever you need," he said, "but please do me the favor of avoiding black. It makes your skin look sallow."

Garrick rolled his eyes. "I'm afraid you're going to have to learn to ignore him."

Elliot glanced at her, as if Garrick's teasing had goaded him into a sense of unease. Liberty gave him a bright smile to let him know she was not offended. "Do not fear, my lord. I never cared for the colors of mourning. It merely seemed simpler to comply than to invite further comment on my person."

"Comment from Millicent Rendell, you mean?"

"There's no need to fret over it," she assured him. "It doesn't matter anymore."

"Damn the hag's hide," Elliot said. "I almost hope she tries to defy me."

"Now, Elliot, your feud with Howard does not have to extend to the other members of his family. You needn't quarrel with Millicent, or Carlton, on my behalf. I'm quite capable of dealing with them." He looked as if he wanted to argue, so she laid her hand on his thigh to distract him. His gaze instantly went to her small hand. Lest she lose his attention, she rushed to say, "But thank you, all the same." She then turned to Garrick. "So, Mr. Frost, what brings you here today?"

Garrick glanced from Liberty to Elliot, then back again. "I had no choice," he finally said. "You should see the street outside my house. The carriages are lined three deep with people waiting to talk to me. Everyone Darewood has turned away, and anyone who didn't have the nerve to see him first, is looking for me. I had to steal out my back door and come over here in a hack to avoid being mobbed. Do you have any idea what a tempest you two have created?" He winked. "Rumor has it that Victoria herself is queued up to see you."

Elliot took a long sip of his coffee. "I received a summons this morning. I'm to call on Her Majesty at four o'clock this afternoon."

Liberty groaned. "Oh no."

Garrick set his cup on the table. "What are you going to tell her?"

"I'm going to tell her that yes, I got married, and yes, I married the woman rumored to be Howard Rendell's former mistress." She did not miss the harsh edge to his tone. "And that yes, Carlton Rendell is furious over it. What else would I tell her?"

Liberty pushed aside a feeling of panic. Elliot's reputation at Court was legendary. The queen had made a practice of surrounding herself with the handsome gentlemen of the peerage. Elliot had held her ear for some time. His ardent defense of the prince consort's plan for the Great Exhibition, set to open in a few weeks, had gained him unparalleled access to the royal seat. The grand plan to assemble within an exhibition hall in Hyde Park called the Crystal Palace some of the world's most interesting and special products and goods had been the source of ridicule and speculation since Prince Albert had first proposed it. She could see now why the idea had intrigued Elliot. He was drawn, almost irresistibly, to projects of large scale and scope. His support had reportedly won Prince Albert sufficient allies in the House of Lords to ensure the exhibition could go forward. Rumors abounded that the queen, in her gratitude, was considering awarding him the Royal Garter, one of the highest tokens of her esteem. "Don't you think," Liberty said carefully, "it would be best to phrase it a bit more gently? The queen doesn't take very kindly to scandal."

"The queen," he said, "wants my continued support of Albert's Great Exhibition. I suspect she'll forgive a few improprieties."

Garrick laughed. "That's true enough. If it hadn't been for you, Albert's plans would have died in the parliamentary scuffle. The day he announced he wanted to build the Crystal Palace, his enemies started stacking up against him."

As Elliot nodded Liberty said with gentle insistence, "With the opening of the exhibition imminent, don't you feel it would be wise to smooth the situation? I'm certain if you explained to Her Majesty that you and I were in agreement, she may not feel as disconcerted."

Elliot shook his head. "Liberty, the only crime you and I have committed is giving the gossips something to discuss. I should think they'd be grateful."

Garrick nodded. "They're more than grateful. They're ecstatic. They haven't had anything this good since Imogene Cutterly appeared as Lady Godiva at Woolrich's masked ball."

With a growing sense of dread, Liberty realized

just how far they'd forged into the public eye. "This is disastrous."

"It's nothing of the sort," Elliot assured her. "In a week or so, they'll have something new to talk about. In the interim, we have so much to do that we won't have time to worry about it."

"Shaker and Hatfield have been here, I take it?" Garrick asked.

"They just left."

Liberty drew a quick breath. "Howard's solicitors?"

"The legal transfer of your property will take some time. Carlton, of course, is protesting."

"Of course," she muttered.

"While Carlton did not say anything about our moving the contents of the library, he is objecting to the removal of anything from Howard's study, though I think we shall have those items in rather short order."

Liberty glanced at him in astonishment. "I cannot imagine how you manage to have your will prevail."

While he showed no immediate reaction, she was certain she saw a flash of satisfaction in his gaze. "You will soon learn that I pride myself on dispatching difficult tasks immediately. Only the impossible requires a bit more planning. That is why we will have to wait until some of the dispute is settled. You may expect the rest of the items within the week."

Garrick let out a low whistle. "What will that leave at Huxley House?"

Elliot lifted one shoulder in a slight shrug. "Most of the furnishings, I imagine, but almost none of the items used as collateral. Carlton Rendell's extended credit has just run out."

Liberty leaned back against the sofa. "He'll fight you."

"He's welcome to try. Just know that I will win."

There was a finality in his tone that made her feel distinctly nervous. Elliot would not easily let the matter drop, and she'd have to keep constant vigil if she hoped to avoid disaster. She almost sighed in relief when he changed the subject to news of the Crystal Palace's latest problems. She wondered whether Elliot wished her to leave him alone with Garrick, but as soon as she'd convinced herself to go, he enfolded her hand in his. Content, she settled back against the sofa to listen to the pleasant rumble of their conversation.

Within the hour, Mr. Wickers brought them a tray of tea and sandwiches. On it was a sealed note addressed to her. Since that morning, invitations had come in an endless stream as news of their wedding had spread. Uninterested, she ignored it.

Elliot, however, did not seem so inclined. He took her cup, then slipped the note into her hand. Garrick continued, mentioning talk about the complications of the Crystal Palace. During construction, several of the trees in Hyde Park had been enclosed in the massive structure. It seemed a roost of sparrows was reluctant to leave.

"I suggested," Garrick said, "that they try netting them, but Pickford is determined to shoot the bloody things down."

"He'll shatter the glass," Elliot pointed out. He glanced at Liberty. "Are you going to open that note?"

She looked at it. "I suppose I could, but I'm sure it's just another invitation. You're better liked than you believe, Elliot. We've received over forty this morning. I'm tired of answering them. Can't this one wait until tomorrow?"

"I'd like you to open it now," he insisted. He looked at Garrick again. "I hope you told Pickford that I'm not paying to replace that glass if he blows holes in it."

"I did indicate that the project was considerably over budget, and I saw no harm in trying the nets first."

Liberty broke the plain wax seal on the invitation while Garrick and Elliot continued to debate the issue. The folded parchment was wedged too tightly in the envelope, and she had to work it loose with both hands. Finally, it slid free.

"Why don't they try sparrow hawks?" she suggested. "They could turn three or four loose in the structure and let nature have her due. I'm certain it would work."

Garrick snapped his fingers. "That's brilliant. I'm

going to let Pickford know this afternoon. I wonder if he'll be at the club?"

"Liberty," Elliot leaned closer to her, "why are you avoiding reading that?"

She gave him a disgruntled look. "I wasn't avoiding reading it. I was absorbed in the conversation."

He shook his head as he plucked the paper from her fingers. "You don't want to read it because you know what it is."

"Don't be ridiculous."

Garrick seemed to catch the underlying tension of the conversation. "Bloody hell. It can't be."

Elliot snapped open the note with a flick of his wrist. "I'm afraid it is," he said. "It seems whoever is threatening Liberty hasn't been deterred after all."

Chapter 11

Agitated, Elliot paced the dimly lit room. Over the past three days, his frustration and anxiety had evolved into rage. He only had to remember the note Liberty had received that afternoon to feel his blood heating. Given half a second, he'd strangle the bastard who had sent it. "Damn it, Frost, where is he?"

"He'll be here."

The interior of the Velvet Hell left much to be desired. Flocked floral wallpaper covered the sagging plaster. Grime dimmed the glare of the gas lamps. Fringe dripped from every conceivable angle, and the overstuffed furniture resembled the brothel's clientele: fattened, as it were, by too much of Society's indulgence. Elliot's lips turned down in disgust. "The bloody little bastard. I should have known we'd find Rendell in a hellhole like this."

"When a man goes looking for rats," Garrick pointed out, "he spends a lot of time in the sewer."

In the eerie stillness of the secluded Velvet Hell,

an occasional scream echoed through the walls. Here, weak men like Carlton found ways to vent their frustration, generally at the expense of one of the harlots. During his long and arduous climb from the pit where Howard's treachery had once cast him, Elliot had seen too much of this side of life. It had always sickened him. By day, the respected members of Society took their pleasure over cards and tea. It was only in the night that the vampires came out to prey on the innocent. His temper escalated with each tick of the clock.

A commotion in the hallway had Garrick on his feet. The door flung open suddenly. Carlton, clad only in a velvet dressing robe, was shoved into the room by the Hell's proprietor. "Will that be all, yer nibs?" the burly man asked Elliot.

Elliot didn't look at him. His gaze remained firmly riveted on Carlton's sweating face. "For now," he said.

"What the hell is the meaning of this, Darewood?" Carlton shouted. "You've no right to do this."

"Haven't I?" Elliot had to clench his hands to keep from attacking. Carlton cowered in the corner while Garrick paced an anxious path in front of him.

In the few days since his marriage, Elliott had searched every possible lead to Liberty's tormentor. Two more notes had arrived, each delivered by a young boy who knew nothing of the man who'd hired him. While Liberty appeared only mildly disconcerted, Elliot was not. Quite to the contrary, and he had deliberately kept the last one from her. He couldn't be certain how she'd respond to the most recent and ugliest one to date.

For the first time, the message demanded a meeting with her.

The same curiosity that had led her to Willis Braxton's library in the middle of the night would, no doubt, have carried her to Vauxhall for a meeting with the cretin who was causing her distress. He comforted himself with the knowledge that she was off visiting Pearl Asterly. There, at least, she'd be safe. The thought of her confronting a man like Braxton made his blood run cold.

The meeting was to take place tonight. After two fruitless days of squeezing every source of information he had, he finally had decided to confront Carlton. Garrick was certain Rendell was the culprit, but instinct told Elliot differently. A piece of the puzzle was still missing. Early that afternoon, as he'd studied the succession of messages, a theory had begun to form in his mind.

He'd finally agreed to confront Carlton with the hope that he could get from the scoundrel the piece of information he needed. "I'll keep this short, Huxley," he said. "My wife has been receiving threats. I want to know if they're coming from you."

Carlton staggered forward and collapsed onto

one of the stuffed chairs. "You must be joking. Surely you've heard that I'm a ruined man? You have what you want, Darewood. You've destroyed my life. Why in hell would I threaten the tart? It would do me no good."

Elliot surged forward to strike him, but Garrick intercepted him. "Not yet," he warned. "We're not sure. When we're sure, then you can hit him. I'll even help you."

Reason momentarily subdued his anger. "I'll give you one chance to keep me from killing you," Elliot told Carlton. "Did Willis Braxton pay your uncle a visit in the days before he died?"

Carlton's bleary eyes drooped. "Willis Braxton? How the hell would I—"

Elliot grabbed the lapels of his dressing gown and jerked him to a standing position. "Did he, or didn't he?"

Carlton's breathing was shallow. His eyes darted fearfully to Garrick. "Don't let him hurt me, Frost."

Garrick shrugged. "If you want to survive this, I suggest you tell him what he wants to know."

"All right, all right." Carlton clutched at Elliot's wrists. "I don't know anything about Braxton except what Shaker and Hatfield told me. He and Howard had some type of agreement—there are special sets of books." When Elliot jerked his lapels again, Carlton screeched. "I don't know where they are, I swear it."

"But was he there before your uncle died?"

"I can't say. He—"

With a swift upward thrust, Elliot buried his knee in Carlton's groin. He held fast to the robe as Carlton slumped forward, gasping for breath. "He threatened me. He said he'd cut off what little money I have left."

Disgust poured through Elliot as he watched Carlton struggle for breath. He felt soiled and repulsed. And as he considered that Liberty might have been forced to marry this man, a murderous rage sprang up in him. He grabbed a fistful of Carlton's thinning hair and jerked his head back. "That's better than dying, isn't it?"

Carlton looked nervously at Garrick, who shook his head. "See here, old boy, if you've got any brains left in that muddled head of yours, you'll just tell him what he wants to know. Believe me, angering Braxton isn't nearly the folly of angering Darewood."

Carlton's eyes drifted shut in resignation. "Yes. Braxton visited with my uncle before he died. All I know is that they quarreled about something. Braxton has been on my heels ever since to give him access to the library. Now that the contents have been moved, he's threatened to kill me if I don't recover a book he wants." When Elliot gave him a final jerk, he shook his head in terror. "That's all I know. I swear, that's all I know."

"And the title of that volume?"

"*The Treasure,*" Carlton said quickly.

Elliot felt a burst of satisfaction as he threw Carlton to the floor. At last, he had what he needed. He gave Garrick a knowing look. "Now," he said quietly, "we can leave."

Liberty checked the pocket of her cloak to ensure that the bound copy of *The Treasure* was still there. Finally, Braxton had taken her bait and demanded that she surrender the novel to him. The night she'd paid the visit to his library, she'd left him a carefully worded message. Had Elliot not interrupted her, he might have found it sooner. As it was, the note had no doubt gotten buried in the papers he'd thrust into the safe.

She'd been anxious ever since, until she'd discovered Braxton's note on Elliot's desk, requesting a meeting with her. Fortunately, Elliot and Garrick had been out. She assumed that Elliot had intended to hide it from her—something she determined to take up with him at the first opportunity. She'd discovered the note while searching for an ink bottle among his supplies.

It had taken her a while to slip undetected from the house. She'd been several minutes late arriving at the designated spot, and now feared that she'd missed Braxton altogether. Amidst the raucous noise and gaiety at Vauxhall, it would be painfully simple to avoid detection. From her secluded station near the arbor, she scanned the colorful crowd.

He had to be here. He desperately wanted what she possessed. He would not miss this appointment.

"Lady Darewood. What a pleasant surprise."

She turned to find Willis Braxton and Peter Shaker watching her. "Gentlemen. I wasn't expecting both of you."

Willis Braxton gave her a beady-eyed look. "No? How unfortunate. I assume you have the book?"

"I assume you have the ledger?"

Peter Shaker coughed. "Now, see here, Viscountess, I do not perceive a need to surrender the late earl's personal records to you. Braxton has offered you a perfectly reasonable price for *The Treasure*. Be a good girl and sell it to him so no one will get hurt."

"Not until you give me the ledgers."

"What can you possibly want with twenty-year-old records?"

"That is my affair." She met Braxton's gaze. "You're hardly in a position to argue, my lord. I am well aware of why you want *The Treasure*."

The two men exchanged worried glances. She saw the slight shake of Braxton's head as he sent Shaker a silent warning. Liberty continued, "There are two sets of ledgers. One set reflects Howard's legitimate business pursuits. The other is a record of the illegal profits you and he have been running through the accounts for the past two decades. Those ledgers are encoded within the pages of *The Treasure*. I doubt that Howard's investors would be pleased to find that they have been cheated out of their money." She looked at Peter Shaker. "Or that Mr. Hatfield would be happy when he discovered his partner has been instrumental in defrauding a good number of his clients." Slowly, she extended her hand to Peter Shaker. "Give me the set of ledgers I've requested, and I'll give you the volume. No one need know about this."

Shaker looked at Braxton. "How could she have known, unless that imbecile Carlton told her?"

Liberty had trouble hiding her annoyance. That she might have learned the truth on her own had obviously never occurred to either of them. Peter Shaker was in no way prepared to admit that she knew far more about Howard's business practices than he did. Her fingers tightened on the book in her pocket. "How I know is immaterial. What concerns me now is that we make the exchange and be done with it." She looked over her shoulder. "The viscount doesn't know I'm here, and if we're all lucky, he won't find out. I can't imagine he'd be very happy to learn you've been threatening me."

Braxton's eyes narrowed. "Threatening you?"

"Don't pretend you don't know what I'm talking about. I assure you, the notes were a quite effective, if cowardly, means of getting my attention."

Shaker looked at Braxton. "What notes?"

Willis Braxton seemed to grow annoyed with the conversation. "You believe I've been threatening you?"

"I believe you were very determined to get what you wanted."

"Bloody hell, you stupid chit. You're the one who broke into my safe—though I've no idea how—and told me you knew the secret of *The Treasure*."

"Howard kept the combination to your safe in his files. It seems he didn't entirely trust you, either. That's why he kept *The Treasure* carefully hidden among his own books. Should you choose to betray him, he had all the evidence he needed to expose you."

"The bastard. Without me, he never could have attained what he did. He owed me."

Liberty felt the familiar pain in her heart. Over the past two weeks, her study of Howard's records had shown her just how naive she'd been. She exhaled a long breath. "The earl rarely worried about what or whom he owed. He was more interested in what and who he could possess."

Shaker mumbled something beneath his breath. Braxton ignored him. "You know, he always regretted that he couldn't bring you along with us."

Liberty's breath caught in her throat. "I beg your pardon?"

"He told me once that if he could get you to trust him fully, he would induct you into our little circle. Something about your brain, he claimed, would have made it possible not to keep any records at all, which I always found odd." He lifted one hand as if to touch her. "I never thought your brain was what held his interest."

Repulsed, Liberty stepped quickly away. "That is none of your affair, Braxton. What was between the earl and me is my business alone."

"Perhaps, but I'd be willing to bet Darewood isn't prepared to learn that Howard has won the war after all."

"What—what do you mean?"

Peter Shaker nodded. "He's correct. Howard didn't leave you with a great financial empire—he left you near ruin. The estate is in so much financial turmoil, you'll bankrupt even Darewood within two or three years. Most of the holdings are designated as collateral, so you cannot sell them, and the debts are too enormous to service, despite the flow of cash. Even Darewood, rich as he is, can't dig his way out of this one. If Darewood hoped to get revenge on Rendell by marrying you, he'll be sorely disappointed. Howard suspected you'd turn to Darewood. He planned to use your inheritance to destroy the viscount. If Howard excelled at one thing, it was creating the most unlikely solution to a problem by using the most obvious strategy. Generally, his solutions were so obvious, no one would even dream he'd have the nerve to carry them out. In Darewood's case, he accomplished what he intended by making you an enormous liability."

Liberty felt a band of panic squeeze tight around her heart. Suddenly, her business here seemed that much more urgent, that much more necessary. She extended her hand to Peter Shaker. "What you say may be true, but let's not forget that I am still holding *The Treasure*. Without it, I could destroy you all, not just Darewood."

"Bloody tart," Braxton muttered. He pulled a leather-bound volume from beneath his cloak. "Here it is. This is a complete copy of the second ledger from 1833 to 1836. I cannot think why you should want it. It won't do you any good now."

Liberty handed him her copy of *The Treasure*. "And here is your salvation, at least for now. I trust this completes our business."

Braxton looked her up and down again with that insolent gaze. "For now, but when Darewood tosses you out on the street, feel free to come to me. I'm certain I can find something useful for you to do."

Liberty sensed the dangerous slant of his mood. For the first time, she wished she'd waited until Elliot had returned to keep this rendezvous. Sternly reminding herself that she'd kept her wits through plenty of scrapes before, she fingered the small dagger she'd slipped into the pocket of her gown before leaving Darewood House. Braxton was unpredictable at best, and while she didn't think he would actually hurt her, she couldn't entirely rule out the possibility either. Her fingers closed on the handle of the dagger as she tucked the ledger into her cloak. "I assure you, Braxton, should my marriage to Darewood end, I will have no difficulty finding suitable employment."

He leered at her. "I'm sure you won't."

Peter Shaker seemed to sense the volatile nature of the exchange. He laid a hand on Braxton's arm. "Willis, there's no sense in this. We have what we want. Let's go."

She saw the anger flare in Braxton's eyes. His face grew florid as he studied her in the garish cast of the gaslights. The sound of exploding fireworks bled into the seclusion of the arbor, creating a sense of unreality for it all. "I must be going," she said. "If my husband discovers I'm here, he won't be pleased."

"Are you worried he might beat you?" Braxton drawled.

"No. I'm worried he might beat you."

The angry retort set flame to his cinder-dry temper. His hand shot out to circle her wrist. "I don't like to be threatened."

"Neither do I," she said through clenched teeth as she tried to wrench her arm free.

Braxton pulled her close to his body. "Come now, Liberty, don't you want to give old Braxton a taste of what made you so valuable to Howard? I could never get him to tell me."

With a strength amplified by her fear, she jerked the dagger from her pocket and thrust it at him. She felt it sink into his flesh, felt warm blood spurt onto her hand, and in the same instant, heard his angry cry of pain.

Clutching the ledger to her, she fled into the night.

"Gone? What the bloody hell do you mean gone?" Elliot threw his cloak onto the chair as he confronted his butler. "She's supposed to be with Pearl Asterly." He had returned with Garrick from the Velvet Hell in a dangerous temper. Though he now had an additional piece of the puzzle, he was certain that something still eluded him. While Garrick insisted that Braxton must be behind the threats after all, Elliot was beginning to unravel the threads of a more sinister scheme. The idea that formed in his head left him feeling uneasy. By the time they'd reached Darewood House, an unsettling notion clutched him.

"Now, Elliot," Garrick said smoothly, "I'm certain there's no cause for panic."

"I don't know, your lordship!" Wickers exclaimed. "She was here one moment and gone the next. The last time I saw her, she inquired if I might know where she could find a bottle of ink. I suggested she look in your study."

Elliot froze. "My study?"

"Yes, sir."

"On my desk?"

"Yes, sir. The only thing I know for certain is that

she took her cloak. No one on the staff knows when she left, or how. She didn't take the carriage."

"Damn it to hell, she read the note."

Garrick dropped into a chair. "Dear God, you don't think she went to Vauxhall, do you?"

"Where else?"

"Without a carriage?"

"She's had years to practice the art of slipping from a servants' entrance undetected." He scrubbed a hand over his face. "My God, how could I have been such a fool? I should have destroyed the thing."

"You couldn't have known," Garrick insisted.

Fear sliced through Elliot like a knife as he considered the implications. Didn't she realize what was at stake? Didn't she know how much they could hurt her? Stark terror momentarily immobilized him. What in God's name was he going to do if he lost her? Suddenly the door flew open and Liberty raced into the library. Elliot almost crumpled to the floor. "My lord," she said, breathless, "you've returned."

There was blood on her hand, her gown. He couldn't take his eyes from it.

"I hadn't expected you back so soon," she said in a rush. "Mr. Wickers, would you please bring us some tea? Yes. Tea would be quite nice."

Wickers withdrew. Garrick took Liberty's arm and eased her into a chair. "Are you all right?" he asked her. "There is blood on your gown." Elliot virtually roared the statement.

"Please stop shouting." She pulled her cloak over the bloody area. "It's only a small stain. It will come out."

It wasn't small at all. It was monstrously wide. Even with her cloak pulled across her lap, he saw where the incriminating red stain reached the hem of her dress. He rushed to her and swept her cloak aside to reveal the six-inch swath of blood that had ruined the pale satin. It smeared her hands as well. He grabbed them, searched them for wounds. "Are you all right?"

"Of course. I'm fine."

Garrick had crossed to the beverage cart. "I'll get you a brandy, Liberty."

"I'm not in need of alcohol."

"You'll drink it," Elliot insisted as he pushed the hem of her skirt to her knees.

Liberty's hand stayed him. "Elliot, what are you doing? Garrick is here."

"I want to know where this blood came from."

She shoved her skirt back in place. "Don't worry. It isn't mine."

"Madam, I swear"—he cupped her face in both his hands—"either you tell me what happened right now, or the phrase 'God help you' is going to take on a whole new meaning."

She'd begun to tremble, but Elliot couldn't keep the anger from his voice. She'd scared the life out of him. She couldn't possibly expect him to remain calm when she'd entered the room coated in blood. "I will gladly tell you, my lord, but I fear I'm perilously close to tears. If you keep shouting at me, I won't be able to get it out at all."

Garrick returned to her side and pressed the brandy snifter into her hand. "Drink this," he said. "You'll feel better."

Elliot took the glass and held it to her lips. When she'd taken three swallows, he set it aside. Color was beginning to return to her pale face. He scooped her into his arms and carried her to the sofa, where he settled her firmly on his lap. She snuggled close to him with a contented sigh that did strange things to his gut. "Liberty," he said, "tell me what happened. You went to Vauxhall, didn't you?"

She glanced at him in surprise. "How did you know?"

"I reasoned it out." He tucked her head against him once more. "You were snooping about my desk and found Braxton's note."

"You shouldn't have kept it from me."

He couldn't believe she was scolding him. "I kept it from you because I was utterly certain that you'd go racing off in the middle of the night to meet him."

Wickers entered the room with a tray of tea and sandwiches. Liberty tried to squirm off Elliot's lap, but he held fast. There wasn't a chance in hell that he was going to let her go. Not until his heartbeat slowed to a normal rhythm and his mind accepted that she truly was unharmed.

Garrick had taken a seat across from them, and once Wickers withdrew from the room, he pressed Liberty for more information. "That was where you went, was it not?"

"Yes." She nodded. "I knew Braxton wanted Howard's copy of *The Treasure*. He also had something I needed. I had been waiting for him to contact me about it since that night Elliot interrupted my visit to his library."

Elliot went utterly still. "Liberty, are you saying that you deliberately provoked him?"

"Now, Darewood, don't get angry." She raised her head from his shoulder. "I didn't provoke him. I suggested a perfectly reasonable exchange. After I discovered the discrepancies in his records, it didn't take long for me to determine that Braxton was the one sending me the threats."

Garrick nodded at Elliot. "You see. After Carlton . . ."

Liberty narrowed her gaze on her husband. "You don't believe it was Braxton?"

"What I believe isn't important. I want to know what business you had challenging the man when you suspected he was dangerous."

"I didn't think he was really dangerous, just a bit desperate."

He felt a renewed sense of panic. "Liberty," he

said with strained patience, "desperate men are nearly always dangerous."

She was moving her fingers along his shoulder in an absent rhythm. "But I didn't think Braxton would actually hurt me. He wanted *The Treasure*, and I wanted something he had in his possession."

"What could you possibly have wanted that was worth this risk?" Garrick asked.

From a large pocket inside her cloak, she produced a leather-bound volume. "I've suspected for weeks now that Willis Braxton was somehow involved in Howard's more unsavory business practices. I was certain they were keeping two sets of books. I didn't know how long the arrangement had persisted, but I had a niggling suspicion about it. I traded him Howard's copy of *The Treasure* for the secondary ledger." She pressed the book into Elliot's hand. "Do you know what this means, Darewood?"

He couldn't breathe. The magnitude of it shook him to the core. "My God," he said.

She nodded. "The evidence you need to exonerate your father will be in these accounts. I'm sure of it."

He was trembling; then his entire body shook as he struggled for control. That she had taken so great a risk threatened to fell him. He could do nothing but stare at her.

"But Liberty, what about the blood?" Garrick asked. "Whose is it?"

She finally turned her gaze from Elliot, as if she could no longer bear the intensity in his eyes. "I'm afraid that's the bad news," she said. "It's Willis Braxton's. I think I killed him."

Chapter 12

Three hours later, Liberty pulled the blankets closer to her chin and sank down in her bed. She was beginning to doubt that she'd ever be warm again. It didn't help matters that, following her confession about Braxton, Elliot had placed her in the bed, given the sternest possible order that she remain there, then promptly left the house.

He'd gone in search of Braxton's body, she supposed.

In his haste, Elliot had left the ledgers in the library. Anxious to divert her mind, she'd fetched them, along with Howard's primary books, and spent the next several hours comparing the figures. A grim web of deceit had begun to emerge as she calculated the numbers.

She'd been torn between an insatiable curiosity for the truth and an emerging fear of what that truth might mean. With insidious certainty, Willis Braxton's charge that Howard had used her to destroy Elliot took root. If what she was learning from the

ledgers turned out to be true, he would suffer personally as well as financially by the time he was
done with her. Her only hope was to find the Cross
of Aragon as quickly as possible. Once she was
no longer Elliot's wife, he would be free of all
responsibilities.

And in that instant, she realized that she'd
allowed the unthinkable to happen. She'd fallen in
love with Elliot Moss, and now she was faced
with the sure knowledge that she could destroy
him. Once, she'd feared giving him power over her.
Now, however, she realized that loving him had
made her stronger than she'd ever imagined.
Loving Elliot wasn't about losing her freedom. It
was about becoming her own person. She could not
allow harm to come to him. If it meant tearing
Howard's cursed collection to pieces, she'd find the
cross for him. It was the only hope they had.

That thought drove her from the bed. Thrusting
aside the ledger, she swung her feet to the floor. The
cross must be among the items in Howard's desk.
Otherwise, she'd have seen it. Driven by fear and
anxiety, she made her way to the chilled ballroom.
The enormous shelves, filled with books and trinkets, loomed like specters in the near darkness.

She lit several candles, then began a systematic
search through the contents of Howard's desk. When
it yielded nothing, she turned to the bookshelves.
Where, she wondered, would he have hidden it?
Her mind sorted through all the things she'd known

of him. While she checked the obvious places, she thought of the many times she'd seen Howard plan a strategy. If, indeed, his plan had been Elliot's downfall, where would he have placed the object?

As she grew more desperate, she began tearing items from the shelves, searching the pages of books and the contents of crates. By the time Elliot entered the room, she was covered in dust and surrounded by a pile of debris. He looked worn, she noticed, as he shut the door with a soft click. "Hello, my lord."

"I told you to stay in bed." There was no rebuke in his voice. He frowned at the books strewn on the floor. "I thought you'd be sleeping."

"I couldn't." She dropped the books in her hand onto the growing pile. "Is he dead?"

Elliot didn't flinch at the question. Oddly, it made her feel better. He would be in more of a temper, surely, if she'd murdered the man. Calmly, he finished removing his gloves, then tossed them to the desk. "No. He has a nasty gash in his shoulder, but beyond that, he's quite well."

Relieved, she sucked in a much needed breath. "I'm glad."

Elliot impaled her with a glittering look. "I am not." The finality in his tone made her shiver. "Frankly, I wish you'd killed the bastard."

"Elliot, you didn't do anything rash, did you?"

"Rash? Madam, I would like you to explain to me what you would possibly consider rash, given your propensity for sneaking about in the dead of the night to consort with characters like Braxton."

"I did not consort with him." She pulled several more books off the shelf, inspected their bindings, then set them on the floor. "I negotiated a trade."

An angry sound escaped him. With a wave of his hand, he indicated the books. "For what—evidence of a scandal fifteen years past? You risked your life! Have you any idea what lengths he might have gone to in order to procure *The Treasure*? God Almighty, he could have killed you."

And you would have been better off, she thought, feeling suddenly bereft and miserable. "He might have anyway," she reasoned. "He was already threatening me. I felt it best to give him what he wanted."

"But you've known he wanted *The Treasure* since the night you went to his library?"

"No. I didn't know which book he was after until later. I discovered it only when I was unpacking the contents of Howard's collection. It must have been among the items in his desk. I hadn't seen it before the other day."

"Still, you could have sent it to Braxton and been done with it. Instead, you risked your life, and for what? More evidence of Howard's treachery?"

"It was my life to risk," she asserted.

"Damn it, it was not." He faced her, his expression an unreadable combination of emotions. "The day you married me, it became mine. Don't ever forget it again."

Liberty stared at him. The primitive possession she saw in his gaze had her trembling. She'd always known that Elliot was a driven man, but until now, had never seen such stark evidence of the power in him. He reminded her more than ever of a predatory jungle cat. "Elliot—"

With a frustrated oath, he stalked toward her. "You've no idea what you're dealing with, have you?"

"I—I don't know what you mean." She couldn't take her eyes from his face.

"You think that the threats you've been receiving, that Braxton's interest in *The Treasure*, are a simple case of some misdirected funds."

"Aren't they?"

"No. They are not. Braxton wanted *The Treasure* to protect himself, but did it never occur to you that someone else stood to gain from Braxton's ruin? As badly as Braxton wanted the evidence, someone else didn't want him to have it."

She swallowed. "What do you mean?"

"I mean that Willis Braxton wasn't merely after a book with some encoded figures in it. He wanted far more than that. He wanted the power to consolidate Howard's financial empire for himself." His hair, windblown from the long night's activities, lay in disarray on his shoulders. He swept a hand through it as he watched her in the pale light. "He would have done almost anything to ensure his success."

"Would have?" she questioned.

"Yes. I don't think he'll be bothering you again."

Terrified, she asked, "What did you do to him?"

"Do you want to know if I killed him? I thought about it."

"I will not see you hanged."

"Don't worry yourself. Garrick persuaded me to take a more reasonable course of action."

"Remind me to thank him."

"I convinced Braxton that his future would be better spent out of the country. If he left his fate in my hands, I'd see to it that every banker and investor in London knew the truth."

"But he had the evidence."

"Which you'd memorized before you gave it to him."

As usual, he knew her too well. "You told him that?"

"I told him he didn't have the only copy of the information in *The Treasure*, and if he doubted me, I could procure any of the figures for him by sunrise. I believe he thought I might be bluffing, but he wisely decided not to risk it."

"Then the threats will stop." She looked inside an Egyptian burial urn, then set it aside. "I'm sorry to have worried you, but you must see that everything has come right now. With Braxton gone, there will be no more threats. I'll be able to find the Cross of

Aragon for you and you will be free of me." She peered inside a Ming dynasty vase.

With a dark oath, Elliot crossed the final few steps between them, wrested the vase from her hands, then hurled it against the wall. It smashed. Liberty stared at him. He had never been violent before. When she thought of it, she realized she'd never seen him yield to his more passionate nature. Even in their stormiest moments in bed, he had always remained firmly and utterly in control. Now, it seemed as though something primitive in him had been unleashed. "Elliot—"

He grabbed her shoulders in his large hands. "Is that what you want, Liberty? Your freedom?"

"It's your freedom that interests me, my lord. I thought it's what you wished."

"What I—" He bit off an oath as he bent his head to kiss her. "Obviously, madam, you've no idea what I wish."

The kiss was hard, devastating. She flowed into him as he took complete and utter possession of her mouth. His hands were everywhere at once. He was pulling at her wrapper, cupping her breasts. With a swift tug, he rent the fabric of her thin nightgown. The feel of his cool hands on her heated skin inflamed her. With the realization that she loved him had come a deeper, more consuming passion to ease the unrest she sensed in him. If, even for a moment, she could offer solace to the young man who'd once felt cast aside, it would make her loss more bearable. She clung to his broad shoulders, tilting her head to give him better access.

With a low groan, he hooked her leg over his hip. "Don't ever, ever frighten me like that again."

In answer Liberty brought his mouth back to hers and sucked his lower lip between her teeth.

His hands shoved what remained of her clothes to the floor as he plundered her. She felt him mold her body to his from shoulder to hip, as if he couldn't hold her close enough.

She was becoming frantic to be close to him. "Please, my lord," she begged him. "I need you within me."

Elliot wrenched his lips from hers. His face was a mask of desire and intent. "Liberty?"

She threaded her fingers in his too-long hair. "Please. I cannot wait."

In a few short strides, Elliot had her pressed against the door. Her fingers were already tearing at his trousers. When the buttons stubbornly clung, he covered her hand with his. "Here," he said, popping them loose with a swift jerk.

The hard length of him spilled into her waiting fingers. She gasped as her head fell back against the wall. "Now," she whispered. "Please, now."

He wasn't inclined to argue. "Put your legs around my waist."

She lifted her trembling thighs, locked them at his hips. With a harsh groan, Elliot surged into her. "Never," he said as he withdrew to thrust more deeply. "You will never—scare me—like that—again." He punctuated each word with a possessive thrust. "You're mine."

Liberty could no longer think. The feel of him had consumed every part of her, until she felt she would burst with his presence. In her passion, she found his name ready on her lips, and with it, the words that drummed through her blood in rhythm with her heartbeat. "I love you."

He groaned as he pushed into her a final time. "Mine," he said as he buried himself to the hilt. When she felt him explode within her, she melted around him in a shattering climax.

Minutes later, Elliot finally raised his head. His eyes took on an odd glow as he watched her for long, breathless seconds. He adjusted his trousers, then asked, "Did I hurt you?"

"No." She could barely move.

He retrieved her wrapper for her. When her nerveless fingers failed to clutch the material, he gently inserted her arms into the sleeves. "You're certain?" he asked as he tied the belt.

"Yes."

"I regret my lack of restraint."

"I don't." She felt him withdrawing from her again—just as he did each morning when he left their bed, she realized. He was shuttering himself mentally. It never mattered how tempestuous their passion during the night hours; by dawn he was lost to her again. Had she said the words aloud? she wondered. He didn't seem to have heard them.

He stood, staring at her, as if he'd read her mind. When finally she began to feel vulnerable, stripped bare by the intensity of his gaze, she crossed her arms over her breasts. The protective gesture broke the spell. Elliot rubbed his hands over his face. "You have my apologies, Liberty. I assure you this won't happen again."

She reached out an imploring hand to him. "Elliot, please—"

Without looking at her, he took his gloves from the desk. "I think perhaps you are right. The sooner you find the cross, the better off we'll be." When he strode from the room, she felt a permanent chill settle in her heart.

He had heard her. She was certain of it. And having heard her tell him she loved him, he'd rejected the one thing she had left to give. She'd never imagined she would be able to love someone as she loved Elliot. Her body felt weak with it. Her heart ached as she considered the responsibilities of her newly discovered feelings. In recent days, she'd begun to feel that they'd managed to develop a certain kinship. She understood Elliot, and he, remarkably, seemed to understand her. They'd found a rare pleasure in that.

Braxton's claims that she would be the source of Elliot's financial ruin had frightened her, it was true. But more startling, more disturbing, had been the evidence she'd found in the ledger and the dark picture that had begun to form in her mind. The same force that had sent her fleeing from her bed in a desperate search for the missing cross now had her fighting tears.

At once, she realized the magnitude of her mistake. Unwittingly, she'd contributed to Howard's plan for Elliot's destruction. If Howard had planned to bankrupt him, she could not have prevented it. With her own stubbornness, however, she'd unearthed the key to his complete devastation. Elliot had maintained his sanity with the certain knowledge that Howard had unjustly destroyed his father. When he learned, as she had, that Elliot's father had known of the illegal transactions—had, in fact, facilitated many of them—he would have nothing left. Even the honor on which he'd rebuilt his life would be stripped from him. And she would be to blame. The force of the realization stole what remained of her strength. With an exhausted sob, she sank to the floor amid the growing pile of books.

Howard, it seemed, had been intent on destroying them both.

Over the next two weeks, they settled into an alarming pattern. Liberty spent her days desperately looking for the cross while trying to stay the rising tide of impending disaster. As Braxton had predicted, the drain on her financial reserves was severe. Daily, she saw them dwindling.

With Braxton's sudden disappearance, Howard's associates had become anxious, paying her frequent visits. Only Elliot seemed undisturbed by it all. In the days since their confrontation, he had withdrawn from her almost completely. In fact, except for the subdued evening meals they inevitably shared with Garrick Frost, he seemed to have forgotten her existence altogether.

Occasionally, when she passed him in the corridor or sat across from him at the dinner table, he looked at her with an odd expression that made her pulse quicken. Twice, she'd caught him standing in the ballroom, watching her. The enigmatic look in his green eyes had threatened to make her melt. But when she had met his gaze, he had abruptly quit the room. A depressing loneliness marked her days, and more regularly, her nights, and her only relief from it came through her increasingly frequent interaction with Garrick Frost. Somehow, it helped to be with someone else who loved Elliot.

One rainy afternoon, as she sat searching yet another set of books, Garrick picked up a large copper urn. "What's this?"

Liberty glanced up from her ledger. "The remains of King Mahatmut Khan Maden."

He frowned as he plunked it down on the desk. "I see."

Liberty laughed. "Never fear. I don't believe

they're really in there. Human ashes are notoriously white. Those are an ordinary char gray. I believe Howard was taken on that particular purchase."

Garrick thrust his hands into his pockets as he watched her. "Liberty, I hope that in the past two weeks, I have gained some level of your confidence."

"You have, of course. I like you very much, Garrick."

"But do you like me better than Elliot?" he probed.

She set her pen down with measured calm. "That doesn't seem an entirely appropriate question."

He flung himself into the chair across from her small desk. "It isn't. But now that I've ventured this far, may I ask you something extremely personal and probably equally inappropriate?"

"I suppose."

"What has happened between you and Elliot?"

She couldn't hold his gaze. "He hasn't discussed it with you?"

"Not directly, no. I'm aware that you quarreled the night of your meeting with Braxton."

"Quarreled isn't precisely the word I'd use."

"Argued, then. He hasn't told me the substance. I only know he's been in a towering rage ever since."

"Elliot was quite upset that I confronted Braxton without consulting him first."

"Did he tell you we'd been to see Carlton that night?"

She looked at him, stunned. "No."

"We had. Elliot had been searching for the source of the threats for days."

"Did he think that Carlton was behind them?"

"No, but he didn't believe it was Braxton, either. I think you should know," Garrick continued quietly, "that Elliot is still not convinced Braxton is your culprit."

"But the threats have stopped—it's the only reasonable explanation."

"From the beginning, there's been nothing reasonable about this. He still believes you're in danger."

Liberty considered the information. "Has he told you why?"

"No. He's notoriously closedmouthed these days."

"I see."

"Which brings me back to my original purpose." He leaned closer to the desk. "I would like to know if you and Elliot are lovers."

Liberty hoped he wouldn't notice her blush. "I don't think I should answer that."

"Then the answer is yes?"

"Garrick—"

"Damn." He leaned back in his chair with a low exclamation of disgust. "I knew it." Rubbing a hand over his face, he seemed momentarily lost inside himself. "I feel I've gotten to know you quite well in the past two weeks, and I'm prepared to wager real money that you were never Howard Rendell's

lover. In fact"—he leveled a knowing look at her—
"I'd wager that before Elliot, you were never any
man's lover."

Liberty stilled. "You would?"

"It's true. Isn't it?"

She paused for long seconds before she nodded.
"Yes. It's true."

His breath came out in a harsh sigh. "It's no
wonder Elliot is in such a state. Hell, you should see
him. He's won so much money at the card tables,
only fools will play with him now. If I thought he'd
hold me to my losses, I'd have quit long ago. I think
I owe him eighteen thousand pounds."

"He's gambling?"

"Where do you think he goes every evening?"

She didn't want to discuss what she thought. "I
wasn't sure."

Garrick didn't believe her. "You think he has a
mistress, don't you?"

"His reputation is somewhat formidable."

"He doesn't. He was involved, for a short while
before you were married, with a woman named
Marie Claire Ponchez, but he ended it the day he
proposed to you."

"Oh." She didn't know what else to say.

Garrick studied her for a moment. "May I
have your permission to ask another inappropriate
question?"

She spared him a slight smile. "We've come this
far. I see no point in turning back now."

"Did you really tell Elliot that night that your only concern was to set him free of this marriage?"

"Yes."

"Why?"

She carefully chose her next words. Garrick was Elliot's closest friend. It would be unwise to reveal too much. "He made it clear from the start that he views our marriage as a temporary business arrangement. I thought he would appreciate my cooperation in facilitating its end."

"Do you want it to end?"

"I want my life to return to normal," she said quietly.

"The way it was before your marriage to Elliot?"

It was the last thing in the world she wanted, but she dare not reveal it to Garrick. She raised tortured eyes to his. "Yes." Her voice was barely above a whisper.

"Then tell me something. Why would you surrender the one piece of evidence that could guarantee your personal security in exchange for a ledger that serves no purpose other than to restore Elliot's reputation?"

He had struck too close to the truth. Liberty deliberately dropped her gaze. "I didn't surrender anything. I memorized the figures. I can re-create them if I wish."

"Yes, yes." Garrick waved his hands. "I'm aware of all that, but you know, as I do, that simply re-creating the numbers won't have the power that

Howard's personal records would have carried. It
would be your word against Braxton's, rather than
the written proof in Howard's own hand."

"It would be enough."

"I don't think so." In three easy strides, Garrick
rounded the desk to take her hand in his. "You're an
exceptionally intelligent woman, Liberty, with a
deep capacity for caring. Don't lie to yourself. You
know why you did this."

"You don't understand. It's far more complicated
than that."

"You're protecting him, aren't you?"

"It's—difficult."

"You know, if Elliot weren't my closest friend,
and if I didn't know for certain that he'd kill me for
it, I'd be half tempted to try and seduce you
myself."

Her gaze flew to his. "Garrick, please."

"It's true, you know." His thumb rubbed the back
of her hand. "But once again, Elliot has discovered
the treasure first." His smile was rueful. "It is something I'm getting used to."

"You're a good friend to him, Garrick. There
aren't very many people who care for him the way
you do. He may soon need that."

"And it's precisely because I do care for Elliot
that I want to see the two of you succeed. There's
something between you. I'm sure of it."

"The only thing between Darewood and me is
anger."

"Liberty, listen to me. You have no idea what this has been like for Elliot. I know he's told you what Howard did to his father."

"Yes."

"Has he also told you that no one—not a single one of the men his father counted as his friends—would help him?"

"He told me he was forced to take a job with a shipping company."

"Where he spent five years working for slave's wages in India. My God, they wouldn't even give him a decent job. He had nothing. He went to each of them in turn and humiliated himself, begging them to help him."

"I thought he went only to Howard."

"No. First there was Braxton, then Addison Fullerton, and then Virgil Constantine. No one would help him."

Her heart squeezed into a tight ball. She recognized the names from *The Treasure*. In his innocent desperation, Elliot had turned to the very men who had betrayed his father. "That's why he hates them all, isn't it?"

"He has no respect for any of them. Now that he's back among the powerful, they fear him. They know what Elliot can do if he wishes it."

"Has he spent the last fifteen years planning his revenge?"

"For a while, it was all that kept him alive. Anger

is a potent force, Liberty. Elliot needed it during those days following his father's death."

"And now?"

"Now, I don't think he knows what he wants. You've changed everything. When you went to Braxton for that ledger, Elliot didn't know what to do. For years, he could rely on no one but himself. When he married you, he *expected* you to betray him. You were Howard's mistress, for God's sake. How could he hope for anything else?"

The question stung. She'd given Elliot no reason at all to suspect her of betrayal. "He should have known better."

"Perhaps, but nothing could have prepared him for the fact that you'd confronted Willis Braxton on his behalf. He's still reeling from it. Surely you realize that?"

"I learned many things that night. Among them was the fact that Elliot wishes to be free of me."

"It's not true, Liberty. I beg you, carefully consider the evidence before your eyes. What has he done to make you think that?"

She thought of the ice-hard look she'd seen on his face after she'd confessed her love to him. "He has rejected everything I can give him, Garrick."

Elliot chose that moment to enter the room. He stilled when his gaze fell to Garrick's hand, which was still enfolding Liberty's. "I see you're entertaining my wife, Garrick."

Garrick frowned at him. "I see your temper is

just as rotten as it was when I left you earlier today." He dropped Liberty's hand as he rose to his feet. "Liberty, please think about what I've said. I trust I'll see you again soon?"

She glanced nervously at Elliot. "I'm certain you will, Garrick. I promise I'll consider it."

Elliot's frown remained firmly in place. He stood in silence until Garrick had left the room. "What did Frost want?" he asked the instant the door clicked shut.

Liberty wiped her palms on the skirt of her gown. "He stopped by to inquire about whether you'd be joining him at the club tonight. As you were occupied with your solicitors, he asked me to pass you the message that he will be there at the usual time."

Elliot strode toward her desk. "I see. I'm not sure I know why Garrick is suddenly so concerned with my social schedule."

"He's your friend. I believe he's worried about you."

His laugh was harsh. "I assure you, he has nothing to fear. I am well on the path to having everything I ever wanted." His gaze swept over the makeshift library. "As you've so efficiently pointed out, once you have procured the cross for me, my collection will be complete."

"My lord, I never intended to anger you. I was under the impression that you wanted me to procure the cross as quickly as possible."

"Naturally." His voice held all the chill of a winter afternoon. "Any progress?"

"Not yet."

"I see." A tense silence fell between them. Liberty twisted her hands in front of her as she sought a way to ease the strain. Elliot's gaze roamed the ballroom in a restless search through the clutter. Finally, he looked at the fishbowl on her desk. "Those fish are yours, aren't they?"

The unexpected question startled her.

"Not part of Howard's collection, I mean. They belong to you personally?"

"Oh. Yes. Yes, they do."

He watched them for several seconds. "They seem an unusual choice for a pet. They aren't very affectionate, are they?"

She had the distinct impression that they were talking about far more than her fish. "I understand them," she said quietly. "That's why I like them."

"Yes, so I imagined." A series of unreadable emotions showed on his face as he continued to watch the fish. Finally, when she thought she might crack under the strain, he sat in the chair across from her desk.

When several seconds passed and he still hadn't spoken, she carefully asked, "Was there something you wanted?"

This time, she knew precisely what the look in his gaze meant. As clearly as if he'd said the words aloud, she saw "I want you" written in the clear green depths. The thought sent a rush of strange and forbidden excitement through her blood. His jaw seemed to have set into a harder line. Those long, elegant fingers that had given her such pleasure, here in this very room, had looped around the arms of his chair. Though he remained utterly still, she felt the sudden tension in him.

"Yes." His voice held a wealth of meaning. "There is something I want."

Nervous, she deliberately concentrated on straightening the items on her desk. "What can I do for you, my lord?"

"As you know, the opening of the Great Exhibition is just a week away."

"Of course." She aligned three ink bottles along the edge of the blotter. "I've followed the exhibition's developments for some time."

"Then you realize that I have certain pressing social obligations in conjunction with the event."

"Of course." Still, she did not look at him.

"I can no longer avoid the responsibilities, much as I might wish to, and I would like for you to accompany me."

That brought her gaze back to his. "You would?"

He lifted one eyebrow. "Naturally. You are my wife. I wish to have you at my side."

She studied him for a moment. Whatever emotion she'd seen in his eyes was now gone. "I see."

"I trust you've had time to procure an adequate wardrobe?"

Liberty hesitated. She had purchased several items, but none with the idea of accompanying Elliot to formal events, all invitations to which they had declined. And she had called off the appointment with the seamstress. In the last two weeks, she'd thought of nothing but matters of business. "I have several gowns. I can, of course, order more if you think I will need them."

"Are they black?"

"I beg your pardon?"

He scrutinized her dress. "Your gowns. Are they black?"

The question startled her. During the day, she had taken to wearing the dresses she'd brought with her from Huxley House. Examining the contents of Howard's estate was an untidy task. She'd seen no reason to soil her slightly better gowns in the process. And Elliot hadn't given her any indication that he was aware of her presence in his home, much less her attire. "No. They are not."

"Thank you for that, at least. I would not like to have to explain to my colleagues why my wife is mourning the state of our marriage."

"My lord—"

He held up his hand. "I wasn't being critical. Merely practical. You'd feel out of place wearing black. I was attempting to save you the embarrassment."

"I see."

He continued as if he hadn't heard her. "I have

asked Wickers to hold several invitations for your response. We needn't attend everything, but I'd appreciate it if you would handle the details. Wickers can guide you in your decisions if you wish him to."

"I'm certain he'll be quite helpful."

Elliot rose from his chair. "And if it's all right with you, I would like us to attend a party this evening."

"What time would you like me to be ready?"

"Eight o'clock."

"I won't keep you waiting."

He glanced again at the fishbowl, then left the room.

Chapter 13

Liberty spent the rest of the day in a haze of activity. Poor Wickers had almost suffered apoplexy when she'd chosen the Fullerton affair for this evening. No one in Elliot's personal circle could be unaware of his dislike for the man.

With Garrick's words playing in her head, the invitation to the Fullertons' ball had made her livid. Was it any wonder that Elliot didn't want or even need her love? If the truth be told, he didn't seem to need much of anything.

He'd made himself into the man he was because of men like Addison Fullerton.

When she thought of how hypocritical they'd all been, a hot rage burned in her soul. Elliot's father may not have been innocent, but his only folly, so far as she could tell, was that he'd suffered an attack of conscience. The very men he'd trusted became his worst enemies, and had destroyed him to protect themselves.

That was when they created *The Treasure* as a

record of their activities. They had realized that
they needed insurance against one another. Each
held a copy, and with it, assurance of the other's
complete loyalty. So long as one could destroy the
others, none would dare break ranks.

She alone knew the truth. According to Garrick,
Elliot suspected that the circle of treachery reached
beyond Willis Braxton, but she was certain he didn't
know how far the tentacles spread. Tonight, she
would ensure Addison Fullerton's cooperation. Once
she had it, she could end Howard's tyranny. Elliot
would be whole again.

She spent an exhausting day augmenting her
meager wardrobe and trying not to think of the evening ahead. She found energy for the task by recol-
lecting her conversation with Garrick. A picture of
Elliot—young, grief-stricken over the loss of his
parents, perhaps even a bit naive, wandering desti-
tute through the streets of London—drove her as
little else could. She had only to remember the look
in his eyes when he'd told her the story the night of
their wedding to feel deep anguish. She wondered
what he'd looked like before the hardened edge had
entered his expression.

For all his far-flung accomplishments and wealth,
Elliot had never known the sheer joy of being loved
for who he was rather than what he was. And he no
longer trusted the world to give it to him.

As she dressed that night, she vowed that if she
could give Elliot one thing, it would be the undeni-

able truth of her respect for him, the man. He seemed unable to trust her enough to let her love him, but she could give him this, just as he'd given it to her. Under no circumstances would she allow anyone to question her loyalty to him. Society, in their trite foolishness, had rejected him, though he stood among them as more honorable, more decent, more dignified than they could ever hope to be.

Tonight, she vowed, she would show them their folly. Once again, she and Elliot would be the focus of the evening's gossip. No one would expect them to attend the affair. But she would dance with Elliot in the midst of his enemies, and the two of them would rise above Fullerton and his like. Howard had considered Addison Fullerton among his closest friends. With what she now knew about Howard, it didn't surprise her. The whole lot of them deserved one another.

By evening's end, Elliot would never again doubt that she held him in the highest possible esteem. She was about to make an irrevocable step away from Howard's circle and into Elliot's lonely fortress.

And she'd never felt better.

Elliot flipped one end of his cravat over the other as he expertly executed the intricate knot. Garrick sat sprawled in a leather chair on the far side of Elliot's bedchamber. "Name of God, Darewood. I cannot believe she committed you to attending the

Fullerton affair. What the bloody hell was she thinking?"

He'd asked himself that same question a half-dozen times. "I have no idea what she was thinking," he muttered, "but I am tired of having to explain myself to bastards like Fullerton. If Addison is anxious enough to see my wife on my arm to actually invite me to this damnable thing, the least I can do is accommodate him." He gave Garrick Frost a shrewd look. "I'm certain my wife has an excellent reason for taking me into the jaws of the enemy."

"You know"—Garrick downed a hefty swallow of his scotch—"I envy you that arrogance of yours. You don't care a whit that every sharp tongue in London is whipping the story of your marriage into some kind of legend, do you? Never mind that the queen virtually smacked your hand over the matter. You'd flaunt all of them to get what you want."

Elliot concentrated on his lapel pin. Garrick couldn't possibly know what the evening was costing him. Every second of the day, it seemed, he heard the sound of Liberty's soft voice telling him she loved him. She loved him, and because of his own stupidity, he was losing her. The knowledge was killing him.

Once he had the emerald lapel pin in place, he turned back to Garrick. "As I suspected, the queen and the prince consort wanted my money. Her Majesty showed an exceptionally high tolerance for my indiscretion. She actually offered me her congratulations."

"How long do you intend to pretend you don't care what they think of you?"

"I don't care what they think of me," Elliot insisted. "You, of all people, should know that by now. I have no fear that I shall soon become socially ostracized. Besides, it isn't as if I don't know what to do when Society isn't smiling on me."

"Must you make life so hard on yourself? There's something to be said for the easy path."

"There certainly is. It's boring." He leaned close to the mirror to inspect the quality of his shave. "I probably should have shaved again." He tipped his head to brush his fingers over the line of his jaw. Liberty had sent him a note to inform him she had several stops to make before she could join him at the Fullertons'. He was to meet her there at his convenience. His secretary had been little help; he was only able to tell him that Liberty had said she needed to make a few purchases in preparation for the Fullertons' ball. Not knowing where she was, or what she was doing, had made him edgy for the better part of the afternoon. Though she was confident that Willis Braxton had posed the only threat to her person, he was not. The more he'd contemplated the pieces of the puzzle, the more certain he had become that Howard's treachery went beyond a few misdirected funds.

Then there was the question of Liberty's insistence

that they attend the Fullerton event. She could not be unaware of his dislike for the man. Their feud was nearly as legendary as his feud with Howard. For the better part of the day, he'd struggled with a growing irritation. She would not betray him; he was certain of it. She might not know, or understand, why Fullerton was so dangerous, but he was sure that Liberty would honor her commitment to him.

She loved him, after all.

If she had a reason for tonight's fiasco, she'd explain it when he arrived. In his agitation, however, he'd allowed too much time to slip away before he'd retreated to his room to change. He hadn't had time for a shave, and his dark whiskers, as always, were making a nuisance of themselves. "Is the shadow too visible?" he asked Garrick.

"For once in your life, you could follow fashion and grow a beard."

"I don't like beards."

"You don't like the fact that every fop and dandy in the city is cultivating one."

"That either." Elliot stepped away from the mirror to give his appearance a final look. His black evening clothes were impressively immaculate, if several years past the fashion. He gave his jacket a tug to settle it more comfortably on his shoulders, then turned to face his friend. "Garrick, one of these days, you will quit trying to rescue me from my own folly."

Garrick set his glass on the small reading table as

he rose to his feet. "I'm not sure I consider your marriage to Liberty a folly."

"You seem quite taken with her." The sight of Garrick holding her hand had seared a permanent spot into his memory. He didn't like the unsettled feeling it gave him, or the slow-burning anger he felt when he considered the easy way Liberty and Garrick seemed to communicate.

"I am." Garrick gave him a narrow-lidded look. "What man wouldn't be?"

"She is *my* wife."

"So she is. Still, as you seem intent on treating her more as your employee, I'm wondering just what the boundaries are here."

Elliot paused in the act of reaching for his cloak. "What?"

"You heard me."

"Garrick, if you even consider seducing my wife, I'll kill you. Make no mistake about it."

"I would, you know," Garrick said. "Except that she has an annoying personal habit I cannot seem to overlook."

"What the hell are you talking about?"

"She's in love with you. I find that damnably unattractive in a woman."

Elliot's breath lodged in his throat. Lord, even Garrick knew. His destruction seemed imminent. When he lost her now, he'd have nowhere to go. "You are being ridiculous. What Liberty and I have is a business arrangement. Nothing more. Once she procures the Cross of Aragon for me, she'll be done with me. I'll have what I want, and my revenge on Rendell will be complete."

"And then you'll be happy?"

"Naturally."

Garrick swore beneath his breath. "And what of Liberty?"

"What of her?"

"Will she be content to take your five thousand pounds and disappear?"

"That is the deal we struck. I assume she is satisfied with it."

"Good God, Moss, are you this intent on destroying yourself?"

Elliot squelched a surge of panic. "I've no idea what you're talking about, Garrick."

"You've spent so many years isolating yourself, you can't admit what you feel for her, can you? You're afraid that if you care for her, she'll betray you, just like all the rest."

Elliot felt his heart slam an unsteady rhythm against his ribs. Garrick couldn't know how the fear had consumed him in the last two weeks. For the first time in fifteen years, the cauldron of rage in his soul had been replaced. In its stead was a knot of fear that she would take from him the one thing that had become more important than breathing. "You're being ridiculous."

"Am I? Think about it. Why have you been so angry these past two weeks?"

"Someone is threatening my wife, Garrick. She could have been killed. Forgive me, but the incident seems to have put me in a bit of a temper."

"It isn't because Braxton threatened her. It isn't even because you think she's still in danger of some sort. It's because she scared the hell out of you. Face it. You believed that she'd betray you at the first opportunity. When she didn't—when she gave up *The Treasure*—it scared you to death. You yourself said that she could have used the book for profit. Braxton wanted it badly enough to pay dearly for it. Yet she used it for your benefit, not her own. And now, you're angry because she's made you care for her."

Liberty was many things—complex, intriguing, even innocent in her views of the world. She was not, however, the manipulative young woman he'd once judged her to be. The image of the bill his secretary had shown him that afternoon popped into his mind. In the weeks since she'd been his wife, she'd spent less on her own wardrobe than he spent on his servants' uniforms in any given quarter of the year.

Garrick, he realized, was still watching him expectantly. Elliot cleared his throat. "I suppose you're going to give me your opinion on this whether I solicit it or not."

"Of course. I think you have shown your usual stubbornness and have, perhaps, missed the point.

She is not a business to be raided and possessed, Elliot; she is a person."

"A person who once aligned herself with Howard Rendell," he pointed out as he reached for his hat.

"Have there not been times when you would have lain in bed with the devil himself to advance your own cause? Consider for a moment what her choices likely were."

"Everyone has choices." He settled his hat on his head. "Sometimes, they make the wrong ones."

"And you're making the wrong one now."

"What is it you want me to do, Garrick?"

"Think about her rather than yourself, for a change. I don't say this easily. God knows, no one wants to see Rendell exposed for what he was more than I, but if you want to be the better man, you will consider her feelings. Don't you know what it will do to her when she realizes you're using her to wipe out Rendell's empire?" Garrick paused while Elliot swung his cloak over his shoulders.

"She has no idea how precarious Howard's financial position was when he died. She wouldn't believe me if I told her."

"But you want her to?"

Elliot carefully considered his next words. "I have plotted a course, and I will stick to it." He gave Garrick a piercing look. "Now, if you will be so kind as to abandon this conversation and make your way to Fullerton's, I've a stop to make before I can join Liberty there. I'd prefer to know that you're keeping an eye on her."

"Are you certain about that?"

"I will repeat my earlier warning. If you proposition her, I will call you out."

"What have I done to make you think I'd betray you?"

"Nothing," Elliot admitted as he tugged on his gloves. "But I know you well, and I have learned to recognize that particular look in your eyes. You want her."

"So do you."

He clenched his teeth in a tight line. "It doesn't seem to matter what I want, does it?"

Twenty minutes later, Elliot's coach rolled to a stop near the portico of Fullerton House. As he considered the evening ahead, his temples ached with tension. Society was still agog with news of his marriage to Liberty, and Fullerton could no more resist the urge to test his patience than he could have resisted a promising investment. The entire lot of them, Elliot knew, were waiting for Liberty to betray him.

The idea had him seething. What was his, he kept.

Never in his life had he felt this relentless need to possess another person. That passion had always been reserved for things. Finally, he had begun to understand the irresistible pull he felt toward

Liberty. Anger and resentment had given him the ruthless energy he needed for his pursuits. While he had lived, Howard Rendell had been the focus of that energy. Without Howard to keep the feeling alive, the fire had begun to dim—it no longer had the power to drive him. Like a starving man, he'd flailed about for a new sense of purpose, and he'd found it in Liberty Madison.

She loved him. It was a rare and incredible gift.

With that thought firmly in mind, he gathered his formidable calm and entered the den of his enemy. His gaze found Liberty almost immediately. At the sight of her, a surge of desire as fierce as a winter wind ripped through him. She was dressed in white and sparkling with diamonds. Her dark hair lay in soft tendrils around her face and was secured at the crown with a glittering cross of gold and garnets. She looked irresistibly and undeniably beautiful—and his.

And she smiled at him.

As if it were the most natural thing in the world for her to face him across the expanse of Addison Fullerton's ballroom, she smiled at him. Never mind that an uneasy hush had fallen on the crowd. Never mind that Addison was glowering at him from across the room. Liberty gave him the poised smile of a woman completely in control of her situation. He surrendered his cloak and hat to the butler, then made his way across the room toward her.

The crowd parted before him like stalks in the wind. In her blue eyes, he saw amusement twinkling. She was enjoying herself, he realized. She knew exactly what a scene they were creating, and she was reveling in it. Yet another side of the complex woman he'd married made itself apparent to him. Garrick Frost, he noted, was observing her bare shoulders with far too much interest for his taste. When he reached her, the look on her face made him forget his frustration with Garrick. No one could look into that face and doubt the woman's integrity. "Good evening, Liberty."

"My lord." She inclined her head to him. "I trust you received my message."

"I did." He felt vaguely foolish for staring at her like some ill-mannered fop, but he couldn't take his eyes from her. This was, he realized, the first time he'd seen her elegantly attired. Her simple gowns, while flattering, lacked the sophistication of her glittering white satin ball gown. The dress gave her an allure he found singularly intoxicating. He had the strongest urge to touch her, to feel her melt against him. When he heard the distant strains of a waltz, he sent a silent prayer of thanks heavenward. For once, someone seemed to be smiling on him. Slowly, he extended his hand to her. "I have only now realized that you and I have never danced. As long as we are creating this scene, will you share this waltz with me?"

Garrick cleared his throat. "I'm next on the card, Moss. You'll have to wait."

Without looking at Garrick, Elliot placed his hand on Liberty's waist. "Go to hell, Frost," he muttered as he led her toward the dance floor.

Liberty laughed up at him. After the many days of strained silence between them, the sound threatened to undo him. Her fingers softly stroked the fabric of his jacket sleeve. "You shouldn't be so rude to Garrick. He'll stop taking care of you."

"Garrick Frost is the last thing on my mind at the moment." He turned her into his arms. "You look extraordinarily lovely, by the way."

"I pass inspection, then?"

"Do you doubt it?"

"I wasn't certain you'd like the gown. The bare shoulders are somewhat daring."

Elliot pulled her close as he began to move on the floor. The feeling was indescribable. "I prefer daring," he whispered against her hair. "In fact, I can categorically say that on you, daring is nothing short of devastating."

She favored him with a bright smile. "Are you paying me another compliment?"

"Have I been so remiss in giving them to you?"

"In fairness, you have seen a good bit of me at my worst in recent days. I'm sure you've begun to believe that dust and grime are my favorite fashion accessories."

"In case you hadn't noticed, I'm not exactly a slave to fashion myself."

"My lord, while your tailoring may not be the style of the day, you are possessed of an elegance that any man would envy." Her fingers moved along the width of his shoulders. "I feel most fortunate to be dancing with you. I'm sure every woman in the room is envious."

He spun her in a deftly executed move intended to throw her off balance. When she leaned into him, he pressed her tightly against him. "I believe, madam, that you are teasing me."

"I believe you are right." She met his gaze. "Don't you think it is ever so much nicer than arguing?"

He turned suddenly serious. "Have I been such a nuisance these past few days?"

"I think we have both made several mistakes. I would like us to find a way to regain the comfortable footing we shared in the days following our wedding."

He felt his mood lifting with each step. "As would I." He eased his hand from her waist to slip it into his pocket. "In fact, I was late this evening because I stopped to retrieve something for you."

Her eyebrows lifted. "For me?"

"Yes. I realized this afternoon that I have been remiss in some of my duties toward my wife." He tugged a slender gold chain from his pocket. On it hung a blue-and-green cloisonné cross. The gold filigree pattern glistened in the candlelight. "I should have given you jewelry long ago. I regret the delay."

Her eyes appeared to dampen slightly. "My lord, really, it's not necessary."

"It is." He held the cross in his hand as they continued to move about the floor. He wondered if she would realize the significance of it—he felt as if he were putting his mark on her. He *wanted* to put his mark on her. "I hope you like it. I thought you'd prefer something unique."

She looked at the necklace. "It's beautiful."

"Would you like to wear it?" He held his breath for her answer.

She seemed to sense the importance of the question. Her fingers tightened in his. "Yes. I'd like that very much."

The chain was long enough to slip over her head without unclasping it, so he gently settled it on her neck. When he adjusted its position, the backs of his fingers brushed the soft skin of her shoulders and throat. The cross lay against her flesh just above the hollow between her breasts. He had to tamp down a cry of exultation as he returned his hand to her waist. Briefly, he shut his eyes. "It's perfect."

"Yes." At the sound of her whisper, he looked at her again. Liberty moved her hand in the barest caress on his shoulder. "Thank you, my lord. Nothing could have pleased me more."

"Or me."

The air seemed to have thickened. He was having trouble breathing, and as if she sensed the momentous nature of what had passed, Liberty's face flushed a delicate pink. "Are you warm?" he asked her.

She seized on the chance to change the subject. "I find I am. There's quite a crush here. And I fear we're giving them another scandal."

"No one expected to see me in the home of Addison Fullerton. Certainly no one expected to see me dancing with my wife."

"Or giving her jewelry."

"Quite so. Fullerton and I aren't the best of friends, you know."

"But you were invited."

"*You* were invited. There is a distinction."

"Constance Fullerton should know better than to invite me without my husband. No matter what they think of me, I would not be running about London unescorted."

"I believe Addison thought your loyalty to Howard would stand him in good stead. You are aware, are you not, of Fullerton's ties to the Rendell properties?"

"Of course. You do not think I could have been so involved in Howard's businesses for so long without recognizing Addison Fullerton's name, do you?"

"Then you *knew* of my long-standing feud with Addison?"

Mischief made her eyes appear a deep ocean blue. "My lord, I am most aware of your opinion of Addison Fullerton. That is precisely why I wanted you to attend this affair with me tonight."

"I would ask you to explain yourself, Liberty. You have no idea how I felt when Wickers told me you'd insisted on attending this one."

Her smile faded. "Oh, Elliot. You didn't think I came here because I desired the company of the Fullertons, did you?"

"They were among Howard's closest friends. It occurred to me that you might find it easier to grieve his death when surrounded by his companions."

"His companions treated me most poorly. Surely you realize that."

He should have realized that Howard's social circle would have been singularly unforgiving of the woman they believed to be his mistress. In his refusal to give her respectability, Howard had isolated her from any hope of decent companionship. For the first time, Elliot saw how truly alike he and Liberty were. She was, perhaps, the only person in the world who could understand the extent of his loneliness. "I am sorry, Liberty."

"Don't be. But you do understand why I wanted us to be here together, don't you?"

"I am beginning to believe that you enjoy creating a scandal."

"I would hasten to point out that you orchestrated

the last two—both the cigar and the wedding were your ideas."

He noted the astonished looks of several of the guests as they circled the room to the final strains of the waltz. "My dear, the rumor that you were caught smoking a cigar with me, and the extraordinary circumstances of our marriage, cannot begin to compare with the events of this evening. Not only are we in the ballroom of a man who would just as soon shoot me as look at me, but we are giving every impression of being pleased with the entire matter."

"Aren't we pleased with it?"

He studied her face for long seconds. "What are you about, madam?" The waltz ended and Elliot guided her to a partially secluded spot near one of the terrace doors.

Liberty straightened his lapel pin before she met his gaze. "I think it is high time, my lord, that your associates understand that I am no longer the mistress of the Earl of Huxley—I am the Viscountess of Darewood. And if there are any questions at all where my loyalties lie, tonight will settle them."

Something seemed to explode within him. She couldn't possibly know the effect the simple statement had on him. He was having difficulty breathing as he looked at her. "Liberty—"

She shook her head. "I realized today that I have been most unfair to you, Elliot. It was only after my conversation with Garrick that I saw what I had done. You have made every effort to be fair and honest in your dealings with me, and I, in turn, have given you reason to doubt my intent. Given the confrontation with Braxton, it's no wonder you questioned me."

"That's not true."

She pressed her fingers to his lips. "I never wanted to give you cause to question my honor. I have every intention of being a good and dutiful wife to you, Darewood. I know things have been difficult between us, and I know I have not always been the easiest person to manage, but I did warn you that I don't take direction very well. Still, I hope you realize that I would never betray you."

Her impassioned speech left him feeling breathless. At the moment, he wanted nothing more than to toss her over his shoulder, carry her home, and take her to bed. He drew a ragged breath as he mentally fought for control. "Madam, you have a deplorable sense of timing, do you know that?"

Her eyes sparkled at him. "You do believe me, don't you?"

"I do."

"And you know I'd never allow Addison Fullerton to use me against you?"

"I never doubted it."

Her eyes widened. "You didn't?"

"I'll confess I was unsure of why you wanted to attend this damnable party, but I never once considered that you were conspiring against me."

To his very great astonishment and delight, Liberty wrapped her arms around his waist. "Thank you, my lord. You have no idea how much that means to me."

Garrick interrupted the tender moment. "I say, Moss, is it your intent to monopolize the woman for the rest of the evening?"

"She is *my* wife."

"I'm glad to see you realize that." Garrick extended his arm to Liberty. "Now, if you don't mind, I've been promised a dance."

She glanced at him. "Are we quite through, my lord?"

He raised her hand to his lips. "I believe that we are just beginning. Enjoy yourself. I have some business to conduct."

He waited while Garrick led her away. A new exhilaration pumped through him as he considered the impact of her words. Finally, the fear he'd felt since that evening in the ballroom had begun to abate. He needn't worry about losing her at all. She'd given him her loyalty. Perhaps he could allow himself to trust the priceless treasure of her love. If he guarded it closely enough, there was no reason why he should lose it.

He had been very wise, he was just now realizing, in his choice of bride. But, he realized, he'd made a tactical error these past few weeks with his withdrawal. Had her declaration not unsettled him so completely, he might have recognized it sooner.

If he wanted to possess her heart, she had to know that he trusted her.

That thought firmly in mind, he set about the task of clearing the final obstacles that stood in his way. Through the course of the long evening, he occasionally caught sight of her in the crowd. She seemed to be enjoying herself. Society had initially been reticent to accept her as one of their own. But Elliot had insisted that she be given every advantage as his wife. He would not, under any circumstances, tolerate a direct cut.

Now he had but one problem left to solve. His hand slipped into his pocket and closed on a crumpled piece of parchment. That afternoon, Liberty had received another threat. Once he ferreted the bastard out, he'd be free to concentrate on getting his wife to tell him again that she loved him.

Chapter 14

"Viscountess?"

Liberty felt a chill slide down her spine at the oily sound of Addison Fullerton's voice. She gave Garrick a reassuring smile, then turned to face the older man. "Good evening, sir." Addison extended a plump hand to her. When she shook it lightly, his palms felt clammy. She suppressed a shudder. "I haven't seen you in some time. I trust you've been well."

"Quite well. I was delighted when my wife told me you'd be in attendance tonight."

His beady eyes swept over her in insolent appraisal. Garrick slipped his hand to her waist as he stepped beside her. "Fullerton," he said, "I'd say it's nice to see you, but I'd wager you wouldn't believe me."

Addison laughed, a cackling little gurgle that left Liberty feeling unsettled. "I imagine you're right." He looked at Liberty again. "Mr. Frost and I go back several years."

"So I understand." She scanned the crowd beyond his shoulder but saw no sign of Elliot. At least, she thought, she wouldn't have to worry about a brawl. Elliot seemed to have momentarily disappeared. With any luck at all, he'd remain absent until after she had had an opportunity to confront Addison. "I was most pleased to receive your invitation, my lord. There is a small matter I have been wishing to discuss with you." She felt Garrick stiffen at her side.

"Something about Howard's business affairs?" Addison asked.

She shook her head. "It's a matter of a small volume I found in his collection. Perhaps you know it." She deliberately lowered her voice. "It's titled *The Treasure*."

His face paled. He drew himself up and narrowed his gaze on her. "What do you know of that?" he asked sotto voce.

Beside her, Garrick had drawn an anxious breath. Deliberately, she linked her arm with Addison's. "It's a long story. Perhaps you will honor me with a dance, and I'll tell it to you."

Garrick's fingers clamped on her forearm. "Liberty—"

"Don't fear, Mr. Frost. I know what I'm doing."

Garrick began to protest, but Liberty steered Addison quickly away, then toward the center of the room. He turned her roughly into his arms. Deliberately, Liberty eased a good distance away. "Not so close, my lord. This is a cotillion, not a waltz."

He glared at her. "You will tell me what you know of *The Treasure*. Now."

She executed several of the complicated steps, then waited through the rotation of partners until Fullerton stood across from her once more. "I know that each of you has a copy. I know who you are, and what it means."

"Rendell was a fool. He never should have told you."

She didn't bother to tell him that she hadn't gleaned the information from Howard. "There is, however, a slight problem."

He began to sweat. Again, the dance had them exchanging partners. She waited until she faced him once more. His eyes looked hunted now. His face was as colorless as his shirtfront. "What problem?" he demanded.

"Howard's copy is missing."

"Dear God."

"In the exchange of properties from Huxley House to my new home, it has been misplaced."

"Misplaced?" His skin looked sallow. "Do you know what this could mean?"

"I'm not certain," she said carefully. "Why don't you tell me?"

"My God, we could lose everything. Everything."

"Surely you exaggerate, my lord."

"You stupid chit. You've no idea what you've done, have you?"

"I happen to have a very good idea. I know that in that volume was enough information to destroy a good number of people. None of you trusts the others enough to tell the truth. If one of you has it, he'll never confess."

"Damn your hide." When the music ended, he linked a hand under her elbow. His fingers bit into her flesh as he hurried her off the floor. When he had her cornered, he loomed over her. "What do you want?"

"Have you been threatening me?" she asked him.

Surprise registered on his face. "Threatening you? Good God, no. Do you think I actually wanted you to know *The Treasure* even existed? As long as you believed it to be just another book, there was nothing to fear. Now that the information is in the open, God alone knows what will happen."

"There is one man who can save you, you know."

"Who?"

"Darewood."

She saw the shock in his gaze, saw the way his lips went slack and his mouth dropped. "Are you mad? Darewood wouldn't cross the street for me."

"Because of what you did to his father." It wasn't a question. She noted with no small amount of satisfaction the way Fullerton's eyes began to shift nervously back and forth.

"What do you know of that?"

"I know that Howard, and Braxton, and you, and even Constantine, allowed the Viscount to take the blame for your own activities."

"He was spineless. We all could have been rich."

"You *were* all rich. You just weren't honest."

His face flushed with anger. "What do you want? You can name your price, and you bloody well know it."

"I want you to return to Darewood what you stole from him."

"That's impossible."

"No. Together, you conspired to ruin that man. If you had the power to destroy him, you have the power to fix the deed."

"It was fifteen years ago."

She shrugged. "Then I see no reason to put off reparation for even an instant more."

"What gall." He glowered at her. "Just who do you think you are?"

"I'm the woman who knows the secret of *The Treasure*. Either you find a way to remove the stain from his father's reputation, along with restoration of what's rightfully his, or I'll see to it that the information in that book not only finds its way into the hands of your investors but that Braxton and Constantine know you gave it to them."

Before she could react, he grabbed her shoulders and pressed her to the wall. "Listen to me, you tart. I don't know what business you think you have meddling in this. You were Howard's strumpet. We all knew it. He may have trusted you, but I don't. If you don't recover that volume for me, your husband may find your body in the Thames."

Liberty clutched at his wrists as she tried to pry away his fingers. "If you hurt me, Darewood will kill you."

"Will he? He's got what he wants from you. Surely you know the state Howard's affairs are in. I'll wager you've had your hands full trying to keep your chin above water."

She renewed her struggles against the imprisoning grip of his hands. "It won't matter," she bluffed. "Darewood will never allow you to get away with this."

His fingers tightened. "Darewood can't stop me."

"Drop your hands." Elliot sounded like an avenging angel. To Liberty, he looked a bit like one, as well. She had a fanciful notion that his eyes were shooting flame, and wondered if hysteria was making her hallucinate.

At the sound of Elliot's command, Addison stiffened for a moment, then abruptly released her. She stumbled forward and would have fallen, except that Elliot pulled her to him. His arm circled her waist in an inflexible band. Liberty felt the anger in him, sensed impending disaster. An unnatural hush had fallen on the crowd. She placed a beseeching hand on Elliot's chest. "Here you are, my lord." Heavens, how she wished she didn't sound so breathless. "I was just thinking that I would like to go home."

Elliot didn't take his gaze from Addison. He didn't speak, either, which had the other man squirming like a worm on a hook. Liberty tried again. "Where is Garrick? Perhaps he can fetch the carriage for us. I must confess I'm not feeling at all well."

Elliot's only noticeable reaction was to tighten his fingers at her waist. Addison finally seemed to regain some of his composure. He coughed to clear his throat. "Now, see here, Darewood. No need to do anything rash." Several curious onlookers passed near enough to eavesdrop on their conversation. Addison beamed at them, greeted each by name, then waited until they walked away. Elliot still watched him with a murderous glint in his eyes.

Liberty wedged herself between him and Addison. "That's right, Elliot. No need to do anything rash. I'm certain his lordship meant no real harm."

Addison wiped the sweat from his florid face. "No harm at all. Just wanted to ensure that my position was understood."

Liberty glared at him. The man obviously didn't understand that she was trying to save his wretched life. The fact that Elliot had seen him physically threatening her, she knew, was enough to send him into a towering rage. She could feel the raw power in him circling her like a cocoon. "Elliot, please."

She deliberately kept her voice at a low pitch. "I want to go home."

Whether Addison believed her comment meant that he'd sufficiently frightened her or whether he was merely a monumental fool Liberty didn't know, but when she saw the look of triumph on his face she realized her first moment of real dread. He glanced at her, then met Elliot's gaze once more. "You'll find your social entrée more easy to manage, Darewood, if you learn how to control that woman."

"Oh dear," she said with a touch of sarcasm.

With a slight tug, Elliot moved her back to his side. She tried to stand her ground, but her soft slippers were no match for him. He merely slid her out of the way. She gave Addison a warning look. He seemed utterly unaware that he'd just released the hounds of hell. Elliot took a step closer to him. Liberty frantically searched the room for Garrick. He was the only one who could help them now.

Most of the crowd had abandoned the pretense of indifference to the drama unfolding in the corner. Now they watched openly, their faces masks of curiosity and comic horror. Liberty knew there was no point in arguing with Elliot. His anger had become a living force. In a move so rapid that she sensed it rather than saw it, he pinned Addison to the wall with a hand at his throat. "How is it we're supposed to go about this, Fullerton?" His voice was almost a growl. "I tell you you'll hear from my seconds? Is that the procedure?"

Liberty knew a moment of panic. She would not have him fighting an illegal duel. "Now, Elliot—"

He ignored her. "As you well know, I'm not particularly well versed in Society's manners." His fingers tightened until Addison's flesh puffed around the edge of his hand. "Arranging a duel seems a bit of an inconvenience to me. Particularly that annoying bit about drawing blood rather than actually murdering one's opponent."

The color drained from Addison's face. "See here, Darewood—" His voice was a hoarse whisper.

"So let's leave it at this, shall we? Touch her again, and I'll destroy you. Is that succinct enough?"

Liberty was pulling at his other arm now. He was going to strangle Fullerton if he didn't release him. "Elliot, I do believe he's gotten your point. Look. You can see it in his eyes." The only thing she could see in Addison's eyes was fear, but she was becoming a bit desperate.

Elliot's hand increased the pressure until Addison was gasping for breath. "Do I make myself clear?"

"Yes," he choked. "Yes."

"And for the record," Elliot said, "that woman is my wife." He gave Addison a final shove before he released him. "Don't ever forget that again."

Addison crumpled to the floor, clutching his throat and gasping for breath. Elliot seemed unconcerned by the reaction of the crowd. He took Liberty's elbow and started for the door. She didn't even think of resisting him. His hand exerted only the barest pressure on her elbow, but she knew she hadn't a prayer of stopping him. She bravely smiled at a young couple who were forced to hurry out of the way lest Elliot plow into them.

When it became apparent that he was fully prepared to knock down anyone who stood in his path, Liberty attempted to reason with him. "Now, Elliot—"

His fingers tightened in silent but perceptible warning. She didn't speak again until they'd cleared the room and were walking steadily across the foyer. Garrick stood near the door with their cloaks. "Well, Garrick, I see you've finally put in an appearance. Where were you when I needed you, I'd like to know?"

Garrick gave her an apologetic look, then handed their cloaks to Elliot. "The carriage is waiting. Any details you need me to attend to?"

Elliot threw her cloak around her shoulders with an impressive flick of his wrist. "Make absolutely certain that Fullerton understands," he muttered. "And while you're at it, see that Constantine heeds the same warning."

Liberty looked at him in astonishment. "Elliot, you knew about Constantine?"

"Madam, I would strongly advise that you hold

your tongue. I fear I am in danger of losing my temper."

He glanced at Garrick. "Good night, Frost."

Garrick inclined his head, then lifted Liberty's hand for a brief kiss. "Don't fear, my lady. He's not nearly the tyrant he sounds."

Elliot ignored him, then turned and escorted Liberty to the door.

They didn't speak during the short carriage ride home. Seated across from him in the open coach, Liberty could feel his tension.

In less than five minutes, they reached Darewood House. Elliot threw open the door of the carriage, then helped her to the ground. Silently, he ushered her up the steps, where a startled Wickers held open the door for them. "You're home early, your lordship."

"So I am," he said. "We'll be retiring, Wickers. Feel free to lock the house for the night."

Liberty gave the butler a reassuring smile. "Thank you, Mr. Wickers. We had a lovely evening." The last was delivered from the foot of the stairs. Elliot was dragging her along behind him at such a rapid pace that she had to run to keep up.

In seconds, he had her up the stairs and through the door of his bedroom. Jonathan Stanley, his valet, wisely withdrew from the room without comment. He gave Liberty a pitying glance as he passed, then shut the door behind him with a decisive click.

"Elliot, really. You needn't be so abrupt. You have the staff thinking you're going to beat me."

"I might." He bit the words out.

"No, you won't, and you and I both know it. I'm sorry that scene with Fullerton got out of hand, but—"

"Out of hand?" His expression turned thunderous. "Out of hand? I glance across the ballroom and find the man threatening you, and you think it is out of hand? My God, what next? Did you plan to stab him, too?"

At the reference to Braxton, she sucked in an angry breath. "It wasn't like that."

He stalked toward her. "Did I, or did I not, hear you mention *The Treasure* to Fullerton?"

"You did."

He was so near her now, she had to tip her head back to hold his gaze. "Damn it, Liberty, have you no sense at all?"

"I've quite a lot of sense."

"Then perhaps you will explain to me this fascination you have with danger. First there was your midnight visit to Braxton's library, then that utter disaster at Vauxhall, and now you are taunting Addison Fullerton with your knowledge of his misdeeds."

"If you will let me explain—"

"This isn't a game. These men are dangerous. You've been receiving threats, for God's sake. I would think you could understand the seriousness of the situation."

"I do."

"Then you're no doubt aware that Fullerton would just as soon see you dead as have the information in *The Treasure* exposed."

"Of course."

His expression turned livid. "So, knowing that, you naturally decided to confront the man with the fact that you know enough to destroy him."

"It wasn't like that. I—"

Elliot's hands closed on her shoulders. "Damn you, Liberty. Are you determined to drive me insane, or are you simply incapable of making a rational decision?"

"I resent that."

"Not nearly as much as I resent the fact that you're intent on destroying yourself."

Irritated, she pushed his hands from her shoulders. "If you will give me a moment to explain, I believe I can make you understand the entirety of it."

"I already understand it." His voice sounded tight. "I understand that you exchanged Howard's copy of *The Treasure* with Braxton for a ledger you thought would prove my father's innocence. I understand that when you examined the ledger, you found that he was not so innocent as I led you to believe."

Her eyes widened. "Elliot. You knew?"

"Of course I knew. Don't you think Howard showed me the proof of my own father's treachery?"

"But you also knew that Howard, Fullerton, and Constantine were intimately involved. That's why you hated them so much."

"Yes."

"Your father wanted to set things right, and they destroyed him for it." In the dim light, his face was an unreadable mask of shadows. "And then you decided you'd get revenge."

"The best way to do that was to become a man they had reason to fear."

It was all becoming frighteningly clear to her now. "So you married me," she reasoned, "knowing that *The Treasure* was in Howard's collection." Her eyes widened with the realization. "You knew from the beginning that they'd come after the book."

"I did."

"And you saw no reason to enlighten me?"

"Had you done as I asked, you would not have been involved. The only reason you've been dragged through this is because you insisted on inserting yourself. I would have handled them."

She found her first spark of anger. "You used me."

A slight hesitation. "No."

"Yes, you did. You wanted revenge on all of them, so you used me to get it. You weren't angry because I confronted Braxton the other night. You were angry because I gave him the book."

"That's not true."

She stared at him, agape. "I cannot believe that even you would stoop this low, Elliot. To think that I believed the world had misjudged you. That story about your father, it was all a part of your strategy, wasn't it? You elicited my sympathy in order to ensure my loyalty."

"You are making this all sound far more sordid than it is."

"Am I?"

"Yes. I knew about *The Treasure*. I knew that Braxton, Fullerton, and Constantine would be desperate to obtain it. But that is not why I married you."

"Oh yes, I forgot. You married me for the Cross of Aragon."

"You don't understand what it means to me, Liberty."

"Then tell me." To her horror, she heard the thread of tears in her voice. She would not cry in front of him. Not now. "Make me believe you. Because at the moment, I cannot see that what you've done to me is any better than what those men did to you."

He stared at her then. She felt the conflict that warred in him. Instinctively, she sensed how difficult this was for Elliot. He was unused to explaining himself to anyone. "The cross isn't just a missing piece of my collection. It's the reason Howard destroyed my father. You read *The Treasure*. You know that most of the information in it is encoded."

"Yes."

"How much of it were you able to decipher?"

"Most of it," she said.

"But not all?"

"No."

He drew a deep breath, as if he needed the fortitude. "And the information you have is enough to cast suspicion, but it's not proof."

"That's correct."

"Because," he said grimly, "to complete the information, you need the key. The placement of the stones on the Cross of Aragon provides the missing information. With it, *The Treasure* becomes more than a log of activities. It becomes enough evidence to convict, and probably hang, the men involved."

Her eyes widened. "How long have you known this?"

"Since the day I found the letter from my father explaining what he'd done. He was the one who encrypted *The Treasure*. The copies are each in his own hand." His expression turned bleak. Her heart wrenched as she realized just how alone Elliot really was. She knew, with utter conviction, that he had never repeated this portion of the story to another soul, not even Garrick. He'd carried the burden alone, too ashamed to let anyone share it. "I didn't need Howard's copy, Liberty. I have my own. To complete it, I needed the cross. It wouldn't help me prove my father's innocence, but it would help me ruin the men who killed him."

She stared at him. Though his body was completely still, she sensed the storm of conflict that tore at him. He had laid himself bare for her. In a few brief moments, he'd given her the power to hurt him. The feeling pouring through her was extraordinary, strangely close to euphoria. So many things made sense now. He'd been angry that she'd traded *The Treasure* for the ledger because he didn't want her to know the truth. He'd withdrawn from her that night in his fear that she'd reject him. The impact of that painful lesson of his youth had shaped the man. She'd known that he trusted no one to love him, that he had faith only in himself. To keep his heart safe from the unbearable pain of humiliation, he'd encased it in an unbreachable wall of stone.

Until now. That Elliot had shared this with her was far more telling than any declaration of affection he could ever make. He might not love her, but he trusted her. "Why didn't you tell me?"

He held her gaze for long, painful seconds. "I have spent a lifetime cultivating a disdain for other people's opinions of me. Like you, it became necessary for my survival. But with you, it was different."

"You feared that I'd use the knowledge against you."

"I had believed, remember, that you were the mistress of my enemy."

She crossed the room until she stood directly in front of him. "What now? Can you trust me?" She searched his face.

"Now," he said, his voice oddly hoarse, "I find I am helpless on that point. If you want to destroy me, then you will. It can be no worse than the hell of the last two weeks."

"Oh, Elliot." She wrapped her arms around his waist. For a moment, he stiffened in surprise; then he crushed her to him with a low groan that was half pain, half triumph. "How can you believe that I would do anything to hurt you?"

He buried his lips in her hair. "You won't be sorry, Liberty. I swear, I'll never allow you to regret this."

She gave him a secret smile. "I know you won't." With all his complexities and enigmas, Elliot was a remarkable man. One day, she'd make him believe it. Rising up on tiptoes, she placed a soft kiss on his lips. "As we have the rest of the evening before us, and no plans to fill it, do you think I might possibly persuade you to take me to bed?"

Chapter 15

Elliot wasn't about to question the extraordinary turn of fortune that had Liberty back in his arms, back in his bed, where she belonged. For some reason he'd never understand, God had forgiven him one more time.

He slanted his lips over hers in a kiss that told her, fully, how very desperately he needed her. "Dear God," he breathed against her mouth. "I'll make you believe me."

Liberty's hands slipped inside his jacket. With gentle insistence, she pushed it from his shoulders. "I already believe you, Elliot." Her fingers went to work on his buttons. "The trouble here is that you don't believe me."

He had the vague feeling that she was trying to tell him something important, but he couldn't seem to concentrate. Liberty had worked his shirt loose and was now nuzzling his chest. He remembered, in excruciating detail, everything about the way it felt to make love to her. With no effort at all, he could recall precisely what it felt like to be buried in her warmth. He went wild just thinking about it. After two weeks of lying alone in his bed while she slept next door, he was dangerously close to exploding. He cupped her bottom in his hands to lift her against him. "I need to feel you," he muttered.

"And you will." Her hands reached the waistband of his trousers. He would have torn her dress from her then, but she captured his attention by skimming her fingers along his stomach. His shirt joined his jacket on the floor.

With a soft groan, Elliot reached for the hem of her skirt. Again, she eluded him. Finally, he tore his lips from hers. "Liberty?"

She was concentrating on his trousers. "I don't want you to undress me."

"What?" His chest ached with the effort it took just to breathe.

She met his gaze with alarming frankness. "I want to undress for you."

His ears started to ring. She couldn't possibly know what that announcement had done to him. His mouth went dry; his heart momentarily stopped beating. A rush of white-hot desire left his limbs trembling. He watched, utterly powerless, as she knelt before him to remove his shoes, then stood again and tenderly pushed his trousers over his hips. "I don't think—"

"Please, Elliot. It's been so long since you touched me. Let me do it this way."

Tonight, he could deny her nothing. He stood naked before her, emotionally, he realized, as well as physically. He could not refuse her request, even if it killed him. Which, he thought ruefully, it just might. Liberty seemed unaware of his inner turmoil. With steady hands, she was pushing him toward the bed. "Sit, Elliot," she commanded. "Let me show you."

He dropped silently to the bed. Liberty gave him a smile filled with seductive promise as her fingers went to the buttons of her white gloves. This was not the sophisticated seduction of a skilled courtesan. He could tell by the way she studiously avoided looking at his arousal that she was embarrassed, and it seemed to amplify the effect on him. She kicked off her slippers, then tugged her gloves from her fingers. As the soft silk whispered down her arms and over her hands, he closed his eyes in a shuddering prayer for control. With a soft *plop*, her gloves fell to the carpet.

Elliot opened his eyes again. The flush in her cheeks told him she was no less affected than he. The sight of her arousal forced him to ease his body back against the pillows to relieve the growing pressure in his groin. Without comment, Liberty reached for the buttons of her gown. As she struggled to unfasten the silk-covered nubs at her back, he grew harder, longer. His body clamored for release. His blood ran hot in his veins. Each twist of her arms had him gasping for much-needed breath.

When the dress finally slid to the floor, she stood before him in the thinnest of petticoats and undergarments. Above the stays of her corset, her breasts swelled in lush invitation. Vividly, he remembered the taste of them, the feel of them cushioned against his chest. He reached for her again.

Liberty frowned at him. "I'm not finished."

"Then let me help you."

She shook her head. "Don't you like this?"

"Oh, I like it. If I liked it any better, I'd probably die."

"Then let me finish it."

"You're torturing me," he groaned.

"You'll survive." She pulled at the ties of her petticoats. They puddled around her feet in a whoosh of soft lawn and lace.

She held his gaze as she undid the tapes of her pantalettes, but when they dropped to the floor, she lowered her eyes in a sudden burst of shyness.

"Liberty," he whispered. "Come here."

She walked slowly to him, her bare hips swaying with each step. When she reached the curtained shadows of the bed, she looked at him once more.

In her eyes he saw a naked longing that wrenched a groan from his chest. He saw the love for him written so clearly in her gaze that he was forced to look away. "Liberty, please," he said.

He felt the bed dip as she knelt beside him. "The stockings and the corset," she said. "Do you want them on or off?"

With a guttural oath, he pulled her on top of him. The weight of her cloisonné cross felt cool on his heated skin. "I can't take this," he said. His lips moved feverishly across her face. "I need to feel you."

Her stocking-clad legs drifted open so she straddled his hips. The moist heat of her cushioned him between the exquisite softness of her thighs. How had he forgotten how soft her thighs were? "You will," she promised him as she pressed a light kiss to his throat.

Before he could stop her, Liberty was moving over his body, tasting him. She nipped at his shoulder, kissed the center of his chest. "Your skin tastes salty," she observed.

He couldn't answer. When she took one of his hands to her lips and pulled a finger into her mouth, his back arched off the bed.

Liberty sucked at his index finger, then pressed his hand to her breast. "Have I told you how much I like it when you touch my breasts?" she asked him. "Do you like it as much?"

All he could do was nod as he flexed his hand against the full curve. "They feel strange when you touch me. They tingle."

"Liberty," his voice sounded strangled.

She pressed his dampened finger to the tip. Again, he reached for her. Again, she eluded him. She pressed a kiss to his flat nipple, laving it with her tongue in the manner he'd taught her. "Does it feel as good to you?" she probed.

"Yes." He hissed the word.

His body thundered for him to roll her to her back and be done with it, but the pleasure he saw on her face as she explored him was enough to keep him pinned to the bed while she continued the tender ministrations. Her lips found his ankle. "What about here?" she asked. "Is it sensitive?"

Her mouth moved to the tender flesh behind his knee. "You're so different from me. You're hard where I'm soft."

That had to be the understatement of the century. If he got any harder, he was going to turn to granite. "Let me show you," he whispered.

"Not yet." She pressed a kiss to the curve of his hip bone, then slid along his body to nuzzle the skin behind his ear.

Her corset pressed into him. The hard stays contrasted sharply with the softness of her breasts, her skin. He went through every mental exercise he knew, but nothing took his mind from the pulsing intensity in his groin. Only barely did he manage to remain still, save for the involuntary flexing of his muscles and skin wherever she touched him.

When she moved lower and dipped her tongue into his navel, he could no longer remain passive. His hands clenched in her hair. The dark silk twined around his fingers like a satin bond. He twisted his hands in it, would have pulled her to him, but

the hazy passion in her heavy-lidded eyes held
him back.

Sensing the incredible effort it cost him to surrender to her, she rewarded him with a loving smile.
Then, without warning or preliminaries, her lips
closed around him like a liquid glove of heat.

He sat up in the bed, tremors racking his body,
and clutched at her head. He could take no more.
With a rough groan, he rolled her to her back. His
fingers tore at the laces of her corset. His hands
pushed and tugged until she was bare, save for her
stockings and the gleaming cross between her
breasts.

With heated lips and unintelligible words of
praise, he lavished her body with the same attention
she'd given him. He trailed wet kisses over her
breasts, down past the flat of her stomach. When
he nuzzled through the damp curls at the apex of
her thighs, she cried out his name. He slid both
hands beneath her bare bottom, lifted her to him for
the most intimate of caresses, then plundered her
with his tongue while she melted into a shattering
climax.

Her body was still shuddering when he rolled to
his back seconds later. She tried to pull him on top
of her again, but Elliot resisted, instead linking a
hand behind her nape and crushing her mouth to
his. He parted her thighs with his hand, eased her
atop his hardened shaft, then buried himself in her
satin warmth. She cried out when she was fully

seated. With her on top of him like this, he could fill her more completely, give her more pleasure. She was whimpering as he pressed her hips down on his. Swiftly, he opened his eyes to gauge the sound. Nothing but rapture showed on her face. He moved in her once. At the exquisite feel of it, her own eyes flew open. Holding her gaze, he emptied himself into her. She joined him at the edge, calling his name in a breathless cry as they toppled into the vortex.

Moments later, he was still trying to find the energy to move away from her. He couldn't stop caressing her, couldn't make his hands stop moving on her flesh. With her body draped over his, he was as near to heaven as he'd ever been. Her skin felt damp against his cheek. The steady beat of her heart tickled his ear.

Her fingers traced a slow path on his sweat-slick shoulders. He'd have marks in the morning, he thought, as he recalled the way her nails had bitten into his flesh. And he found the idea that she'd marked his skin oddly pleasing. He was almost tempted to have his shoulders permanently tattooed.

The sheer barbarism of the thought gave him the energy to roll away from her. Something, he realized, was amiss, but he couldn't quite put his finger on what it was. Liberty seemed blissfully sated. When he rolled to his back, she followed him and turned into his arms like a flower to the sun, laying her cheek against his chest. "Thank you, Elliot."

He searched his mind for the source of his unease. "I believe that if we're going to be strictly correct, I'm supposed to say that."

"You were never interested in being strictly correct before."

The soft comment made him realize what bothered him. Tonight, Liberty had given him another priceless gift, but she had not told him again that she loved him. The thought had him frowning.

Liberty wriggled against him as she pulled her corset free from the tangled sheets. "I think you ruined this."

He sent it sailing to the floor with a flick of his wrist. "I'll buy you another," he promised.

Liberty pulled the sheet more comfortably around her breasts. Her hair lay in tangled disarray across his skin, so he threaded his fingers through it, gently working free the knots as he considered his jumbled feelings. It shouldn't matter so much that she say the words. She'd shown him in a hundred different ways that she still loved him. Her innocent seduction should have been enough for him.

But it wasn't. He needed the words from her to keep the loneliness that lurked just beneath the surface of his soul from creeping back. His mind raced as he considered how best to broach the subject with her. He couldn't simply demand that she tell him. Could he?

He glanced down at the top of her head where it lay pillowed on his chest. Her even breathing told him she had fallen asleep. He'd have to spend one more night, he realized, with his fears. He'd survived this long with the chill in his heart. With her warm body snuggled against him, he could keep the fear at bay until sunrise.

Liberty awoke to the sound of an insistent rain striking against the windowpanes. She stretched, reveling in the delightfully stiff feeling in her limbs. Elliot had awakened her once in the night to make love to her. This time, he'd been the one to torment. He'd paid loving attention to every inch of her body, telling her in a thousand ways how much she meant to him, carrying her with him to new heights. The sheer pleasure of it had been breathtaking.

But in the aftermath had come the depressing reality that Howard Rendell had indeed had his way. Elliot stood on the brink of financial and personal ruin, and she was the cause. She felt a profound sense of loss as she moved to latch the windows. The chill in the air had her reaching for his discarded shirt. It smelled musky and male—like Elliot. As she slipped it on, she glanced at his naked form, sprawled on their bed.

The lithe lines of his body, each well-formed muscle, bore testament to his self-discipline. The rigorous exercise he did each morning, and even the way he moved, reflected the total harmony of his mind and his body. Naked, the effect was amplified. He looked like a dark god. She could picture his catlike stride as he descended from Mount Olympus.

Once more, sadness overtook her, and she turned to watch the rain stream down the glass. More than ever, she wanted to find the Cross of Aragon for him. Now that Fullerton and Constantine knew she had the secret of *The Treasure*, Elliot was vulnerable. Howard's plan was well on its way to fulfillment, and it was her fault.

"Liberty?" His voice sounded from the bed.

She started. "I didn't mean to wake you."

"What are you doing?"

"It's raining."

She heard him toss the covers aside and pad across the thick carpet. His arms wrapped around her from behind. With her breasts pillowed on his forearms and her head fitted neatly against his shoulder, she could almost forget the sorrow that weighed so heavily on her heart. "You're cold," he whispered.

"Now I'm not."

He met her gaze in the reflection of the window. With one hand, he caught the tear that had spilled down her cheek. "You're crying." She saw the concern in his gaze. "Are you all right? Did I hurt you?"

"No. Not you," she whispered. Angrily, she swiped at the tears. "I'm sorry, Elliot. I don't know what's come over me. I'm not generally this emotional."

"That makes us even."

At his quip, she managed a watery smile. "I was just thinking of what a horrible mess we're in."

He rubbed her stomach and hip. "We're not in a mess, sweetheart. Things are just a little complex. It's nothing we can't handle."

"You don't understand. This is what Howard planned all along." She felt a new wave of misery as she watched him tenderly lift her hair aside so he could nuzzle her neck.

"I rather doubt it," he mused.

Liberty's head fell naturally to the side to give him better access. "You're not listening to me."

"Of course I am." One of his hands worked its way inside the open neck of the shirt to cup her breasts. "Howard planned this. If he weren't dead, I'd thank him."

When his fingers grazed her nipple, she gasped. "Not this." She moaned when he stabbed his tongue into her ear. "He planned the mess we're in."

Elliot stilled. "Liberty, have I told you how much I dislike talking about Howard? Especially when I'm making love to you?"

She turned in his arms. "It's what he wanted all along, Elliot. He knew you'd come after the Cross of Aragon. He knew you'd have to marry me to get it. He did what he did to ensure that I'd have no choice. And now, you're burdened with me."

An enigmatic smile played at the corner of his lips. "I can think of worse fates."

"No. I don't think you realize just what he's done."

His hands came up and gently cupped her face. "Tell me why you're so sad," he urged.

"And you'll fix it?"

"I will." He sounded so completely sure that he could, as if he were promising to build a railway or open a factory.

"You can't fix this," she told him. "Howard used me to destroy you."

"You're being overdramatic, I assure you."

"No. No, I'm not. I should have realized it sooner." She drummed her fingers on his chest as she sought a way to make him understand. "How much do you know about the ancient Persians?" she finally asked.

"Enough to know that I'd rather be here with you than listening to a history lesson."

She ignored him. "In their culture, the white elephant was considered sacred. It was against the law to kill it, or even allow it to die. At any cost, it had to be fed, protected, and tended."

"You're going somewhere with this, aren't you?"

"Yes. When a Persian ruler wished to subtly destroy an enemy, he gave him a white elephant. In their culture, it would be an unforgivable insult to give the animal away, so the new owner was forced to care for it. The cost was generally enough to bankrupt him. Howard has an entire book on the custom and its ramifications in his library."

"I'll have to read it sometime."

"Don't you see? That's what Howard did to you. He schemed to get you embroiled with me, knowing that I would ruin you financially."

His breath came out in a long hiss. Gently, he pushed her hair away from her tear-dampened face. "I will never be able to tell you," he said quietly, "how much it angers me that he hurt you in this way."

"You've no cause to worry about me."

"I've every cause." Elliot picked her up and carried her to the bed. "Liberty, Howard didn't *force* me to do anything."

"But—"

He covered her lips with his fingers. "And he isn't the only one capable of devising a strategy. I've known what I was doing from the beginning. No matter how carefully Howard planned to orchestrate my downfall from his grave, he won't win."

She pulled his hand away from her mouth. She must make him understand. "But Howard's estate is in financial ruin. As my husband, you're legally responsible for it now. You'll never be able to maintain the expense. It will bankrupt you."

"Howard planned it that way, true, but with a little help from Fullerton and Constantine, it won't be a problem."

"Elliot, I don't understand."

"I know you don't, sweetheart. I didn't understand it myself until earlier this evening." He shifted so he could prop his back against the headboard. "When you were talking to Fullerton, I realized what I'd been missing all along."

"Missing?"

"The threats," he explained. "Had you been thinking rationally, you would have immediately jumped to the conclusion that they were coming from me."

"But they weren't."

"No, but whoever sent them wanted you to think so."

She wrinkled her nose, confused. "That makes no sense at all."

"Yes, it does. Consider this. If you'd believed I was sending them, would it not have forced a confrontation between us?"

"Of course."

"And I could easily have proven I was not the culprit. Who, then, would have been the next logical candidate?"

"Carlton."

"Correct. I believe that the person who sent you those notes wanted you to believe Carlton was behind them. He was trying to force you into making a decision. As you and I would already have established that I was not to blame, I would have been the most logical person for you to turn to for help."

"But who could possibly have wanted me to turn to you?"

"The one person who had the most to gain from it." He raised her hand to his lips for a gentle kiss. "Howard."

Liberty sat straight up in the bed so she could stare at him. "Howard?"

"Think it through," he urged. "First, he sent the posthumous letter to me, virtually guaranteeing that I would go after you and the Cross of Aragon. Then, in case that plan failed, he arranged for a series of notes to be sent that would force you to take action."

"My God."

"But he also knew that once we were wed, Braxton and the others would begin to pressure you for *The Treasure*."

"Do they know about the cross?"

"No. Howard was the one who arranged for *The Treasure* to be encrypted. He hadn't planned on my father creating his own personal insurance by using the Cross of Aragon as the key."

"Clever man, your father. Since no one's actually seen the cross, no one could re-create the key unless they found it."

"That's right. There are no drawings of it in existence."

"What did Howard tell the others?"

"He couldn't very well confess that his plan had gone awry. To disguise the flaws in *The Treasure*, he told them that each copy was useless without the remaining ones. None of them knew that my father had kept one for himself."

She had the feeling that she had somehow missed a crucial bit of information. What was it? It seemed so close, yet it eluded her. She urged Elliot to keep talking. "Only you knew of the other copy of the book."

"Yes. I also knew it was useless without the cross."

"Which is how I came into the picture."

"Yes. You reasonably assumed it was Braxton who was sending you those notes. At first, he seemed to have the most to gain. I even entertained the notion myself, especially after Carlton told me Braxton had been to see Howard in the days before his death."

"But you never actually believed it?" she asked absently. Somehow, the truth lay in her conversation with Willis Braxton and Peter Shaker. Braxton had been to see Howard just three days before he died. He'd taken with him the second set of ledgers, from which she'd retrieved the crucial volume with the evidence against Elliot's father, but he hadn't retrieved *The Treasure*. She should have thought of that herself.

"No," Elliot continued. "I knew that Braxton, Fullerton, and Constantine would not go to extensive lengths to obtain *The Treasure*. Each believed their copy was useless without the others. There was simply no point in obtaining Howard's copy while the other volumes remained in the open."

"I suppose not." It was something Peter Shaker had said, she decided; something about the way Howard had drafted his will. What was it? He had said that Howard excelled at finding the most unlikely solution to a problem by employing the most obvious strategy.

What could the words have meant? She toyed with them in her mind while she listened to Elliot explain how he'd known Braxton wasn't the culprit when he learned he'd visited Howard but hadn't taken *The Treasure* with him.

The most obvious strategy. If Howard was truly using her to orchestrate Elliot's ruin, what would have been his most obvious strategy?

It came to her in a flash of insight. Elliot was in the middle of telling her how he'd wanted to tear Fullerton's throat out that night when she suddenly tossed aside the covers. "Good heavens," she said beneath her breath.

Elliot stopped in midsentence. "Where are you going?"

Liberty tossed him his robe, then reached for her own. "I know where it is, Elliot. I know where Howard hid the Cross of Aragon."

Chapter 16

Elliot waited with barely restrained patience while Liberty lit the lamps in the ballroom that now served as her makeshift office and archive. In the shadowy light, the enormous room resembled a museum warehouse. Howard's treasures—the possessions he'd counted on to make him immortal—lay in disarray around the perimeter. Once the prized objects of his estate, they now represented shackles to the young woman who'd worked so hard to preserve them.

Elliot watched her as she moved about the room. There was a rare grace in Liberty that never failed to touch his soul. She absently dropped a pinch of food into the fishbowl as she passed the desk. With her hair still tangled from his hands and her skin still flushed from their lovemaking, she looked elemental and real to him. He wasn't accustomed to real people.

But there was no artifice in Liberty. What she did, she did fully, without thought or worry about the circumstances. He supposed he could have chosen a more peaceful existence for himself, one that wouldn't be interrupted by midnight jaunts and an endless stream of curiosities, but as he watched her fish circle in the small bowl, he was struck again by how uniquely suited they were. They were a perfect pair: two parts of one whole.

Only she, he thought as he watched her pull a leather volume from the bottom of a stack, was the better part.

"Here it is." She blew the dust off the ledger.

"Liberty, are you certain this can't wait until morning?" He wanted to take her back to bed, get her to tell him that she loved him, not go searching through Howard's possessions.

She shot him a surprised look. "Elliot, didn't you hear me? I know where to find the Cross of Aragon."

"I'm sure you do, but it's cold down here. I'd rather be in bed." He gave her a meaningful look. "Warm."

Liberty pushed her hair over her shoulder. "Really, Elliot, how can you think of lovemaking at a time like this?"

"I believe it would shock you to know just how and when I manage to think of making love to you. In the past two weeks, I think I've discovered a hundred new fantasies."

She blushed but didn't drop her gaze. "Come

here, Elliot. Give me five minutes, and then, I promise, you may have your wicked way with me."

"Such an enticement," he drawled as he strolled across the floor.

Pointing to the shelf just beyond his right shoulder, she said, "Would you hand me the knife?"

He fetched it for her. "What are you doing?"

"Getting your treasure." She set the leather-bound ledger facedown on the desk, then pressed her fingers along the padded spine until she found what she had been seeking. Using the sharp point of the knife, she slit the binding. "It was something Peter Shaker told me the night I retrieved this volume from Braxton."

Elliot watched the intent look on her face. How long, he wondered, would it take him to arouse her to readiness again? Remembering the night he'd taken her here, in the ballroom, he felt a glow of satisfaction. Not long. In a very few minutes, he could have her gasping his name. A few seconds more, and she'd run hot for him.

She seemed blissfully unaware of his scrutiny as she worked the knife into the leather. "He was explaining to me how Howard had planned to destroy you. That's when he said Howard always found the most unusual solution by employing the most obvious strategy." She bit her lip as she pried the leather away from the backing.

Elliot propped one hip against the desk as he considered just how ready she might be to try a few interesting variations in the pattern of their lovemaking. She'd responded beautifully when he'd helped her ride him earlier. Perhaps tonight, he would attempt something else. She was so incredibly responsive to him. She trusted him so readily that he didn't, for a moment, believe he'd shock her.

Liberty's face had grown flushed from the exertion of tearing the thick leather away from the book. "Don't you see, Elliot? With the cross, we can use the information in your copy of *The Treasure* to force Braxton and Fullerton and Constantine to tip their hands." She pushed her hair away from her damp forehead. "I suppose I needn't have bothered memorizing it. It would have been helpful to know you already possessed a copy."

"I'm certain it would." Yes, a few minutes at best and he'd have her saying his name in that delicious raspy whisper of hers. Then, when he entered her, she'd tell him she loved him. He was sure of it.

"Shaker's words told me precisely where Howard would have hidden the cross." Liberty gave the leather a final cut and pulled the rest of it away. Inside the padded backing of the ledger, resting in its own satin bed, its diamonds and rubies gleaming, was the Cross of Aragon. Liberty looked at Elliot.

Her efforts finally had his full attention. "And that's not all," he said. He pulled a folded piece of parchment from behind the satin. "It looks as if

Howard left us a final memento." He glanced at it. "It's addressed to you."

Her eyebrows lifted. "It is?"

He pointed to her name. Liberty stared at the folded parchment for long seconds, then deftly slid it into the pocket of her robe. "I've had enough surprises for one night." She pulled the cross from its resting place. "I think I'd like to go back to bed now."

Narrowing his gaze on her, Elliot took the cross from her and set it carefully on the desk. It amazed him that he had no immediate desire to examine the thing. It represented the most painful part of the last fifteen years of his life, yet he couldn't seem to concentrate on it. His mind was preoccupied with the misery he saw on Liberty's face. "Aren't you going to read that?"

"No."

"Why not?"

She glanced away from him then. "Please, Elliot, you have what you want. If you like, I'll help you decode the rest of *The Treasure*. Now that you have the key, you'll have those men at your feet. Isn't that enough for you?"

"It probably should be, but I'm selfish when the notion strikes me. I want to know why you won't read Howard's message."

The look she gave him threatened to tear his heart out. "Because," she whispered, "for ten years, Howard was the only family I had. Given that all the evidence suggests he used me against you, I'd prefer to hold on to whatever illusions I can, at least until tomorrow."

"Ah, Liberty." His gaze went again to the fish-bowl. "I think I'm finally beginning to understand you."

"You are?"

"Yes. We're very much alike, you and I."

"I could have told you that."

He watched her fish butt up against the glass, as if they yearned to leap from the water to their freedom, even if the journey would destroy them. He reached for her hands. "Just like your fish, you've always felt trapped. First by your circumstances, then by Howard, now by me. Isn't that so?"

She wouldn't meet his gaze. "Please don't, Elliot."

"You wanted Howard to care for you the way you cared for him."

"I don't want to discuss this." Her small hands fluttered in his.

He felt like a bastard for pressing her, but the selfish part of him wouldn't let her cling to her loyalties to Howard. He had to have all of her. "But he didn't."

"I don't know what Howard felt anymore."

"And you don't want to find out?"

When she finally raised her eyes to his, tears filled them. "Not tonight I don't."

He hesitated. Instinct told him they'd both be

best served if the matter were settled now, but a vision of the completely selfless way she'd given herself to him earlier intruded on his thoughts and he realized that he couldn't push her any harder. Liberty had helped chase away the chasm of loneliness in his soul. For tonight, at least, he would do the same for her. "You're right." He pulled her into his arms. "There'll be time enough tomorrow."

Late the following afternoon, Liberty sat alone at her desk. Her fingers trembled as she pulled Howard's note from her pocket. She'd delayed the inevitable as long as possible. At least part of her had wished to forestall this moment because she knew the words Howard had written would become indelibly stamped on her mind. She wouldn't even have the luxury of allowing the image of them to dim.

Sometimes, she thought, her memory was a curse. She glanced at her fish and thought of Elliot. He'd been right last night. The fish reminded Liberty not only of her relationship with Howard but of her relationship with Elliot. He was unable to give her the one thing she most craved—his love. Elliot would never make himself that vulnerable. Too many people—people like Howard—had wounded him too deeply.

Once again, she'd placed herself in a situation where she could never have what she wanted beyond all things. Like Elliot, she'd spent her life looking for someone to love, someone who would love her in return. With an aching heart, she realized that nothing Howard could say to her in this note would hurt her as deeply as the knowledge that Elliot was more interested in protecting his heart than he was in sharing it.

She broke the seal on the letter, then gingerly unfolded it. Laying it open on her desk, she began to read. Howard's script was steady and sure, as if he'd written the letter far before the waning days of his life. Her focus blurred for a moment as tears threatened to spill, but she brushed them away.

My dear Liberty,

If you are reading this, it is because I am no longer alive. I cannot help but wonder how long it took you to find it. I have the utmost confidence in your power as I do in Darewood's. Though I felt the need to help the two of you along a bit, I'm quite certain you will have found the Cross of Aragon by now. Tell Darewood he has my blessing to do with it whatever he must.

I am an old man now, and as old men do, I have begun to realize the folly of my ways. Things that once mattered deeply to me no longer seem important. Unlike Darewood, however, I lack courage. I don't doubt that you will have experienced great sorrow at my passing. Things will not have been easy for you, and in many ways, I have not made them so. I hope you will

*find it in your heart to forgive me, and know that
I wanted only the best for you.*

*The story I am about to tell you will likely
seem most unremarkable, yet it amazes me how
long I have carried it with me. Liberty, I cared for
you more than you will ever know. That night we
met at the auction was no chance passing. I knew
you would be there. I knew you'd want the
powder casket. I had given that casket to your
mother sixteen years before as a token of my very
great esteem. I loved your mother deeply, but in
my youthful pride, felt I could not marry her. She
was a ballet dancer, and at the time, my title and
station mattered more to me than my heart.*

*It has been my profound joy, however, to see
that you, my daughter, have become a person so
much stronger than I ever could have been.
Where I have failed you, I grieve. But it is my
hope, my fondest desire, that finally you are at
rest. If everything has gone according to my plan,
you are well married to Darewood. He is a fine
man. For all our differences, he is twice the man
I ever was. He has honor, courage, valor. You
may rely on him always.*

*If he now has the Cross of Aragon, then you
know the secrets of* The Treasure. *You know that
I, in my foolish pride and greed, committed many
acts of which I am deeply ashamed. In life, I
lacked the conviction to reverse the choices I'd
made. In death, however, I am free to see the*

world righted. That is why I give you this final bit of advice. Darewood is everything I would have wished for you. Cherish him. Treasure him. One day, he will learn to love you. He cannot help but love you.

And if you love him, as I dearly hope you do, then do this one final task for me. For years, I allowed everyone, including Darewood, to believe his father played a role in his own destruction. By now, you will have seen the ledgers and the evidence. But the truth is not in the numbers. Elliot's father was innocent of all wrongdoing. You will find the proof of it in the hidden compartment of my desk, behind the left top drawer. Fetch it for Elliot, Liberty. It will set him free to love you.

You will never know how much I regret that I cannot be there to share your life, but I suppose all sins, even the sins of the very rich, eventually exact their due. If I know that you are well, then my soul can rest in peace.

Your loving if foolish father,
Howard

For long moments, she stared at the letter. The implications of it seared her. Somehow, the terrible sadness she'd felt since Howard's death began to lift. In his cowardice, he had hurt her, but the sheer vulnerability she saw in his final words to her helped ease some of the pain.

Her mind drifted to the many happy times she'd spent with him. She had loved him—loved him like a father, she realized. And he, in turn, had done what he could to return her affection. He'd been far from perfect. She would, perhaps, always regret that life had taken them where it had. But as she considered the incredible revelations of his letter, she found a watery smile. Her gaze strayed to the humidor on her desk.

With little effort, she could picture Howard strolling into the library at Huxley House. Whether to hide from his secretary or merely to pass a few pleasant hours in conversation with her, he would sit in the chair across from her desk and light one of the cigars. She opened the box and sniffed the spicy aroma of the tobacco. Those had been good times, times when he'd given her all he could of himself.

Tears of regret formed as she considered all that she'd never known about him, could never know. On impulse, she pulled one of the cigars from the box, snipped the end, and lit it, then perched it on the edge of a smoking bowl to smolder. Leaning back in her chair, she closed her eyes. Here, surrounded by Howard's treasures and the scent of his tobacco, she could almost picture him in the room.

In her mind, she heard his voice replaying the words of his letter. And in that instant, the last ache of loneliness slid away. Like snow melting beneath a spring rain, she allowed the words to cleanse away the ache. As her tears began to fall in earnest, she opened her eyes to glance at Howard's portrait, sitting near the door.

And she knew that he had loved her. Not well, or endearingly, or even gently, but he had loved her. She wasn't alone after all. She picked up the cigar and waved it in his direction. "Here's to you, old boy," she told him, then took a long draw of the tobacco. The sensation, she decided, was definitely growing on her.

Now she only had to deal with Carlton.

Elliot glanced at the note with a growing sense of horror. "When did she give this to you?" he asked his secretary.

"An hour or so ago. You were out with Mr. Frost. She asked me to convey this to you with her regrets that she won't be joining you for lunch."

"Bloody hell," Elliot muttered.

"What's wrong?" Garrick asked him.

Elliot reached into his desk drawer to retrieve his revolver. "Her note says she has gone to visit Lady Asterly for tea."

"Forgive me, but shooting her seems a bit extreme."

He tossed the revolver to Garrick, along with a box of ammunition. "She isn't with Pearl Asterly."

"How do you know that?"

"Because I know my wife."

"Then where is she?"

He produced another revolver from his drawer. "She's gone to see Carlton Rendell."

"Good God, why?" Garrick began loading bullets.

"Because Howard has finally told her where she can obtain the evidence I need to exonerate my father."

"It wasn't in the ledger she retrieved from Braxton?"

"No. Howard needed my father's guilt to keep Braxton and the others in line. Only Howard knew the truth. And now Liberty has this insane notion that she's got to confront Rendell to get the evidence for me."

"Damn you, Elliot. For once, I'd appreciate receiving information from you in some manner that doesn't shock ten years off my life. How long have you known?"

"Known what?" He slid the revolver beneath the waist of his trousers as he rose.

"That Howard had a second set of ledgers."

Elliot strode toward the library door. "I've known from the beginning."

"How?"

"Because I know a lot about Howard Rendell, and I know he always finishes what he starts."

Fear gripped him as he drove through the congested morning traffic. He'd known from the moment he saw the smoldering cigar in her office that she'd read Howard's letter. He wished to God she'd shared the contents with him. For the last two hours, anxiety had torn at his soul as he considered that Howard may finally have succeeded in driving Liberty from him.

In the long course of the night, he'd begun to consider what the Cross of Aragon meant in his life. According to the terms of their agreement, Liberty was now free to leave him. And despite the tempestuous nature of their passion, she had not given him the words he craved like a lifeline.

When he had awakened alone in his bed, he'd begun to feel the ice reforming in his soul. She was torn, he knew, between him and Howard's will for her. And fool that he was, he'd ruined his last, best chance for happiness. Like all the rest, he'd crushed her. His heart felt sick.

Now, having read Howard's letter, she'd returned to the home of his enemy. He could hardly bear to contemplate what that might mean. He was almost unaware of the hell-for-leather pace he set until he reined in his team in front of Huxley House. Garrick shot him a disgruntled look. "Next time, I drive."

Elliot was halfway up the stairs by the time Garrick got the words out. He pounded on the door with his fist. Huxley's butler pulled open the door with a frown. "Yes, sir?"

Elliot forced his way into the foyer. "Where is he?"

"Who, sir?"

"Huxley. Where is he?"

"He's not home."

Elliot would have grabbed the man then, but Garrick stepped in front of him. "This isn't a game, man. If Huxley is here, you'd best tell us."

"He's not here, I say. He went out. Almost an hour ago."

"Out where?" Elliot demanded.

"I don't rightly know. I don't make it my business to ask his lordship where he's going."

Elliot lost the slender hold he had on his temper. He pushed past Garrick to loom over the butler. "Then may I suggest you tax your memory a bit harder. I want to know where he is, and I want to know now."

"Darewood!" Millicent Rendell screeched his name from the top of the stairs. "What are you doing here?"

Elliot jerked his hand away from the butler. Millicent stood watching him, an expression of utter terror on her face. Dressed in her wrapper, she looked hardened and worn by the years of distrust and hate. "Where is he, Millicent?"

Her chin lifted a fraction. "Why do you want to know?"

Garrick stayed Elliot with a hand at his sleeve. "You'd best tell him. If he gets to your son before he harms Liberty, Elliot may let him live."

Her face blanched. "You wouldn't hurt him."

Elliot could feel his rage threatening to overtake him. "If a hair on her head is harmed—"

Millicent's expression shifted. She looked from Garrick to Elliot. "You fool. Don't tell me you're besotted. Do you know what that woman is?"

Elliot's control shredded. He had heard the last of the insults he would bear on her behalf. With a loud roar, he stalked forward. "Damn you. Tell me where she is, or I swear, I'll kill Carlton when I find him."

The look of sheer rage in his eyes terrified Millicent. Her hand went to her throat. "He said something about a meeting with Peter Shaker, then he was going to the River Club."

Elliot halted. "The River Club? On Front Street?"

"I believe so."

He swore as he headed for the door. Garrick was hard on his heels. When Elliot would have swung into the driver's seat, Garrick pushed him aside. "You're in no condition to drive. We won't do her any good if you kill us on the way over there."

Elliot paused, then acquiesced. Garrick was right. His rage was making his hands tremble. "Hurry, Garrick," he told his friend as he slid aside. "I cannot lose her."

Liberty stood watching the boat traffic on the Thames as she waited for Carlton to join her. In her pocket was the Cross of Aragon. Elliot might not forgive her for this, but she knew it was the only hope she had of obtaining the volume she needed from Carlton. Carlton was desperate to salvage whatever he could of Howard's estate. The cross would give him the key to *The Treasure*. With it, he could ensure that Braxton, Fullerton, and Constantine helped him rebuild some of the empire he'd lost. And Elliot would no longer need the cross for his case against the three men once his father was vindicated.

Nor, a small voice told her, would he need her.

"I see you're prompt, as always." There was nothing but malice in Carlton's tone.

She stiffened, then turned to face him. He looked far worse than she remembered. His skin was blotchy, his eyes puffed and red. His mouth, always a bit slack, sagged at the corners from too many sleepless nights and too much debauchery. Liberty deliberately met his gaze. "Good evening, Carlton."

He snorted. "I'm not sure I know what's good about it. You'd better have a decent reason for demanding that I meet you. I'm not interested in playing any more of your games."

"I assure you, you'll be most pleased I came."

"I will have you know that I have just left Shaker's office, and he assures me I am a ruined man."

"Not for long." She pulled the cross from her pocket. "Did you bring the volume I requested?"

He produced it. "Had the devil's own time finding it. Why the hell Uncle Howard thought he had to be so suspicious of everyone and everything, I'll never know."

She almost melted with relief at the sight of the book. She'd half feared it didn't exist. "I'm willing to negotiate a trade," she told him. "I'll give you the cross for the book." She held the cross by its chain so it dangled like bait in a trap.

His eyes narrowed. "What is that?"

"It's the Cross of Aragon," she told him. "Surely, you've heard of it."

"Isn't that the piece Darewood has been after all these years?"

"It is."

"How much is it worth?"

"To you, it's worth a fortune." Quickly, she explained the story of *The Treasure* and how Carlton could use the cross to restore his wealth. She paused periodically to ensure that he was following the story. Carlton would never be the business genius Howard had been, but he was no fool, either. In his dull eyes, she saw the workings of his mind. He was quick to grasp the power the cross would give him. She felt certain he'd agree. "If you use it wisely," she told him, "you can regain much of what you've lost."

His gaze narrowed on her. "What's in this for you?"

"I have personal reasons." She glanced at the volume. "That book is nothing more than a useless set of figures. To you, it has no value at all. To me, it's priceless."

He regarded her for a moment. "How do I know you aren't lying?"

Liberty felt the shadow loom behind her like an ominous specter. "Because," Addison Fullerton said, "I said so."

She moved quickly away from him. "Carlton, did you tell Fullerton you were meeting me here?"

He nodded. "Addison extended a much-needed loan to me some time ago. In exchange, he asked that I keep him informed of my contacts with you."

Addison pulled a pistol from his cloak and waved it in Carlton's direction. "Give me the book," he said quietly.

Liberty laid her hand on Carlton's sleeve. "Carlton, no."

The cock of the pistol hammer was frighteningly loud in the quiet dusk. "My dear Liberty. First Braxton, then me, now Carlton. When are you going to learn that you cannot go about giving orders?" He pointed the pistol at Carlton again. "Give it to me."

Carlton hastily thrust the book into his hand. Addison looked at Liberty. "Now, give me the cross."

She shook her head. "I won't."

"You have no choice," he ground out. "Darewood's ruin is nearly complete. And I want to thank you for this charming little explanation of *The*

Treasure's secret. It's all so clear now. That bastard Howard deceived us all."

"It won't work," she told Addison. "Now that I've seen the cross, I know how to decode the rest of *The Treasure*. Did you know that Darewood has his own copy?"

She had the pleasure of seeing Addison pale. "You're bluffing."

"No, but even if I were, it wouldn't matter. I read the copy I surrendered to Braxton and I can re-create it if I need to. Now that I've had time to study the cross, I know the key. Stealing it won't do you any good. You'll be better off to make your pact with Carlton."

Addison seemed to waver with indecision as he considered what she'd said. She was almost certain he didn't believe her. He pursed his lips as he fingered the trigger of the pistol. "And what's to keep you from exposing us later?"

"Only my word that I won't. Don't you think I want this ended as much as you?"

He shook his head. "That's not good enough. Howard was sure he could depend on your loyalty, but I am not that much of a fool. It's clear that one turn in the sheets with Darewood has swayed your allegiance. Who's to say it won't happen again?"

Carlton, she noticed, was staring fixedly at Fullerton's gun. She'd find no help in that quarter. Sternly, she forced herself to think. "The book can have no meaning to you, Fullerton. I'll make the same deal with you I made with Carlton. Give it to me, and I'll give you the cross."

"Ah, but as you've already pointed out, you don't need the cross to decode *The Treasure*. No, I'm afraid that won't do at all." He took a menacing step forward. "In fact, I believe the only choice I have is to see to it that you're in no position to cause any more damage." He gave her arm a hard jerk and pulled her against him. "I fear that you are about to have a most unfortunate accident—a tragedy, really. I wonder how Darewood will feel when he learns that his wife has drowned in the Thames."

From the end of the bridge, the loud report of a pistol rent the still air. Liberty glanced up to see Elliot, his cape swirling about him in a dark cloud, advancing like a predator. Even in the dim evening light, his eyes glittered a feral green. Once again, she realized, she had failed him. In the book lay his best chance for happiness. She must get it for him.

"Release her, Fullerton." Elliot leveled his pistol on Addison. "Do it now before I kill you."

Carlton gasped when he felt Garrick's pistol press into his back. "Don't move," Garrick muttered. Liberty sensed Carlton's fear but could not take her eyes from Elliot.

"Please be careful," she warned him.

Addison gave her arm another wrench. She stifled a cry of pain, knowing full well that it would add fuel to the fire of Elliot's wrath. Addison was too unpredictable, too desperate. As long as he held that loaded pistol, he posed a threat to Elliot.

"Darewood," Addison said, leveling the revolver at him, "this is becoming an annoying habit."

"Unhand her," Elliot snarled, "or I swear to God I'll send you straight to hell."

"I don't think so. You wouldn't fire that at me as long as I hold your wife hostage. She's made you weak." Addison hauled Liberty in front of him and wrapped his arm around her throat. "She did it to Howard, and now she's done it to you. Tell me, just how good is she in bed to win such undying loyalty from her lovers?"

Elliot's expression turned stone hard. Liberty pried at Addison's tenacious grip. "Elliot, please. He won't hurt me."

Addison gave her hair a sharp tug. "Don't bet on it. It's a shame, really, that I have to kill you. I confess I would have liked a go at you myself."

Liberty renewed her struggles, but his arm held her immobile. With the book in his hand, he applied a painful pressure to her throat. In desperation, she used the sharp edge of the cross to cut a jagged path in the skin of his forearm. When he let out an anguished screech of pain, Elliot moved, faster than lightning. With a swift, powerful extension of his leg, he clipped Addison in the shoulder with the heel of his boot.

Still screaming from the deep cut in his arm, Addison stumbled backward. Elliot fired one well-

aimed shot. A bright crimson stain began to spread
across Addison's shoulder as he teetered near the
edge of the bridge. On reflex, Liberty grabbed the
leather volume from his hand. He, in turn, clutched
one end of the cross while she held fast to the other.
But as he lost his balance, Elliot reached for her.
His fingers closed on her wrist to pull her free of the
edge. When the cross slipped from her fingers,
Addison's tenuous balance failed him. With a final
scream, he crashed through the wooden rail of the
bridge.

The Cross of Aragon glinted in the setting sun as
it sailed through the air to land, forever lost, in the
fast-flowing waters of the Thames. Liberty stared at
it, stricken.

Elliot hauled her to him. He held her with one
arm while the other held his still-smoking pistol at
his side. "My God," he breathed into her hair. "Are
you all right?"

"The cross, Elliot." She still stared at the water.
"You've lost it forever."

He pressed a kiss to her forehead. "It doesn't
matter, Liberty. I don't need it."

"Of course it matters." She glanced at him,
stricken. "I would gladly have given it to Carlton
for the book, but to lose it like this—" Her voice
broke.

Had she not known better, she'd have sworn she
saw the hint of a smile cross Elliot's lips. "Liberty,"

he said, "stop worrying about that damned trinket and tell me if you're all right."

"What? Oh. Yes, yes, of course. He didn't hurt me."

"Good." Elliot glanced at Garrick and Carlton. "Rendell, you have what you want now. I trust I've seen the last of you?"

Carlton hastily nodded. "Your feud was with my uncle. Not with me."

"Make an appointment with my secretary for sometime next week," Elliot told him. "We'll see what we can do about rebuilding your finances."

Carlton evidently knew better than to question his good fortune. He shot Liberty a final glance, then offered Elliot his profuse thanks as he scurried off the bridge. Garrick released the hammer on his pistol, then tucked it back into his trousers. "I must say, Darewood, I used to believe marriage was an interminable hell of boredom." He turned his twinkling gaze on Liberty. "But your wife has inspired me. I believe I'll start seeking a bride at the beginning of next season."

Elliot didn't look at him. "Find one that's biddable, Garrick. Your life will be much simpler."

Liberty frowned at him then, but Garrick's laughter stayed her soft rebuke. "I believe your wife has a word or two to say about that, so I'm going to see to the horses. I'll be at the end of the bridge."

Elliot didn't even wait until Garrick passed to bend his head to hers.

She forestalled his kiss by laying her hand on his mouth. "Are you truly not angry about the cross?" She could hardly credit it. She knew how he felt about it.

"You've run me a fine chase, do you know that? I should have known that day you smoked the cigar with me that I wouldn't have a moment's peace with you."

"I never promised you tranquillity."

"Madam, you haven't even managed to avoid chaos. You've dragged me through one misadventure after another."

"And for your pains," she said miserably, "you've lost the one thing you wanted all along."

Elliot drew a deep breath. "Hear me well, Liberty. You know I have no talent for conversation, so I may not put this exactly right. Once, I believed that if I possessed all the treasures of the world, I would be happy. The Cross of Aragon was a symbol of the man I was."

Her heart skipped a beat. "And now?"

"Do you trust me?"

"Implicitly," she said.

"Do you love me?"

She realized what it had cost him to ask. "I've always loved you, Elliot."

Satisfaction flared in his gaze. "Then you are all the treasure I need."

He kissed her then, and for the first time, she allowed herself to believe that everything would finally come right.

Chapter 17

A month of relative calm had followed the stormy day ending on the bridge across the Thames. Liberty finally finished merging Howard's collection with Elliot's. They sold a good number of the items and even returned a few to Carlton. Elliot had hired workmen to extend his library in order to accommodate the extra books.

The opening of the Crystal Palace had brought a world of new opportunities to them both. With Pearl Asterly's guidance, Liberty had even managed to give several widely acclaimed parties. She was quickly becoming one of the most talked about hostesses in London.

Elliot remained occupied with his financial affairs and even, miracle of miracles, helped guide Carlton through the murky waters of international trade. Their social calendar grew ever busier, and as the eyes of Society turned to new entertainments, Liberty felt free to begin carving out her own place as Elliot's wife. With its usual fickleness, most of

London seemed to have forgotten the scandal of her relationship with Howard and her marriage to Elliot. When the queen had awarded Elliot the Royal Garter in gratitude for his work with the prince on the Great Exposition, Society had welcomed them with open arms.

For her part, Liberty found a sort of solace in the work. It gave her time to reflect on all that had happened, and time to finally say good-bye to Howard. Except for a slight feeling of unease that persisted whenever she dwelled on Elliot's detachment, her life was very near perfect. Elliot had been more solicitous than she could have imagined when she'd shown him Howard's letter. He'd even allowed her to hang Howard's portrait in his library, something she considered a monumental sacrifice on his part.

Still, though they shared the same stormy passion they always had, Elliot held something back from her. She had been certain that day on the bridge that he loved her. She'd seen it in his eyes. More important, she'd seen it in the way he'd dismissed the loss of the Cross of Aragon. But she needed him to say the words.

Except for his brief statement on the bridge, he'd never even acknowledged that he was pleased with the way things had turned out for them. It seemed he was intent on keeping himself safe, and when she allowed it to, the knowledge frightened her.

This day, however, she dismissed the thought. She had made an incredible discovery among

Howard's things and could not quite tamp down the excitement she felt when she thought of presenting it to her husband. It would please him as nothing else could. She'd delivered it to Elliot's jeweler for cleaning and had picked it up just that morning. As the well-sprung carriage carried her back to Darewood House, she clutched the treasured item in her hand.

She dearly hoped he was alone. She would be sorely disappointed if he were trapped in a meeting or out with Garrick. She didn't want to wait to present him with the gift. She never had mastered his own preferences for careful planning. She preferred impulse, and though it often seemed to unsettle him, he swore it kept their marriage interesting.

The carriage rolled to a stop and Liberty hurried up the stairs into the foyer. What she found there brought her to an abrupt halt.

"I see you're home," Elliot said. He stood beside the largest aquarium she'd ever seen. She stared at it. Nearly nine feet tall, the glass structure stood in the center of the foyer on a marble base. Shaped like an enormous crystal elephant, its tusks and toes were trimmed in gold. The glass sparkled in the morning sunlight. At least a hundred fish swam in its voluminous tank.

"Where did that come from?"

He walked toward her. "Do you like it? I remembered that you admired the one in the exhibition."

"It wasn't that large."

He glanced at the elephant. "Well, no, but it wasn't an elephant, either. I had this one specially made."

Her ears were starting to ring. She knew if she didn't get out what she wanted to say, she would soon lose her resolve. "Then, before you explain it to me, may I give you something?"

His eyebrows lifted. "What is it?"

She began to unwrap the parcel. "That day on the bridge, when you told me you no longer wanted the Cross of Aragon. Do you know, I didn't really believe you?"

"I said I didn't need it. I didn't say I didn't want it."

"Yes, well." She pulled the satin away from the treasure in her hand. "I thought you would be happy to know that Howard outwitted both of us." In her palm lay the genuine cross. The markings on the back and the set of the stones bore testament to its authenticity. "It seems he was a step ahead of us the entire time. The real cross was hidden in the bottom of his humidor. The one that fell into the Thames was a fake."

Elliot took the object from her and weighed it in his palm. "I can't believe it."

"I've had it appraised," she told him. "It's the real thing."

He studied it for long seconds. "I never expected to possess it."

She took a deep breath, determined to say what

was on her mind. "You know what this means, don't you?"

"That I have to begin a new collection?"

She ignored his quip. "It means, my lord, that our agreement is completed. I have procured the cross for you. You needn't keep me any longer."

He went completely still. The look he gave her made her heart beat wildly. "Is that what you want?"

"I love you, Elliot. I will always love you. But right now, I'm interested in what you want."

With a flick of his wrist, he sent the cross sailing across the room. The gold chain hooked on one of the elephant's tusks.

"Do you know why I bought this monstrous thing for you?" he asked quietly.

Something began to unfold in her chest. "No. Why?"

He took her in his arms then. "Do you remember what you told me that night we found the cross? What you said about Howard giving you to me to destroy me?"

"Yes."

He glanced at the elephant again. "I have been seeking a way, ever since, to make you understand what I am feeling. I've never been good at this. I'm almost definitely going to muck it up."

Tears burned at her eyes. "Oh, Elliot. Just say it. I promise it won't be nearly as hard as you think."

He drew a deep breath. "That night, you told

me that you believed you were to be my white elephant—the gift that would ruin me if I were forced to care for it and tend it."

"That's right."

He shook his head. "But it isn't true at all."

"It's not?"

"No." His expression turned completely serious. "The truth is, I wouldn't care if all the hounds of hell were at my heels, nothing could make me give you up."

With a soft sigh, she leaned into him. "I love you, Elliot."

"And I love you." He tipped her face to his. She could see the wonder in his eyes, and it filled her heart to bursting. "Never doubt it, Liberty. You aren't my ruin. You're my salvation."

"Oh, Elliot." She hugged him close. "Who in the world ever told you that you had no talent for conversation?"

With a slight sound of triumph, he bent his head to cover her lips with his own. There, amid the sparkling reflection of the water, he kissed her—a kiss filled with all the love they shared. A kiss that told her their love was, indeed, priceless.

BLUE CLOUDS

by Patricia Rice

Phillipa "Pippa" Cochran has a reputation of being a regular Pollyanna who smiles her way through life's tribulations. But when her mother dies, her nursing career fails, and her fiancé becomes abusive, Pippa loses her smile. She flees across the country to live in California and is hired sight unseen to care for the disabled young son of Seth Wyatt, a wealthy, handsome, and difficult recluse.

Unprepared for the altogether-too-attractive hurricane that is Pippa, the troubled Seth and his lonely son begin to blossom under her care. Then a series of "accidents" threatens Seth's life as well as the fragile love that has begun to grow between Seth and Pippa. Determined to protect the man she loves, Pippa is drawn into a dangerous game of cat and mouse that could cost her this precious new love.

Published by Fawcett Books.
Available wherever books are sold.

Coming next month . . .

THE PIRATE PRINCE

by Gaelen Foley

Taken captive by a fearsome and infuriating pirate captain come to plunder her island home of Ascension, the beautiful Allegra Monteverdi struggles to deny her growing passion for her intriguing captor. Lazar di Fiore is a rogue with no honor and has nothing in common with the man of her dreams—the honorable and courageous crown prince of Ascension, who is presumed murdered with the rest of the royal family by treacherous enemies of the throne.

But Allegra has badly misjudged Lazar, a man with a tragic past and demons that give him no peace. He harbors a secret that could win him Allegra's love and restore freedom and prosperity to Ascension, if his sworn enemies do not destroy him first. And the greatest battle of all must be fought within Lazar's own heart as Allegra tries to prove that, prince or pirate, he is truly the man that she has always dreamed of.

Published by Fawcett Books.
Available wherever books are sold.

Want to know a secret?
It's sexy, informative, fun, and FREE!!!

❧ PILLOW TALK ❧

Join Pillow Talk and get advance information and sneak peeks at the best in romance coming from Ballantine. All you have to do is fill out the information below!

♥ My top five favorite authors are: _____
_____
_____
_____
_____

♥ Number of books I buy per month: ❑ 0-2 ❑ 3-5 ❑ 6 or more

♥ Preference: ❑ Regency Romance ❑ Historical Romance
       ❑ Contemporary Romance ❑ Other

♥ I read books by new authors: ❑ frequently ❑ sometimes ❑ rarely

Please print clearly:
Name _____

Address_____

City/State/Zip_____

Don't forget to visit us at
www.randomhouse.com/BB/loveletters

m.kaye

PLEASE SEND TO: PILLOW TALK
BALLANTINE BOOKS, CN/9-2
201 EAST 50TH STREET
NEW YORK, NY 10022
OR FAX TO PILLOW TALK, 212/940-7539